Aggravated Momentum

Aggravated Momentum

Didi Oviatt

Prologue

My hands are as far above my head as they can reach, my back is intensely arched, and my calf muscles tighten, extending to the footboard. My pumpkin orange painted toes point as they join the stretch. The sun beams through a tight crevice in the drapes, challenging my eyes to regain vision. I squint and strain to open them. It's late afternoon, and I've been sleeping for four hours. Sadly, it's the most uninterrupted sleep my taxing life has allowed in over a week.

The sensation of piercing eyes causes the hair to raise on my forearms. After I finish rubbing the sleep from my face I glance around intently. No one is here. Weird. I swear I could feel someone's presence. It must be my nerves. My thick down comforter drops from my shoulders as I sit up for another stretch. It isn't usually this hot in my room, so I'm glad I was able to sleep through my sweat. My body is clammy. The tank top and shorts that cling to my skin are damp and wrinkled.

I'm supposed to meet Markie for a girl's night in an hour. I better hurry. I told that weird friend of hers from work that I wasn't going to make it, but I changed my mind after debating all week. The decision is made, I'm going. Markie is one of my closest friends, but she's changed since Beth died. She's distanced herself. Now, with everything else going on around her, I'm afraid.

As the water heats, steam fills my shower and escapes through the bathroom door that I usually leave open. I like stepping out of the shower feeling clean and refreshed, not muggy and overheated. I think about Markie's situation as I rub an oversized purple body sponge across my skin. A delicious scent of lather forms on my protruding ribs and bony hips. The stress of all these deaths has taken a serious toll on my appetite. My body is shrinking, from its once curvy appearance. I'm beginning to look sickly.

I wonder how I'm supposed to tell Markie that I've been sleeping with the one acquaintance that's off limits. I guess I can't. Not now anyway, it will have to wait. I should feel worse about it than I do, but he's convenient, and I'm lonely. He'll do for now. It must be the guilt of it that's forcing me to go to this stupid club tonight. Any smart woman would stay away.

My fingers scrub harshly into my scalp. I squint my eyes tightly, trying to block out the shampoo as it washes away. Before they can fully open, the shower door slides open. A shocked gasp rises from my throat, and I force my lids open through a painful soapy haze. The air escapes my lungs in a slow, relieved sigh. I take in the sight of him. He stands naked with a grin, ready to join me.

"What the hell are you doing?" I demand.

"What does it look like?"

"You scared the shit out of me!"

"You're pretty sexy when you're startled."

"I really don't have time for this." I snap back at him, "I'm in a hurry."

He pushes his way in anyway and shuts the door behind him. He stays just out of reach of the spraying shower head and watches me wash off. My back tingles and the blood rushes to my skin's edge in reaction to his touch. The last of the soap bubbles disappear into the drain at our toes. He raises my leg at the thigh, and then presses me forward against the shower wall.

With one hard thrust he forces himself inside me. Its a lot rougher than his usual tactic. I gasp and press my hands against the wall for balance. He moves violently, but I like it. His strong fingers are intertwined through my wet hair at the base of my scalp, then he pulls it, hard. My head jerks back with the powerful tug. A quiet, excited, involuntary squeal escapes my open mouth. I can feel his hot breath on the back of my neck.

"You like it hard, don't you Joyce?" His voice is lower than I've ever heard him speak.

"Yes!"

For the first time in my life, I get a thrill from hearing my name. He releases his hold on my hair and then shoves me back against the wall. A firm arm presses against my back. I'm unable to move my chest or shoulders, as am forced to take him in on his terms. Just as I'm about to crumble under his strong hold, a menacing whisper echoes in my ear.

"This is going to hurt."

A shock pools toward my center and a chill runs down my spine. It takes every ounce of strength that I have to pull away from him. He squeezes my body tightly against his own. Then he loosens his grip, allowing me to turn and face him.

"What are you talking ab—"

A sudden pain consumes my neck, cutting me off mid-question. My voice catches in the center of my throat and is unable to escape. Instinctively, I grab hold of the sharp pulsating pain and squeeze. The fluid filling my hands and running down my arms is much thicker and hotter than the shower water. Everything is beginning to blur. I look at him, trying to plead with my eyes. I'm unable to speak. I lean against the wall, to regain balance. Everything is spinning. I pull my bloody hands from my neck and look at them. My vision is distorted, but not enough to disable the sight of color. My scarlet fingers spin and blur.

I feel cold. I want to grab him, beg for his help, but I can't. My body slumps down against the wall. My legs become weaker and weaker. *What have you done to me?* I scramble through the black and red blur, struggling to see his face. For a flash, I see him. His head is tilted to one side and his face is blank. A hint of a smirk forms across his lips. I black out. I can still feel but I can't see. I pull in breath with short shallow pants. I can hear an awkward gurgle coming out of my throat. My body is ice cold under the hot running water.

My life slowly drains away, yet a sharp digging pain reminds me that I'm still alive. One piercing jab after another jolts into my ribs, chest and stomach. I try to kick, throw my arms up in defense and scream, but can't. I can't move. It only takes a few more jolts to realize that I'm being stabbed. Over and over the shock spreads across my body.

After what seems like a lifetime of torturing pain, it finally fades. A faint sensation is left at my neck. There's something touching my midsection, something inside it. That too melts away until there is nothing left. I don't feel anything anymore – no pain, no fear. I give up the struggle for breath and let myself go to the darkness.

Chapter One

MARKIE

"Nice pants." Kam smirks, with an amused lift in her right brow.

I look down at the tight brown shiny leather that's hugging my thighs, as it bunches uncomfortably at the knees.

"That bad?" I ask.

Blood rushes to my cheeks. I feel the heat rise into a thick red blush.

"Not at all!" She giggles, sarcasm is radiating. "I'm quite sure brown leather would be my first choice for a blind date, too."

When it comes to picking out clothing, I find it easier just to stick with basic, simple, and plain. If it were not for my sister, I'd surely be the laughing stock of South Brooke, Florida. Brushing off her sarcasm has become easier throughout our lives. I've come to accept the fact that she will always have quicker wit than me. Although, I do try keeping up with her jokes, I still find myself

coming up short in the playful banter department. For the most part, I have learned to blow
off snide comments, and take them with a grain
of salt. At least she keeps my life interesting. I've
never had to worry about dull quiet moments, or
that 'awkward silence' as she calls it.

"Well then, fashion princess, what exactly
would you suggest?"

It's hard to understand her through her muffled giggle.

"No really, Markie, you should totally stick
with what you have on! I would love to see this
man try to take you seriously… you know… his
sexy date in a pair of cheap rocker chic, vintage
leather pants."

She no longer tries to muffle the humor rising
in her chest. Its now full on rolling laughter, bubbling and rising out of her full, perfectly glossed
lips. The skin around her baby blues bunches
adorably in the corners. Water forms inside her
eyes, threatening to spill over.

"Wait!" She shouts. Her face hardens, and
mouth drops. "Oh my God, Markie."

"What?" I stare at her, my belly is filled with suspense, as I wait for an explanation for her dramatics.

"You have to take a look at your camel toe!" Again, laughter pours out.

My response is flat, "you're a dick."

I scowl and sulk, standing still, with my shoulders slumped, just waiting for her outburst to die down.

"You're trying to embarrass me and it's not going to work."

Not only is the slick leather sticking to my legs, but it makes an unavoidable swishing noise as I shift on my feet. Kam stands up from her seated position, on the corner of my bed with grace and ease. She moves with a smooth, superb athletic motion. Walking tall with confidence across my bedroom floor, she disappears into the closet. My whole life, I have been jealous of her grace. Tall and tan with an hourglass shape, is the perfect description for Kam.

All the while I've spent a lifetime cursed with a pale pasty skin tone, aside from the occasional sunburn that is, when I change to the purple-red shade of a boiled beet. My hair is unmanageable, thick and frizzy, my feet are big, and my legs are short and squat. Kam is right, these pants do absolutely no justice for my distinct shape. I stare down at the ridiculous attire hugging all the wrong curves. I thought they were appropriate for the occasion when I had picked them out. Shit, was I wrong.

Upon emerging from the closet, Kam shoves a pair of fitted black slacks into my arms, along with a tasteful floral print top and a light jean jacket. She grins proudly.

"Here, sweet pea. I'm sure you can find some shoes on your own. Or do you need me to help you with that too?"

I scan every inch of her smug face, straining my thoughts for some equally smart remark. After a few short moments of waiting in silence, Kam lifts an eyebrow and cocks her head to the side sarcastically. Her waiting ear turns ever so slowly, inching its way in my direction. More so disappointed at my own lack of a better response, I grunt.

"I think I'll be fine, thanks!"

"You know that annoyed, blank, 'I'm in deep thought' expression you have? It's one of my favorites."

"Yeah, you've pointed that out before... isn't there somewhere else you're supposed to be right now?" I ask, only sort of teasing.

"Nope." She grins, sitting on top of the world.

I retreat, back into the closet to change. I'm not about to let her watch me struggle out of the brown leather. Thinking about the night ahead holds no comfort for me. It isn't exactly a blind date. I have met this guy before and wasn't impressed. When my best friend was killed last summer, I'd let myself slip into the role of her parent's newfound daughter. Of course, they set up this whole date, and I was too nice to say no.

I've always been close to Beth's family, especially her parents. Beth's mother, Trish, is sweet and her father, Spence, is a comfortable man to be around. Never in the thirty-two years of friendship I had with Beth were they ever rude or unwelcoming to me.

We grew up as neighbors and were completely inseparable since the year we were born. Up until last year, that is, when her life was brutally taken. Not a day goes by that I don't remember the petrified look on her bloody, lifeless face. She was stabbed twenty-seven times and left dead on her kitchen floor. There was so much blood I hardly recognized my dress hanging from her body in torn pieces. I found her the morning after she was attacked. The fear of her killer remaining at large sits on my shoulders, weighing me down to this day.

Kam's loud voice rings in my ears.

"Are you okay in there?"

Crap, I'm spacing out again. I've done this a lot since Beth's murder. Everything reminds me of her, and the thought of her death makes me freeze up like a deer in headlights.

"Um, yeah," I mumble back quietly, as I slip on the floral top.

"You could have told them no, you know. You don't have to go out with this guy if you think he's a creep. You're too nice to them."

"I know, Kam." I appreciate my sister's concern, but my God, I'm tired of this conversation.

"Why do you let them treat you like you're Beth? It's not a healthy way for them to grieve, you know. And by letting them, you're just as bad as they are."

After stepping out of the closet, I hold up two different pairs of black heels. Maybe I really do need her help with the shoes. Kam's eyes roll slowly. She's being far too dramatic. She points to the opened toe choice in my left hand.

"Thanks," I mumble, "and I can't help it. You know that. What am I supposed to say to them? 'I'm not your dead daughter, remember?'"

Irritated, I slip on the heels. This conversation is the last thing I need. It's a bad way to start off what's bound to be an altogether shitty night anyway.

"No, dummy, just say it nicely. Tell them that you appreciate all the crap they buy you, and the dinners, and the phone calls, but that you need your space. Remind them you're Markie, not Beth. This is totally the kind of date they would have set her up on."

"I can't, Kam. Not yet anyway, it's too hard. Do we really need to talk about this?"

"I think we do, yes."

"You are so damn stubborn. How is it that we're related again?"

"Ha. Ha. Real funny."

The concern in her eyes doesn't match the pushy words spewing from her lips. She's a sweet soul. She's honest and straightforward, no matter the cost. I'm constantly annoyed and jealous of both qualities. I never have been able to pull either of them off.

"Anyway," the bunched-up skin on her nose smooths out as she changes the subject. "What if we have some sort of backup plan? For this whole date night? I could call you and pretend there's an emergency of some sort. Or maybe you could have a code word that secretly means come and bail me out."

"That's not a bad idea, actually."

At least she's resourceful, I think, while admiring the clothing choice in the full-length mirror leaning against my wall. Not too dressy, and not too casual. It's a good mix.

"So, what will it be?" She asks, as she holds her fingers to her chin. "What if I say we had a small kitchen fire, or I fell down the stairs and need a ride to the hospital or something?"

"Hmmm," I can't help but chuckle at her plotting. "I like the fire idea. Then I can leave in a bit of a hurry and act irritated. It's not really an emergency he can help me with, but it's one that I still have to leave the date for."

"Deal!" Kam is sitting tall, holding her head high in pride and excitement at the scheme. "When did you meet this guy, anyway?"

"He was at one of those real estate sale things Beth used to drag me to all the time. She spoke to him when we first got there. I guess their parents are friends, so they knew each other as kids."

I fall back onto my bed, letting my arms go limp at my sides, completely relaxed. Kam is so easy to talk to, even if she is a pain in the ass. She's a natural listener, and she always cares about everyone around her.

"I thought he was cute at first, but then he followed us around the rest of the day. I caught him staring at us. I don't know. I guess he just came off as kind of strange to me."

"Are you sure it's the same guy?"

"Yeah, Trish showed me his picture."

"Why didn't you just tell her no then?"

"Here we go again."

I pull myself up and make my way toward the door, not that it does any good. Kam follows me out and keeps at it, as usual. She mumbles and nags. Her toes almost clip my heels with each step, as she crams words of unwelcome advice down the back of my neck, on the way down the hall, past the living room, and to the front door. Having my sister as a roommate has its perks and downfalls.

"Just call me in an hour and get me out of this mess, okay?"

"Fine!" She snaps back in defeat.

Hanging by the door on a small hook are the keys to my black Tahoe. Beth helped me pick it out the week before she died. I hate it now. Not only have I had to replace one thing after another, but it's also a total gas hog. Don't even get me started on the size. In what world would I ever need an SUV? Kam has tried talking me into trading it in on a regular basis. As does my crazy mother, but her motives are just for show. I can't do it though, Beth loved it. She couldn't afford a new car of her own, so she talked me into buying just the kind of vehicle she wanted.

I let her drive the damn thing everywhere we went for that whole week. She even stayed sober to drive us home the night it happened, just so she could be seen leaving the club in it. Trading it in now would feel like I'm betraying her in some way. So, I just deal with its troubles, and try to convince myself that Beth would be right at my side telling me how hot we look in it.

Kam stands in the driveway as I pull out, holding a hand on a popped-out hip with attitude. She glares at the front grill of my car. It wouldn't take a rocket scientist to tell what's on her irritated, concerned mind. Shaking off an eerie feeling, I swallow the bile rising in my throat, and then drive away. *What does Kam know, anyway? The Jones' are good people. They would never send me on a date with a weirdo.*

It doesn't matter that my first impression wasn't perfect. That had to have been at least four or five years ago. Who knows what was going on with him that day, or even myself, come to think of it. I've always considered Beth's dad to be a very down to earth kind of man. Surely, he would know if there was anything wrong with this Vincent guy. It doesn't matter now, I'm going on this damn date whether I want to or not. I continue to convince myself that everything is fine for the remainder of the drive.

17

The first thought on my mind as I pull into the place is lower middle class. The name *Frenchie's* is plastered on the front of the building in bold red paint. Its also printed on all of the windows and doors. It was clearly decorated with care and intention, as if the owners had put their entire life savings into it. Cars are lined in perfectly slanted spaces next to mine. I can't help but notice that not one of them looks to be any newer than five or six years old. The people coming in and out are dressed in the kind of clothing that screams 'desperate date'.

Wives are wearing worn out dresses and forced smiles. Husbands in button up tops, opening doors with their heads down and mouths shut. I imagine these people have boring, average lives, and boring, average jobs. They probably need to get out of their everyday routine so badly they ache, yet they can't afford anything more than two hours with a high school babysitter and a $10 plate of spaghetti. What better place than a small local restaurant named *Frenchie's*? A pang of guilt hits me for the way I am judging these people. Just because I don't want to be here, it doesn't give me the right to break down strangers.

Killing time and spacing out in pointless observation, isn't doing anything but prolonging the inevitable. My chest rises and falls in a deep effort to de-stress. Of course, it doesn't work. I'm so nervous my bowels are churning. Perfect, just perfect, not only am I actually allowing myself to go on a blind date with a possible creep, but I may shit myself while I'm at it.

I whisper lightly under my breath, "Dammit Beth, why the hell did you have to leave me? Next time I'm definitely putting my foot down and telling your mom no."

Finally, I shut down the engine to the hog. I roll down the windows, as usual, secretly hoping it will be stolen. I leave it behind in the surprisingly full parking lot. My shoes make a light tapping sound, as my feet slowly drag my unwilling body up the narrow sidewalk. The hinges squeak on the door as I pull it open. The bell hanging above the door sounds. I've always hated that.

Bells, honestly, what purpose do they serve except to draw unnecessary and unwanted attention? I've always felt bad for employees that work at facilities with these ridiculous bells. I think if I had to listen to that noise all day long, it would likely wind me up so tight that I'd snap.

I search the inside of the diner, looking in every direction. I was told he would be wearing a black button up top and holding a small bouquet of daisies. Trish must have told him that it's my favorite flower; *how convenient.* I spot him quickly. He's sitting two tables away from the door, with the bouquet in hand. He is much more handsome than I remember. Maybe he's just one of those freaks who's actually aged well. Trish told me that he's pushing thirty five, – which is only two years older than myself, but I'd never guess that now seeing him in person. He could easily pass for a good ten years younger.

A grin spreads across his cheeks as he waves me in his direction with confidence. The smile I return to him is as forced as the women I observed from the parking lot. *Take a breath, here we go, I can manage an hour.* Kam better pull through on her promise, or there will be some serious sabotage in order. It's not like I've never put flaming hot peppers in her drink when she wasn't looking. I may even go a step further and put food dye in her shampoo and conditioner. I've been waiting on an excuse to try that one out anyway.

"You look as beautiful as I remember, Markie."

"Thank you, Vincent, that's very kind."

If he only knew the smile on my face is in response to my silent plotting against my sister, and not him.

"Please have a seat." He gestures. "Your necklace is very pretty."

"Wow, thank you." *Strange compliment*, I think. Though it caught me off guard, I still somehow appreciate the sentiment. "It's a locket my mom gave me a few years back."

I'm not about to go into detail on how Beth had one exactly like it, or about her picture that's inside it. I'm especially not going to tell him the reason my mother bought us a matching set. Her words of insult regarding my lack of better accessories flash through my mind. Beth and I actually wore them as a joke at first, thinking it was funny to act out against my mother's uppity attitude.

After a while, the lockets kind of became an ironic symbol of our friendship, go figure. I rub the small golden heart shape between my thumb and forefinger. It dangles elegantly from my neck. It's no lie, the necklace truly is an exquisite piece. Crazy she may be, but my mother sure can accessorize.

I lower myself into the open chair that he so graciously slid out for me. At first the conversation is light. We talk about the weather, and the drink choice on the menu, which is very limited might I add. Vincent has a low, quiet, irresistibly sultry voice. The scent of his cologne is divine. Filling my nostrils every time he moves, I breathe it in deep. Leaning forward, I let the smell consume me. I don't remember him being this desirable.

He speaks with confidence and holds his head high. I even find myself checking out the toned muscular shape of his chest and arms. I wonder if he would look as good with his shirt off as he does with it on. I stare into his soft grey eyes and listen to him explain the ins and outs of his mundane office job. Vincent spends the majority of his time processing paperwork at a large law firm downtown. Apparently, he finds small, family owned restaurants like *Frenchie's* to be comforting, like a home away from home. As he explains the reason for his choice in diner, I kick myself inside for being so arrogant and judgmental when I first arrived.

Time is flying, our conversation flows easily. I tell him about my time-consuming career at the Mix That Movie Multiplex. I've managed the four-theater movie house for several years, and I've loved every single one of them. I started working there when I was nineteen as a regular clerk, selling movie tickets and popcorn. At the time there was only one big screen with a crack down the middle, along with rundown used seats.

I kept at it for a few years until I completed my degree. It just so happened that the very week of my graduation the manager up and left, she quit very unexpectedly. I was instantly promoted into the position, and I've held it ever since. Vincent seems genuinely impressed, and is interested in the details of my theater. He even asks questions about the changes and upgrades that I've overseen along the way.

I'm in the middle of explaining our second expansion when the ringtone of my phone nearly sends me through the roof. I jump an inch off my seat, and Vincent chuckles. His short-lived humor comes out as a choppy high-pitched snort. Cute, and he is even cuter when he laughs. Has it been an hour already? A half consumed, surprisingly delicious French dip sits on a square dinner plate in front of me. The roast beef is fresh, and the bread is melt in your mouth perfection. At this very moment, I want nothing more than to finish this delicious meal.

I'm tempted to ignore the call altogether. Knowing Kam, she'd probably show up with guns blazing, ready to "cap a bitch" – or so she'd say as she storms through the door. After running the likely scenario through my head, I decide it's best to pick up.

"Hello?" I answer as cheerfully as possible, hoping she'll catch the tone.

"Markie, you have to come home right now!"

Panic radiates in her voice. I must admit, I'm slightly impressed with her acting skills.

"I'm sure everything is fine, Kam. I'm actually having a really good time. Is there any way you can handle things on your own?"

I don't want to give myself away. I try to sound as normal as anyone would with a random, panicked sister phone call.

"No really! It's not a fire, or a stair incident, it's our neighbors. The Snyder family, across the street. Something scary is going on. Cops and ambulances are swarming the block, Markie! Get your ass home now, you have to be here with me!"

"Is this for real?"

Adrenaline thumps in my chest. I can feel my face bunch and tighten. Images of Beth's bloody face flash through my memory. Last time I saw a group of police officers with ambulances present, I watched them drive away with my best friend in a body bag. Her murder was too recent not to panic every time I see flashing lights.

"If you're making this shit up Kam, I'm... I'm... I'll..." My voice cracks, and my eyes water.

Fear, panic, and raw memory paw at the pit of my stomach.

"I swear, Markie, just come home now, okay?"

"I'm on my way."

The phone clicks off in my palm, and I shove it into my purse. The look on Vincent's face instantly strikes me as odd. As I search for words to explain my sister's phone call, he seems strangely amused. The corner of his lip curls upward. The wrinkles above his eyes smooth away, and a flat forehead reveals a pleased little twinkle. Is he happy I am leaving, or excited about my concern? I can't tell. *This is awkward.* What is his deal? I kind of want to smack him right now. Not a hard smack. Just a little backhand to the mouth. Enough to knock that smug little grin off his handsome face.

Chapter Two

"I'm really sorry I have to leave like this." Refusing to look into Vincent's excited eyes, I give my apologies to the table.

"No problem, really." He replies with a stomach-churning grin. "Can I call you sometime? I'd love to do this again if you're up for it."

I stumble over myself, "I…um…yeah."

The date has been great so far. After calming myself, I quickly decide that his odd behavior might have been caused by lack of understanding. Against my better judgment, I take the pen he has ready for me. I scribble my number on a cheap napkin and slide it in his direction. Without another word, I turn away. I can feel his eyes piercing my backside like daggers. An uncomfortable chill slides down my spine. I can hear his low, sensual voice over my shoulder. It follows me as I walk away from the table.

"Good luck with your emergency," he whispers.

I decide against any sort of response and speed toward the door refusing to look back at my strange, handsome date. Clicking shoes against the concrete, carry me quickly down the walkway and into my SUV. *Keys, where the hell are my keys?* My shaking fingers fumble through my messy purse. I can't help but think of Beth. I imagine her always calming voice telling me to slow down. I dump the contents of my purse on the empty passenger seat, then I grab my keys as soon as they hit the cushion. A relieved sigh escapes me.

As the engine turns I look up, only to have my heart drop to my toes. The air catches in my chest as we lock eyes. Vincent is staring at me with that inappropriate crooked grin. He stands on the inside of a giant window only a few yards away from me. The name, *Frenchie's*, is printed in the window directly above his head. His eyes are wide, chest puffed, and his hands are shoved deep in his pockets. He holds my gaze.

The moment is creepy, it feels wrong. His smile widens as he pulls a large hand from his pocket to give me a small, childlike wave. I wave back slowly. My face heats up, and my brows bunch together in the middle. Nearly slamming the gas pedal to the floor, I speed away, refusing to look in the rear view.

I'm not usually one to speed or break the law at all, for that matter. Right now, I don't care, I rush home. I'm completely beside myself, lost in thought. My foot is pushing hard. It shoves the pedal into the floor, painfully squishing my toes out of the small hole at the tip of my shoe. Headlights stream by me with a blur. I slow down only for the few red lights along the way, and I make it home in record time.

The neighborhood is a mess, in every sense of the word. Police cars are parked in front of practically every other house. As I look around, I notice flashlights shining in bushes and sheds. My block especially is utter chaos. Streetlights light up the faces of my neighbors as they stand on well-manicured lawns in front of their homes. Confusion and fear fills the air. I'm driving through a cloud of anxiety, with peering eyes staring at me as I pass. It's a struggle, but I spot Kam.

She's standing on the sidewalk in front of our house with her arms crossed. Her face is pale, it's the lightest shade I've ever seen on her. She is staring directly across the road, past the abundance of authorities, and into the open door of the Snyder home. Her posture is hunched over and sickly. I pull into the driveway carefully, waiting for her to run up to me, but she doesn't. She doesn't move or avert her eyes in any way.

With my head down looking only at my feet, I jog to her side. A large part of me doesn't want to see what Kam's so engrossed by. Somehow, I already know. I just know deep inside that it's happened again. Grabbing her by the shoulders, I give her entire body one rough shake.

"Kam!" I yell. "Snap out of it!"

"They...they...they finally opened the door." A quiet slur.

Her stare remains locked in place. I close my eyes as tight as I can. My head turns toward the Snyder home, then after letting out an anxious lungful of air I open them. Fog takes over my mind, and my body ignites in an overbearing fire. It's Breanna. One of the friendliest, most outgoing teenagers I know. She was the oldest child in the Snyder home. She was a beautiful young woman, now lifeless.

Standing next to Kam, peering across the street and into their home, I can clearly see her mutilated body. Their front doors are French, and opened wide, allowing a perfect view into their once tidy entryway. Breeana's mother is a stickler for bleached white floors, and they're now completely covered in scarlet splatters and pools of blood. That must have been exactly where the attack took place. Right inside the front door, for God's sake. I can only imagine her killer's tactic, pushing their way in as she greeted them with an innocent welcome. Sick. Disgusting. This is completely unfathomable.

The once full of life girl is slumped backwards over a round decorative table. Her legs are bare, and full of slashes. A slow steady drip is still running down her arms and escaping into the floor from her fingertips. Clinging to her body are the remnants of a spaghetti strap tank top, and short pajama bottoms. I can't even tell their original color. My mind wanders briefly away from the present. I picture those pj's were a lovely shade of green, and the smile on her face was genuine.

The thought lasts only a second before my mind snaps back to reality. Like a rubber band pulling itself into place, my head twitches and my lips let out a frightened gasp. Breanna must have been relaxing comfortably in what should have been a safe home. Bile rises from my stomach and into my throat. I swallow it and continue to stare. I'm unable to look away, unable to process the scene in front of me.

Just like Beth was, every inch of her is stained in thick red fluid. This killer is bleeding them out. Every drop of life drained from the victims. Its vicious, and it is personal. I look closer. There's a shine on her chest. It reflects light from the bright police LED lights placed a few feet away from her. Something is resting around her neck. Small and gold. I wonder how it is possible that she has jewelry on that could still hold a shine. *How is there no blood on the top of her necklace?*

"Can you see her necklace?" I whisper under my breath to Kam.

"All I see is blood."

Her response comes out flat and dry. I can hear the dehydrated click as her tongue hits the roof of her parched mouth.

"Do you think this has anything to do with Beth?" She asks, even flatter in tone, as the tears finally spill over.

"I don't know, Kam, but it feels the same."

We hold one another's gaze. The moisture of a lone tear runs down my cheek. It rolls slowly over my foundation and hits the corner of my mouth. I can taste the salt as I touch the tip of my tongue to my lip's edge.

"What do we do?" She asks.

I respond only with a hug. She grabs on tightly, and softly sobs into my shoulder. We stand in shock and confusion. A nicely suited man approaches us. He is guarded, moving slowly, with his head tilted toward his chest. It's a relief to recognize his kind eyes as his head lifts, allowing his face to come into focus. Phillip is his name, Detective Phillip Sharpe, but he always insists on just Phil. I had gotten to know him well in the first few months following Beth's murder. He's a gracious, sympathetic man, and very thorough. No detail is too small or unimportant to him. He has been at our home many times, and must have seen me pull in.

"Markie, I'm sorry we have to meet again under these circumstances."

"Detective."

I reach for his open hand, and let him shake my own in a professional manner.

"I know how hard this must be for you to see."

"It's the same killer, isn't it? The same person who killed Beth?" The question slips out.

Still beside myself, I have no control over my mindless words.

"I'm not sure, ma'am. It's too soon to tell, and until the crime scene has been fully processed we can't be certain on anything."

I can only manage a nod in response. I understand the drill all too well. Looking around, I notice the officers asking each neighbor to go back into their houses. Slow moving families herd up their clinging children and retreat into their homes. Porch lights stay on and windows stay lit. There will be no sleep on this once peaceful street. I turn to the detective and attempt to calm my nerves. I need to get as much information as possible. If this is the same guy, then I must know everything. *I have to.*

"I can see she was stabbed just like Beth. It has to be him." I insist.

"Markie, I'm going to have to ask you…"

I cut him off before he has a chance to say anything else.

"No! I'm not going inside. I'm not going to walk away. This man killed my best friend and now my neighbor. She was seventeen!"

My voice rises louder with every word. Kam gives my hand a tight squeeze as I voice my frustration.

"You have to find him. You have to stop this!"

"Ma'am," Detective Sharpe interrupts me softly and respectfully, with a hand raised. "I wasn't going to ask you go in your home, actually quite the opposite." His eyebrows lift slowly in sympathetic caution, as the rest of his face levels. "I know this is a lot to ask, and if you're not up for it I completely understand," he pauses briefly. "With all of the similarities in this crime scene and in Beth's, I feel it might be beneficial for us if you come with me and take a look."

"What do you mean? A look?"

"I mean…" again with the irritating pause. "It is strange that two completely different young women have been killed this way. Beth and Breanna are opposite of each other in nearly every way. The only similarity they share, Markie, as far as we can tell, is you."

The detective's last sentence comes out slow and guarded.

He ducks his head slightly as he pushes out the statement. It hits me like a truck. He's right. They had nothing in common and were nothing alike. As far as I know, they had never even met each other.

"So, what's that supposed to mean?" I ask quietly.

I'm not so sure if my question is aimed at him or myself.

Kam chimes in with a panicked squeak.

"Yeah! What the hell?"

"That's exactly what I'm trying to figure out. We have a lot of work to do, and I feel it best that we do it together."

"Okay." I agree while holding my head high and straightening my shoulders. "Let's do this then. I'll do whatever I can."

I may look brave on the outside, which is exactly what I'm going for, but inside I feel like a lost, hopeless child. Every bone in my body shakes with fear and vulnerability. I'm rocked with an overwhelming sense of helplessness.

"Wait!" Kam yells, holding her ground. "I can't go over there. I can't do this, please don't leave me alone."

"Kam, we have to."

I try to comfort my frightened little sister. She's usually the stronger and more confident of the two of us, yet here she stands, shaking and pleading.

Detective Sharpe whistles loudly, drawing the attention of several nearby officers. He motions one over with a wave of his arm. He instructs the cop to stay with Kam, then he places a hand on the small of my back. His other arm is held out in front of us. The long, well-groomed fingers of his right hand point toward the gruesome truth across the street. I shudder, take a step off the sidewalk, and cross the road. We move in the same motion, one with the other, our footsteps in sync. He leads me through the crowded lawn, and we stop at the door abruptly, so as not to disrupt any key evidence inside the bloodied entryway. My eyes go straight to the necklace I had noticed before. My throat is as dry as sandpaper.

"Oh my God." I croak.

On instinct, my hand reaches to my collar and grabs the gold chain hanging around my neck. I pull the locket out from under my shirt. My fingers tremble and cling to the gold heart, I gasp for a breath. The air around me closes in, I struggle for oxygen. My bottom lip trembles involuntarily. It feels as if I'm being strangled by this cherished item I have clung to for so long. Detective Sharpe watches my display with eyes wide.

"Markie." His voice is slow and steady. "Let me see your necklace."

My quivering hand drops, and I stare into his eyes. He makes the connection. I'm certain that he is reading my mind as his face lightens a shade. Placed on top of Breanna's chest, and dangled around her already bloodied body, is Beth's matching heart locket. He points to the dead body inches away.

"Is that Beth's necklace?" He asks, already knowing the answer.

"Yes." I force out an answer.

Again, I'm beside myself. Talking through a foggy haze of grief. The detective glances back and forth between the dead teen and myself. His lips are pursed. The color returns to his face in full force. He's clearly at a loss for words.

"It gets worse." I continue.

"How could this possibly get any worse?"

"Beth's locket was hanging from the corner of my bathroom mirror this morning."

Chapter Three

After the police are finished with a full sweep of our home, Kam and I decide to stay together in the living room rather than retire to our separate beds. Flashing lights beam into the windows for hours, we stay awake. Our conversation is deep and emotional.

We share memories, of Beth mostly. We even compare Breanna to the friends we had as teenagers. The constant red and blue invasion is surprisingly welcomed, given the situation. It makes me feel somewhat safer to be surrounded by alert and eager law enforcement.

I know the killer won't come close, at least not for tonight. It's the thought of tomorrow, and the day after, that holds my attention. Detective Sharpe assured me that I'll be tailed by at least one officer at all times. Day and night, I'll be watched and "protected."

Surely, it'll get old, but for now the thought of an officer close is comforting. It's a long, restless night. We drink a couple bottles of wine, one cool, crisp glass after another. We laugh a little and cry a lot.

Kam teases, "remember that time Beth locked you in the closet for two full hours, until you agreed to go to some sports bar with her?"

"Yes!" I giggle through my wine flavored, post-cry phlegm. "How she was able to move those dressers in front of the door still baffles me."

"I remember watching her sit at your vanity table, fluffing her hair, and piling on that thick scarlet lipstick. It was no trouble for her at all to completely ignore your pounding on the closet door." Kam huffs with a slightly turned up lip and continues her recollection. "She only looked away from that mirror once until you caved in, and it was to yell at me for trying to move the dresser and help you out."

"It was a horrible bar, too." I fill Kam in on the rest of my cherished memory. "She wanted to meet up with some guy she met the week before. We drove two hours to get there, and by the time we walked in, Prince Charming was piss-ass-drunk." I stop and chuckle, struggling to make it through the rest of the story. "I mean literally! He had a giant wet spot on his chaps, and a chunk of vomit on his ball cap."

Kam catches herself as she nearly falls off her chair. Her rolling laughter is comforting. A cute little snort escapes from the back of her nose.

"Oh my God!" She bellows. "How the hell did he get puke on his hat?"

"I don't know, maybe it fell off of his head while he was barfing."

She stops cackling only to let out a long, drawn-out sigh.

"She sure could pick 'em, couldn't she?"

"Yes." I concur.

That girl had a taste for sweet talking losers. They were always real charmers right out of the gate, but it never took long for Beth to acquire a huge disappointment. I catch myself staring blankly at the black, powered down TV sitting across the room.

"I really miss her." I quietly declare.

"You know, I was always jealous of her."

"What?" I ask, completely taken by surprise at Kam's confession. "Why?"

"Because of how close you two were."

The look on Kam's face is one of loss, regret, and confusion all rolled into one emotion.

"Of all my friends, I've never had one that close. Not only that, but you are *my* sister. I just knew deep down that you liked her more than me."

Wow. I don't know what to say, or what to think. Not a word of comfort for Kam comes to mind. I want to pull her close, to hold her, and tell her that she has always been my favorite. But, I can't do it. Truth be told, I was closer to Beth than her. Beth was my family. All I can do now is blankly gawk at my vulnerable little sister.

"I'm sorry," I whisper.

And just like that, our reminiscing is over for the night. It took months after Beth's attack before I could sleep a full night through. I know this time will be even worse. It's like living the past all over again. Breanna's murder has pulled everything back to the surface. It reopened a wound that will never fully heal, making the pain of losing my best friend feel just as fresh, as if it happened yesterday.

Every fear I've ever had about this creep is surfacing, and it's intensified. Not only is the killer still out there, but they somehow have a personal vendetta for me. *They've been in my home!*

Before my nerve is lost, I make a split decision to send a quick text to Trish. It's impersonal, I know, but it must be done. I can't grieve properly, or move forward with my life, unless I break contact… neither can she. Like a Band-Aid I have rip it off, feel the sting and move on. *God, I hope they understand.* I type the words quickly:

'Trish, I love you so much. You are such an important part of my life, so please understand. Recent events have stirred up the loss of Beth in so many ways. I need to distance myself from you in order to cope. Please don't call or text, I will get ahold of you in a few weeks, when the dust has settled, and I can emotionally handle things. I love you and Spence, thanks again for everything. We have a lot to talk about when I'm capable.'

Gulp. There, I did it. I read the message through a few times and then press send.

As I lie next to Kam, wide awake on the pull-out mattress of our couch. I imagine the killer as a man. He's been in our house, rummaged through my things, and took the most personal

44

item possible. I wonder if he knew it was Beth's necklace, or if he just seen the picture of us together inside of it?

It doesn't matter either way, the fact remains that whoever it was, they'd targeted Beth and Breanna on purpose, and linked them through me. I am sick. Acid churns in my belly, threatening to bubble up. Prickly hairs on my legs are standing on edge. It's a disgusting reminder of the lack of interest I had in meeting Vincent.

I close my eyes tightly. Trying to shake the paranoia running through my brain, is proving itself an impossible task. I'm unable to shut out the horrific images or stop imagining the killer in my home. It's approaching 2:00 A.M. and Kam has finally dozed off. The heat from her sleeping body warms the covers. It's making me sweat. Cold, sultry dampness is pushing its way out. My back and chest are sticky.

Great, as if my racing mind isn't enough of an adrenaline boost, now I'm too hot for my body to relax. My legs offer a short awkward spasm, kicking off the blankets. It helps, but not enough. The fact that I'm still awake is irritating. Tomorrow is going to be a very long day. I picture my mother and her inevitable presence. She'll surely beat Detective Sharpe here, and he promised to show up before 8:00. We have a lot to cover, the detective and me.

My mom is the pushiest woman I know. She was born into a very rich family, in a mostly upper-class community. Her parents were never around, leaving her and my uncle, whom I've never even met, to be raised by a well-paid nanny. She was brought up to spoiled, and down-right rotten. To this day, the only voice she hears is her own. My father was heaven-sent for her. That is, until they divorced when Kam and I were in our late teens. She kicked him out, and he disappeared. For their whole marriage, he was the only person able to put her in her place when she needed it. Once he was cut out of the picture, Kam and I got to know our mother for who she really is. Drama, drama, drama.

My father's common sense and independence rubbed off on us, thank God. We were raised completely different than my mother, and our personality differences are striking. My sister and I stick together on almost every issue when it comes to my mother's opinion, yet she still pushes her way into every event and situation at hand. She makes her voice heard, and her presence known. I dread the dramatics that will surely show up with her in the morning.

I've been lying awake for what seems like hours. My mind is still racing. Thoughts jet back and forth between Beth, Breanna, Detective Sharpe, and my mother. I notice a strange smell. I take a big whiff, and try to pinpoint the odor. I turn toward Kam, and again fill my nostrils. The muggy night air around her seems to be normal. She smells of fresh vanilla, as usual. I turn my head away from her and lean my face toward the edge of the mattress.

The stench is lingering. What the hell? *My God, it stinks.* Urine... It smells like pee! I wonder how we hadn't noticed it before. I try to wrap my mind around it. *Why the hell would my living room smell like piss?* Revolted, I convince myself it must have come from an officer with bad hygiene. I picture a greasy-looking, smelly, uniformed man wandering around and sitting on my furniture. A mental note is made to shampoo the couches as soon as I have a moment to spare.

3:00 A.M. approaches and I'm still awake. I have to get up. I have to move my restless bones before my heart jumps out of my chest, and before my stomach contents end up on the clean, turquoise pillow that my clammy body clings to. Rolling ever so slowly to the edge of the bed, I slip off without waking my sister. My tiptoeing feet guide me into the kitchen. I lean against the thick marble countertop and stare out the dark window above it. The flashing lights are gone.

I wonder if they have taken Breanna's body, or if it is still slumped over that table. The last glance I had at Beth's face was wretched. A thick black bag with a loud zipper shut her away from the world. We didn't even have an open casket at her funeral. Her body was too gruesome to be salvaged enough to show. My shoulders shudder as thousands of tiny bumps rise on my arms. I'm sure they have taken Breanna by now.

I quietly rummage through a thin medicine cupboard next to the fridge, until I find a small bottle of allergy medication. Why hadn't I thought of this hours ago? No one can stay awake when they take these allergy pills! I grin at my epiphany, then swallow two little red tablets. That ought to do the trick.

My muscles begin to slowly relax, and my eyelids are starting to droop. I lift my body onto the counter next to the window. My knees pull to my chest, I wrap my arms around my legs, and peer out at the yard. The neighbor's porch lights shine over the top of my fence, leaving the night much brighter than usual. It's an uncomfortable reminder of the realities surrounding me. After a few more minutes of sleepy silence, I slide off the counter and join Kam on the uncomfortably thin mattress.

The darkness of my eyelids mutes my thoughts and I drift into a strange, disturbing sleep. A giant muscle twitch jolts me awake. My head shoots to the side instantly, and I look at the giant letters on my alarm clock. I had set it on the end table next to the couch, only inches from my face. The numbers scream 4:26 with an irksome red glow.

My stomach knots. Sleep is wearing off, and it leaves me to feel the dreariness of my body. It settles down deep in my knees and elbows, even my toes and fingertips tingle. I'm reminded of the thawing feeling I got as a child when I would go directly from cold winter weather into my toasty bedroom. It was an irritating feeling then, and it is even more so now. It must be because of that damn allergy medication. I sit up involuntarily as if outside myself. Between the drowsy mind and the restless body, I move in a daze.

I wander slowly from room to room. I'm looking for something, but don't know what. Searching through the fog, I move sluggishly. All I want to do is go back to bed, to my own bed, but I can't leave Kam alone. She would wake up petrified if I was gone. I convince myself that this mindless night wandering is completely ridiculous… that is until I pass my bedroom door. It was left wide open, giving me a clear view out the window.

The tingle throughout my body intensifies, and I'm left to stand in shock. Unable to move, I stare at a black shadow of a body outside my bedroom window. With blood boiling, and heart pounding, I open my mouth to scream. Nothing comes out. Only strained air escapes my throat. My voice is completely gone, and my legs are stuck. Unable to run away, scream, or even blink,

I stare at the figure. We stand face to shadow. Kam's voice comes ringing in, loud and afraid.

"Markie! Wake up!" She yells. "Wake up, damn it!"

Chapter Four

I wake in a pool of perspiration. My face is damp and my hairline drips in thick, salty sweat. Kam sits next to me with a tight grip on my arm. She's clearly been awake for a while. She's dressed, and is holding a steaming mug in her other hand. Her eyes are bloodshot, and her hair is a mess, yet she somehow owns the look. It's as if she meant to come off as a naturally tired and stressed out beauty.

"You were screaming and kicking, Markie. Are you okay?"

"I, I… I don't know." I manage through shallow breaths.

"Well, pull yourself together. We better get this bed cleaned up before that cop with the hots for you shows up."

"I just barely went to sleep. What time is it?"

I search for my alarm clock as I speak. It's gone. Had I even put it there, or was that part of my dream? My God, I hate this delirious confusion. I'm still half asleep, and I'm lost in ex-haustion.

"Holy shit, open your eyes!" She snaps. "It's 7:30 and I've been trying to wake you up for an hour! What is wrong with you?"

"Sorry," I mumble.

I squint and shake my head. My neck rolls back and forth, trying to fight an uncontrollable sleep nod.

"I took a couple allergy pills. I really am trying. I dreamed he was here, Kam. He was standing outside my window." Her silence is bone chilling. "And what do you mean the cop with the hots for me?"

Now I'm awake. I'm fully awake, and com-pletely taken back by her statement. Her face is expressionless, downright smooth. Looking like a wax figure, her eyes are empty, staring past my face and into space.

She quietly mutters, "I had nightmares, too."

We sit in silence, I await her return to real-ity. Finally, she lets out a sigh, and turns to face me. Just like that, she's back. The corners of her mouth turn up.

"I think that detective likes you. He's cute, too, you should totally go for him."

"He doesn't like me, dumbass, he has to talk to me 'cause he's the lead detective!"

I can't help but to gripe at her. The nerve of my sister is relentless. No matter what the situation, she still finds a way to exasperate me. She does it on purpose, too, I just know it.

"You're so blind sometimes. You could have anyone you want, yet you turn down the decent guys who really like you and date losers all the time."

I rub my eyes before stretching my arms above my head.

"Whatever, Kam. You want to talk about losers, why don't you take a second look at Brock?"

"I'm serious. We talked about Beth's bad taste, but you're just like her."

Kam instantly regrets the statement. I can see the unspoken apology in her eyes.

"Anyway," she hesitates, and brushes off the guilt before continuing. "You better hurry and get up. If Detective Sharpe sees you like this, he's going to run for the hills." She teases. "And I'm not even with Brock, remember? I broke up with him a long time ago, were just friends and he'll be here in a couple hours." She rushes through the sentence as quickly as possible. The subject is changed before I have a chance to interject. "Hey, speaking of losers, how did things go with that weirdo last night?"

With all the commotion I'd completely forgotten about Vincent. I think about her question while we wiggle and twist at the fold up bed, trying to wrestle it back into its rightful place. Every time I move I can feel the stickiness of my lingering night sweat. We tuck the mattress quickly and neatly into the couch, then I answer.

"I'm not sure." With an awkward struggle I pull my messy hair into a band on the crown of my head and continue. "It was okay, I guess. He was really nice, but I don't know. After you called he acted kind of weird."

"Weird? What do you mean by weird?"

Kam shakes her head in disapproval and throws the cushions back on the couch.

As if on cue, my mother bursts through the door. I'm in no mood to talk about my date, and in even less of a mood for what's to come with our mom. *Here we go.* Kam is clearly as annoyed as myself. She rolls her eyes and lets her head fall backwards, hanging loosely at the shoulders. Her lips expand forward as she pushes a lungful of dramatic breath from them. *'Fuuuuuuck!'* She mouths to me as she lifts her head back up.

The door slams against the wall, my mom nearly swings it off the hinges. Unsurprisingly, she has on the most ridiculous outfit I've ever seen. She wears some gaudy shit sometimes, but this ensemble most definitely takes the cake. A black velvet grieving dress hangs loosely on her body. The shoulders are thickly padded, and the bottom is pleated, stopping just past the knees. Her heels are matching velvet, and her hat seems to take up half the room. A thin lace black veil hangs from the front of the hat, shadowing her face.

I'm almost sure I've seen the exact look in a fifties movie, on a rich, grieving widow at her husband's funeral. Why would anyone in their right mind own such a hat? Her hair is curled in stiff, over-sprayed locks around her chin. Even the makeup on her lightly canopied face is thick and flawless. Apparently, the woman had spent a good deal of time preparing herself for the role she's about to play.

"Oh my goodness!" She yells, flailing her arms about. "You're here and safe. My babies are safe. I have been calling you both all morning!"

The steps she's taking into the room are intentionally slow, allowing her to finish her small speech while walking in. She doesn't miss a beat. *Nice entrance, Mother, how very soap opera of you.* I'm certain that either Kam, nor I, have missed any phone calls.

"I saw what happened on the 6:00 news this morning. I can't believe you two never called me. Why am I not important enough for you to involve me in this? You know how much I loved that girl!"

"You've never even talked to her, Mom." Kam responds.

I'm far too disgusted to give her even a slight reaction. Our mother lowers herself into the loveseat, letting out a long sigh. Her arms dangle, fingertips nearly touching the floor.

"Ohhh, the Lord knows what a sweet, sweet soul she was."

Of course, she didn't hear what Kam said. She has no desire to actually talk to either of us, as usual. She merely wants herself to be seen and heard. We could call her every name in the book, staring right into her face, and she wouldn't even notice. She tunes both of us out as if our voices are an octave above her hearing level. To our mother, we're nothing more than a dog whistle or a tool to be used at her own social convenience. We both stand still and stare at her, a bit dumbfounded, and wholly irritated.

"Wow," I finally break the silence. "I have to go get dressed. Mom take off that stupid hat."

Kam jumps in instantly.

"Yeah, Mom, please. Before anyone sees you in it. It's insulting to the people who actually knew and cared about Breanna."

I slip down the hall to escape the dramatics. I drag myself into the bathroom. What a sight! I swear I'll never take allergy medication again. What was I thinking anyway? It's going to take me hours to get the distressed look from my tense face.

The outside corners of my eyes tilt down, and my tear ducts are swollen and red. Even my lips seem tight, dry, and a shade lighter than usual. Bending over the sink, I splash some cold water on my face. I opt to skip makeup after I decide my look is unfixable. I slap on a lightly tinted moisturizer; that ought to do it.

As I finish scrubbing my teeth, I glance around the mirrors edging. A large silver frame with an antique finish protects the glass. The corner that held Beth's locket just the morning before is now bare. The room feels empty – I feel empty. Without realizing it, I've been spacing off again. I briefly wonder how long I had been blankly gawking. The remaining toothpaste in my mouth swishes between my teeth. I relish the clean feeling for just a moment longer, then spit and leave the room. I should be in more of a hurry, but I just can't seem to function properly.

Hesitation grabs hold of me as I reach for my bedroom door. A flash of my dream leaves the shadow of a man imprinted on the back of my eyelids.

"Pull yourself together, Markie."

Talking to myself isn't completely out of the ordinary. It has become a very frequent occurrence since Beth died. I push the door open and stare out the window, my feet stay planted in the doorway. All that's visible is the trunk of an overgrown palm tree which sits entirely too close to my house.

As I glance around my room, anxiously wondering if anything else has gone missing, the sound of our doorbell rings through the house. It's too loud. It bounces noisily off the walls and ceiling and leaves a deafening ring in my ears.

"Shit."

I quickly step into my room, and slam the door behind me. I don't want to be anywhere close when my mother makes herself known, again, to the detective.

I change out of my yellow sleepwear shorts slowly, letting my sister deal with our guests. It's mean, I know, but what the hell? I'm sure if the situation were to repeat itself, she would do the same to me in a heartbeat. While deciding on an old pair of sturdy jeans and a loose white tee, I prepare myself for the day. A plain outfit, to match my bare face. What better way to tell Phillip Sharpe that I'm definitely not interested?

After several minutes of time killing and mental pep talks in my room, I twist the door's handle and step out to face reality. I'm pleased to see my mother has taken off the hat. I greet the detective with a professional handshake and a faux friendly smile.

"Markie, good morning." He chirps, in a particularly strange and chipper tone. "I'm glad to see your mother could make it over so early. Is there somewhere we can sit and talk?"

Weird. He's far too happy for the experience he had last night. Breanna's blood and body flashes in mind, I shudder. Fingers fiddle at his sides, and wide is his grin. He seems eager and excited. I can understand one's love for their job, but this is not the type of job that should fit that kind of description – for anyone, ever. I am baffled. It appears Detective Sharpe released the guarded, grieving reaction last night. Now he is chomping at the bit for a detective's knack and perspective. He is indisputably a strange man.

"There is nothing you can't say in front of me, sir." My mom loudly interrupts our unfitting moment.

Detective Sharpe's face drops to the floor. With a quick recovery, he flashes me a small gentle smile before turning back to her.

"Evelyn, it has been a pleasure, as usual. Now, if you'll excuse us, your daughter and I have a lot to discuss."

The detective's ability to shut my mom up, and so nicely, is nothing short of a miracle. I give an impressed huff, then I nod my head in the direction of the kitchen. The quiet, closed mouth expression of shock on my mother's face is priceless. I wish someone could take a picture.

"This way, Detective. Would you like some coffee?"

"I would love some. And, it's Phil, please."

It doesn't matter how many times he asks me to call him by his first name, I struggle with it. It's hard for me not to address him with a professional title. I'm pretty sure my sister is crazy. In all the time I've spent around him, I've never noticed him favoring me. Detective Sharpe seems to treat everyone the same. Either way, it makes no difference to me – he isn't my type. I have no reason to impress him.

Kam is sitting on the edge of the bar sipping on her coffee. The extra-large pot barely holds enough to fill a mug for myself and for the detective. I don't dare ask my sister how many cups full she's had, or even if it's the same pot I had prepared in the middle of the night.

"Go ahead and have a seat, Detective." I hope he hasn't noticed my trembling hands, or the stoned glaze of my eyes.

Kam turns to face him as soon as his rear end hits the bar stool next to her. "Sorry about our mom." She bursts.

"Trust me, I've seen worse."

"You say that now, but in ten minutes when she barges in here with another opinion, you might change your mind." She insists.

His chuckle is short and genuine, "that may be."

I join them, standing on the opposite side of the bar. The morning is unusually chilly. I can feel a small draft coming in through the open window. Even the slightest breeze cuts right through me, freezing its way up my backbone.

Without hesitation I ask, "do you know anything new, or have any idea who is doing this?"

I don't care for the small talk, and I certainly don't want to waste any time. My best friend and a neighbor are dead. Who gives a rat's ass about my mother right now, or about her opinion?

I continue. "Please tell me he left a finger-print or some hint. It's bad enough he got away with Beth, we have to stop him before he does it again."

"I'm sorry, we're still not sure on any specifics."

Boring and indirect. I swear, that must be a part of police training. Right alongside shooting their guns, a class to teach talking in circles, taught by some phony politician of the year.

"All the evidence has been taken to the lab to be processed. Whoever is doing this is meticulous. We were unable to find a single fingerprint or drop of DNA at the crime scene with Beth. So far, things look just as unclear with your neighbor."

"Shit," Kam mutters, dropping her head slightly to her chest.

"So, what's next?" I ask.

"Well, we need you to search your things, top to bottom. We need to know if anything else is missing. And I'm going to need a list of men and women that may be upset with you, or even anyone who may have acted out of the ordinary. Think hard, no detail is too small."

"Why women? You don't think a girl would be physically strong enough to do this, do you? I mean, I don't know about Breanna, but Beth was very strong. She worked out every day."

"Well, since neither victim had been sexually assaulted, we have no reason to believe these killings were rooted by any kind of sexual fantasy. Which suggests either different motives, or alternate sexual preferences."

"If it was a girl, she would have to be extremely strong. I just don't see it." I point out.

"Adrenaline can do a lot for a person's strength." He continues.

Kam intrudes. "Kind of like retard strength?"

"Oh my God, Kam!" I'm shocked at her insensitivity.

Detective Sharpe chuckles under his breath, but only one short huff. His lips straighten, and eyes grow serious. Obviously confused, he asks, "excuse me?"

"You know, like how special people are really strong. Adrenaline can do the same thing, right?"

She acts completely relaxed and normal, as if her comment was like a regular question. Detective Sharpe's gaze holds no humor, and my eyes widen in shock. My sister's lack of empathy is completely inappropriate. Knowing Kam, she had no intention of coming off as ignorant or careless. She's just the type of girl to declare whatever random thought comes to mind, no matter the time or surroundings. Along with the quick wit, she holds nothing back. She wears her heart on her sleeve, and is completely confident about whatever stupid thing bursts through her mouth.

"Well, yeah, I guess." he answers.

"To be completely honest, I can't think of a single person off the top of my head," I veer the conversation back on track.

Kam's crude outlook is thrown instantly back in the mix.

"You mean you can't even think of one really big woman? A fatty that you might have stolen her guy at a bar? Or some jealous bitch that comes into the theater? I know for a fact you've fired some freaks, and I'm sure at least one of them had to have been a giant, right?"

"Kam! Are you freaking kidding me?" I snap.

"No, not at all." She's stone faced.

"She's right, Markie," Detective Sharpe chimes in again. "I might not put it in those particular words, but your sister has a good point. Think hard. Even random people in passing may hold some information, if nothing else. Anything you can come up with will be helpful." He hesitates, and blushes slightly before continuing, "It would be a good idea to include any men you may have been involved with in the past." He clears his throat, and his face flushes into an even deeper shade, "or now."

He ducks his head, and buries his face in the tightly clutched cup of coffee. Great, now I have to share every single person who's seen me naked with an entire office full of strangers. Isn't that going to be attractive?

"What about that Vincent guy you went out with last night?" Kam pushes. "You said he was weird."

Again, I had forgotten about my date, and again, Kam's throwing it back out there. The reminder of him leaves an acidic taste in my mouth. She's right. Instinctively, I reach my hand up and rub my fingertips around my neck, feeling for the chain of my locket. I wear it ninety percent of the time, but I removed it the second I got home last night. Seeing Beth's matching set draped over my neighbor's dead body freaked me out, to say the least. I'll probably never wear it again.

"He did make a comment about my locket."

Staring at the wall behind them, I think of the kind little twinkle in Vincent's eye as he complimented me and slid out my chair. What came off at the time as gentlemanly, now seems dark and sinister.

"What?" Kam all but shouts. Her nose crinkles in the middle. "How the hell could you forget that?! What kind of comment?" She demands.

This sparked the detective's attention as well. He sits straight up on the edge of his stool, eyes wide. If it were possible for hair to stand on end from astonishment, then his surely would be. His handsomely aged features bunch up, and it looks as if he is eating a sour hard candy.

"Well, it was more like a compliment. He just said it was pretty."

I trip over my own tongue, and a bad taste swipes across the roof of my mouth. *How could I forget?*

"I… I… I guess it was such a small gesture at the time, I never gave it another thought until now."

"Who is this man?" Detective Sharpe asks.

"Yes, who, Marketta?! I demand to know!" My mom throws herself into the room, pressing both hands on her chest, just above her bosom.

She holds herself as if having a heart attack, and then she takes the same slow dramatic steps as she did when she first arrived – each one lands in sync with her visibly deep breaths. I hate it when she calls me by my full name. I guess it could be worse, my name could be Kambriella. Who would come up with this shit, aside from our mother? Why my father allowed her to write such ridiculous names on legal documents, such as our birth certificates, is beyond me.

"Mom, how long have you been listening in?" I ask, wholly irritated.

My head angles downward and my eyes are gazing up past my lowered brows to glare at her. I didn't really need to ask, I already know the answer. I also know she isn't going to respond to my question anyway.

"Who is this man, and why were you out with him at all?" She continues to prod, ignoring me entirely. "You know that none of this would be happening if you would've just listened to me in the first place. You should have bought a nice house in my neighborhood – the one you grew up in, rather than these slums!"

Her arms round in a giant circular motion, indicating our surroundings. The shoulder pads on her dress lift with the motion, nearly touching her ears. It's strange how such a small detail can only add to her drama. I want to rip them out of her dress and fling them in her face. Although I would never dare to act so ruthlessly, the thought still crosses my mind.

"This is a nice neighborhood!" Kam and I respond in unison. I pipe down and let my sister continue. "And, it has nothing to do with where we live!" She yells. "Do you not understand anything at all?"

"Ugh." My mom grunts, and purposely shudders, coming off as queasy. Her shoulders wiggle first, then her hips. She tosses her hair behind her shoulder, and her eyes round a complete circle.

"Let's get back to the situation at hand," the detective interrupts the tense start to what is soon to be an all-out family feud. "Please explain to me this... Um... Date." Again, his cheeks fill in a pinkish hue.

My mother is hard to ignore. Her face is only inches from mine, with tensed eyes. It's obvious that she's trying to act like she's listening intently. She lets out a hot breath, smelling strongly of orange Tic-Tacs, and places a hand back over her heart. I center my attention toward the detective before leaning back against the counter, as far as I can get from her. Despite her efforts, I'm able to blow her off completely.

"He's a guy that Beth's parents set me up on a date with. He seemed like a really nice man. But yes, he was a little weird. And yes, he did tell me that my necklace was pretty when I first got there."

I take a long swig of my warm drink. It counteracts the cold breeze that's still slipping through the window crack. I remember the look on Vincent's face as he stared at me out the window. The uncomfortable sensation I had in that moment resurfaces now.

"He was a gentleman. I don't really know how to explain it, but he seemed… kind of… happy when I had to leave. Almost like he was glad I had an emergency."

I can practically see the wheels turning in Kam and the detective's heads, each one maintaining the exact same expression. One lifted brow, head cocked to the side, and eyes gawking toward the sky.

I continue. "I'm sure his comment had to have been innocent, right? I mean how could he have possibly attacked Breanna when he was on a date with me?"

"What time was your date?" Detective Sharpe asks.

"Eight o'clock."

"The Coroner's office called this morning and said that her death took place sometime between 6:30 and 8:30."

His statement catches me off guard. That's not at all the answer I was looking for. My heart skips a beat. My mother's powerful gasp could have been heard through the entire town. I'm surprised she didn't faint from lack of oxygen. I wish she would have.

"Shit, Markie," Kam says. "That means we were home when she was killed." Her voice cracks and eyes water. She looks at the countertop blankly and continues, obviously talking to herself more than to anyone else. "How did we not hear or notice anything? We had no idea."

"No one on the block saw or heard anything," Detective Sharpe interrupts her, trying to comfort us. He sets the record straight.

"The rest of the family was in South Carolina visiting some relatives. They were able to get a flight home very early this morning, but were gone for all the chaos of last night. It was actually a boy she was dating that found her. The young man told us that Breanna had stayed home to secretly be with him." He bows his head as it shakes slightly in sympathy. "Poor kid will never forgive himself."

Detective Sharpe goes on to explain, and to apologize for the painstakingly long details of forensics. I listen to every word, completely engrossed. Every inch of the Snyder home will be studied. The familiarity of the situation leaves me feeling dizzy and nauseous. At least Beth lived alone, so no one had to be there once the dust settled, forced to relive horrific memories.

I can't even imagine what Mr. and Mrs. Snyder will experience if they try to stay in that house. I'm sure their move will be inevitable. The detective leaves me with strict instructions to put together my list of possible subjects, along with a personal inventory of clothing, jewelry, and any valuable trinkets.

Before leaving, he suggests that I return to work as soon as possible. I'm to try and go about my lifestyle as if it were as any other day. He explains how I'll be watched by undercover officers, and they will be paying close attention to any strange onlookers or possible threats. He clarifies that by going to work and attending social events, my admirer will surely be close by, making him or her easier to find. The word "admirer" gives me chills from head to toe. Agreeing to the tactic, I promise to stay at home for the remainder of the day and go through every possession.

"The list of names will be difficult," I inform him, "but I will do my best."

The detective hesitates to leave, but after some time he pushes himself to the door. Beth's parents' house will be his next stop. I wonder if Beth's mom got the text I sent her last night. The *thump* of my heart speeds as I recall the words I wrote. She's either angry with me, hurt, or shockingly understanding. There is no way to tell. I'm sick with worry and wonder. She never did text me back.

Detective Sharpe assures me that he'll call or stop back by to let me know how things go with Vincent's interrogation once they locate him. My life has been turned upside down. I'm totally invaded. I feel naked and vulnerable, like a bad dream. Everything personal is going to be laid out in the open for everyone to see.

My mother leaves shortly after the detective. She has no reason to stay, with nobody around to impress.

Kam stays close by my side all morning. She's afraid for herself, and afraid for me. She tries to help me remember events or times in my life that may hold some importance. It takes three long, stomach wrenching hours for Detective Sharpe to call back with any information about Vincent. The news isn't at all comforting.

Apparently having a strange reaction to my running out on a date and a comment on my necklace isn't enough to take him in. The apartment he lives in has a doorman. The employee on the clock at the time of Breanna's murder vouched for Vincent, stating he hadn't left the building at all since he came home from work. Not until our date, that is. When I ask about any kind of a back door or alternate way out, Detective Sharpe informs me that they checked it all out and ruled it "highly unlikely." *What the fuck is that supposed to mean?*

He assures me that Vincent lives on a high enough floor that someone would have seen him coming in and out of the fire escape. He tells me that the only way Vincent could have possibly gotten in and out undetected, and with enough time to commit the act, was if he were to sneak past while the doorman was on break or hide behind another tenant.

It's such an unlikely scenario that they decided to ultimately rule him out as a lead suspect. Our conversation leaves me unnerved. Vincent's alibi isn't exactly airtight, and any possibility that he could be the killer frightens me.

It is nearing afternoon. Brock shows up with a bang. I hate him. Kam has only had two real boyfriends in her life, and they were each more feminine than her. I tease her about it when she pisses me off, I call her a lesbian. She detests it, but it's really the only thing I can say that will shut her up when she overdoes it herself. She can have some seriously out of line comments. So, naturally, I take advantage of the angle often.

I highly doubt Brock has ever lifted a shovel, swung a hammer, or set up a tent in his entire life. I bought him a power drill for Christmas one year as a joke. He didn't even get the punchline. He just said "thanks, sweetie" with a friendly squeak, and went about his business. I'm willing to bet it has never even been taken out of the box.

He's a pampered little prince, too. It doesn't matter that he and Kam are broken up, he still comes around on a regular basis, and they act like an old married couple. I sit on the couch a few feet away from the front door when he lets himself in. There's no need to knock.

"Hello?" He squeaks. Even his voice is higher pitched than an average young man.

"Nice pink shirt," I greet him. "Is it new? It looks brighter than usual."

Brock always wears feminine clothes. Even his shorts are color coordinated. Lime green, neon blue, and matching bright pink stripes hang from his waistline and end at the knees.

"Actually, yes," his smile is large and proud. He never does catch onto my sarcasm. "Oh, nice flowers on your car by the way."

I jump to my feet. "What flowers?" My heart instantly sinks to my belly button. I know Brock is dumb, *but is he really that dumb?* "You didn't bring them in?" I demand.

"Nope, why would I? Where's Kam?"

Kam rushes out of the bathroom, jogging to my side. She heard our short conversation and is joining me to take a look outside.

"You're late." She barks at Brock on her way past.

He follows us out the door with his head down. He's an ashamed, obedient little pet of hers. Sitting on the hood of my car is a small bouquet of daisies. They look identical to the arrangement Vincent had intended to give me, but I had left on the table at *Frenchie's* on my way out.

A cream-colored envelope made of thick tex-
tured paper is placed under the left wiper.
Snatching it up, I rip the top open and pull the
contents out. Inside the neatly sealed, high quality envelope is an old picture. I stare at the photo
and remember the day it was taken perfectly.
It was the housewarming party that Kam and I
hosted when we moved in.

The smiling faces of my closest friends and
family look up at me from the picture. There were
nine of us total, standing on the lawn in front of
my home, myself in the middle grinning proudly.
My muscles tighten, and I grow faint. I stare at
a red X that has been marked across Beth's face.
Just like that, it's like she is a craft, a meaning-
less face, the first to be picked off in a group of
random nobodies. My eyes instantly fill, blurring
the image.

A tiny figure in the background of the photo
bears the same mark. It is Breanna. As innocent
and as young as could be, she was sitting on her
porch reading a magazine. She was paying no attention to what was going on across the street.
It's obvious now that the simple act of being in
a random photograph by default, years before,

was the reason for her attack. On the back of the photograph is the wrenching question: **Who's next?**

Chapter Five

The faces in that haunting photograph pass through my head. Their eyes lock into mine, over and over, it's like they are screaming at me. Each face holds an innocent look in their eyes. It consumes me, leaving me unable to concentrate on any of the paperwork awaiting my attention. I've been back to work for two days now, and I've accomplished nothing. Folders, documents, and writing utensils are strewn about my desk amidst empty cans of Red Bull and fast food bags.

My computer's keyboard is buried in garbage. The screen is completely covered in sticky notes containing memories and events that may or may not be of help to the detective. He's due to show up at my office any time with some new agent on the case, some kind of personality expert, or some shit. I glance around at the mess with disinterest. I care about nothing in this moment but the women in the photograph. I decide against cleaning. I have no desire to impress anyone, and no ambition outside of finding my "admirer." I read over each neon green note stuck to the screen of my computer. A light, *tap tap tap* sounds on my thin office door.

"Come in." I manage, without an ounce of energy to get up and open it myself.

The handle slowly twists, and the door creaks open. Rather than the detective I was expecting, Tiffany slowly and timidly pokes her head around the corner. She is petite, blonde, and always modest. She is in her early twenties. She takes in a breath, scrunches her nose up tight, and winces with disgust.

"Do you have a minute?" The question comes out quiet and guarded.

"I guess." I mumble, averting my attention back to the notes.

I don't mean to come off as rude to Tiffany, I like her more than any other employee at the multiplex. Trust me, there are a few doozies. I don't know what the hell I was thinking when I voted them in. In a mere two days, I have grown numb and careless to anything and everything aside from the murders. The people employed at my theater are the last thing on my mind,

Tiffany included. I'm completely and utterly en-grossed. I'm sleep deprived, petrified, and en-tirely exhausted. She slowly moves toward the tan-cushioned chair opposite my desk.

"I… um…" She stammers.

"Can you get to the point, Tiff? I'm a little busy."

Apparently, my comment didn't go over very well. Her timid demeanor quickly changes. The once sweet, soft spoken girl I have come to know and like, takes in a large breath and unloads. In a split second she has changed from passive to aggressive. For the first time ever, she's talking to me like a real – and absolutely pissed off – friend, rather than just another friendly coworker.

"Look, Markie, I know your life is shit right now, but my God, take a look at yourself!"

The words, and tone, are unfitting to her sweet voice. The whole scene is uncomfortable. I shift in my seat.

"Excuse me?"

"This place is disgusting. You've let everything go." She hesitates. "You've let yourself go. Hon-estly, I don't know if it's all this nasty garbage and old food that smells so bad in here, or if it's you." The words stream out in awkward waves.

I can only imagine she's been working up to this moment all day. Tiffany stands and shoves an empty trash can from the side of my desk into my hands. It forces me to my feet. I'm temporarily speechless. While holding the can for her, I listen. She keeps up with the ass chewing, and violently rummages through the clutter on my desk. She separates necessities from useless crap and garbage.

"You can't shut out the world!" More trash clanks and clambers into the rapidly filling can. "You can't refuse to shower or brush your hair!" *Slam*, more garbage shoots in. "You need to fight, Markie! You need to keep people you care about close! You can't just take on this beast all by yourself and live your life like a dirty little recluse!"

My desk is quickly cleared. Even my paperwork is stacked neatly in a corner before she moves on to the unkempt floor.

"And to be quite honest, if I'm going to keep running this place from out front, I'm going to need a damn raise by the time this is all said and done."

I follow her around my small mint and cream-colored office and hold the trash can at arm's length. She continues to scold me.

"I mean... I won't mind the extra time on my paycheck, and I know this is the last worry on your list, but the people around here don't listen to me the way they do you. And, not that you care, but it's hard to hold it together without being a complete bitch to everyone around, and I *hate* that. If you're not going to be here when you're here, then you might as well take some time off like any other normal person would!"

I appreciate her concern. I even respect the newfound backbone she seemed to have grown overnight, yet I'm not about to admit it. Guarded defense is my instant reaction. The wall I've built up around myself isn't coming down that easily.

"Thanks for cleaning my office, now please get back to work."

I respond flatly, holding the overflowing trash can out for her to take back. Tiffany's hands stop instantly at her hips. Her eyes are fierce and she refuses to take the can, or to move toward the door.

"That's it?" She asks. "That's all you've got?"

"What do you mean?"

"You're still going to turn me away after all that?" She's talking at me like a seasoned mother would to a toddler.

She refuses to budge or give up. I can tell that no matter what I do or say, I'm not getting her out of my office – unless I cry wolf, that is, to the police guard standing outside the door. At this very moment, it's tempting.

"What do you want me to say, exactly?"

"Just tell me what is going on in your head… I mean, I know you have other friends and Kam, and I know that you're a strong woman, but everyone needs someone to talk to. I think it's a safe bet that you aren't talking to anyone right now, because you have practically locked yourself in this room for two days straight."

"I can't be your friend, Tiffany." I answer quietly and look at the floor.

I lean my weary torso against a filing cabinet that sits between the door, and a rickety printer that's on its last leg.

"My friends die." I whisper through a closing throat.

"I'm not going to die. I wasn't in the picture. I didn't even know you when it was taken."

My head jolts up. "How do you know about that picture?"

"Everyone knows about it, Markie. Everyone knows that whoever left it for you got past the police, that were supposedly everywhere, without being seen."

I haven't told anyone about the picture, and the police took it a couple minutes after we found it. It was supposed to be kept quiet so as not to give this creep any more psychological power than he already has. Now I'm pissed. *How is it out? How does Tiffany know about this picture, and who did she mean by everyone?*

Tiffany moves to the freshly cleared chair in front of my desk. She takes a seat abruptly. Her back is straight, and her posture is perfect.

"See, now we're talking." She says softly with confidence.

I follow her across the room and sit in my own chair directly across from her. I stare at her. I'm a bit annoyed at the professional look in her face.

What is she trying to do, be my therapist? I lock my arms together across my chest and wait for an explanation of her knowledge. I don't have the patience for games, so luckily it doesn't take her long to spill the beans.

"Brock came in a couple hours ago to check up on you." She explains. "He told us everything. It's the weekend too, if you haven't noticed, so everyone is working tonight. All of the people in line for their popcorn could hear him too, I'm sure."

"He's such a loudmouth. I swear, I'm going to strangle him myself."

"Well, I think you should cut him some slack."

Her kindness returns as her temper tantrum subsides.

"He seemed truly concerned. He wanted to go straight back and check on you, but I told him that you said you didn't want to talk to anyone but Kam or the detective. Plus, everyone was asking him questions, you know how Brock cracks under pressure."

Tiffany talks about my sister's boyfriend like they have known each other for years. He really does wear his heart on his sleeve. Not only does he dress like a girl, but he chats and makes friends like a girl would too. *What a wimp. What a stupid, idiot, wimp!*

"I'm not cutting him slack just because he doesn't have the balls to tell people to shut up. He had no right to share that information! It's bad enough that Breanna's parents officially un-invited me to her funeral, but now everyone in town will know that everything roots back to me." It hits me instantly. "Oh my God, the press!" I struggle for breath, drawing in shallow pants. "They have been like vultures in my neighborhood. I can't deal with them. I can't handle my emotions as it is."

I can't help but to let my guard down and open up to her now. I'm panicked. I know the rumors will spread fast. It'll take no time at all before word will officially be out about the picture.

"Shit!" I stress.

I bury my face into the palms of my hands. Tiffany is no longer chatty and overbearing. She must understand my paranoia, seeing it first-hand.

"I'm so sorry." She offers. "I didn't even think about all of the attention."

"It's not just that." I set the record straight. "I can't get Beth's face out of my head. I keep picturing everyone I know, dead. I play out their murders in my mind over and over. It's as if they've already happened. Everyone in that picture has been notified, and has a watch on them, but if he can get past the cops at my own house the day after he killed Breanna, then who's to say he can't get to any of my friends and family?"

A tear rolls down my cheek. I lift my head from my hands to make eye contact with her. Tiffany listens intently, her eyes are wide.

"Who all was in it?"

"Kam, Beth and her mom, my mom, my dad's sisters, a few other friends I have known since we were kids." I think for a moment on whether Tiffany has ever met any of them here at the theater. "Meagan and Joyce come here on double dates every couple of months. You may have seen me talking to them a few times. Meagan has even stuck around for a while after the movie. She's waited for me to help lock up."

"If I saw their faces, I might remember." Tiffany is soft spoken and seems thoughtful. "Have you talked to any of them since you found the picture?" She asks with a genuine tone of concern.

Tiffany doesn't seem at all like a gossip queen or a meddler. That may be why I like her so much. She has always come off as a real, down to earth kind of girl. She engages in conversations with real meaning. She cares more about life, and the world around her, than she does about her daily outfits or her hair. Not that it's bad to care about one's appearance, but she doesn't.

"No, I don't dare." I take in a breath, looking her square in the eyes, "I'm afraid he'll attack whoever I talk to or spend time with. I'm scared that he meant the question he wrote on the back literally. I know it sounds dumb, but I feel like he was actually asking me who he should go after. Like, he's watching to see who I pick."

I sigh, and look down at my oak finished desk, no longer cluttered with trash and food.

"Does that make sense?" I ask, wondering aloud if I'm coming off as crazy as I feel.

Before Tiffany has a chance to answer, possibly the deepest voice I have ever heard speaks in her stead. "Nope, not dumb at all."

The source of the low voice steps out from behind the door, followed by Detective Sharpe. I hadn't realized the door had been left ajar. They may have listened to our entire conversation. I swear, police are the biggest eavesdroppers. I wonder if they heard Tiffany's rant as well as my own emotional outburst. Oh well, I'm going to have to tell them everything anyway.

This new man on the case is the tallest, darkest man I have ever seen. His skin tone is as deep as his voice. His eyes are big, and his teeth are perfect. Large, but perfect nonetheless. I can't help but stare, open mouthed and everything. I am in awe of him. He continues to speak, unfazed by my childlike reaction to him.

"You must be Marketta." He bellows.

"Yes." I stand from my chair to greet this giant. "I go by Markie, though, please."

Before I have a chance to say anything else, Tiffany excuses herself, practically running away from his gargantuan presence.

"I... I... had better get back to my rotation at the reels." Her stutter is no louder than a whisper, "gentlemen."

Her head nods kindly to Detective Sharpe and the new guy. Her hands scramble, pawing at the full bag of trash. She quickly ducks past them, and the lingering smell of my garbage follows behind her like a lost pet.

"Sorry to barge in, Markie." Detective Sharpe says professionally, with a high head and straight shoulders. He maintains the same excited twinkle in his eye from the other morning. He is aglow.

"This is Agent Reese. He's with the FBI and will be working alongside me."

The agent reaches his ample arm toward me to shake my hand. Feeling like a child, I place my tiny hand into the center of his enormous palm. Fingers fold around the back side, engulfing it entirely, as well as half my wrist. It looks like my arm is being swallowed whole. After gulping down the lump in my throat, I offer him a seat. He thanks me politely and takes the only chair. Detective Sharpe is left to stand at his side. Even while sitting down, Agent Reese reaches the detective's shoulder height. His awkward size makes my office feel like a can of sardines. I'm tempted to ask why he chose this career path, rather than playing a professional sport. I decide against the notion, it may be a tad inappropriate.

"You have a good point, and I hate to say it, but you may be right."

His deep voice echoes against the walls. He continues with the conversation without missing a beat. He didn't even seem to notice Tiffany's exit or the disgusting bag she left with.

"Most stalkers tend to watch their victims for quite some time before they act out their fantasies."

He expels thousands of rays of confidence with every word. Agent Reese speaks with serious authority. His facial expression is flat and unchanged.

"Once they do start acting rather than watching, they tend to build momentum based on their victim's reactions."

"Stalker?" I croak. My mouth feels dry, as if it's full of dirt.

"Yes."

His response is direct and precise. There is no question in Agent Reese's mind of the situation at hand. He explains that everything I do, or don't do, will determine the psycho's next move from here on out. This guy is watching me closely. He's feeding off my life and every action. He's getting off on seeing me live with the pain he causes. These murders had nothing to do with the women he actually killed, and everything to do with me, according to the agent.

"How do you know this?" I inquire.

"It's what I do." He answers without hesitation. "And concerning the photograph, you have every reason to worry."

"So, you're saying he will go after who I choose?"

"Perhaps... Or it could be the exact opposite."

"What do you mean?"

"What I'm trying to say is that at this point, he is in control. We don't have much to play on. The question written on the back of his photograph—"

"Mine." I interrupt to correct him. "My photograph."

"Yes, ma'am, your photograph." He adheres to my correction and continues. "The question may have been meant in a literal sense, as you fear, but it may also be a distraction. Our suspect is careful, and very intelligent. It wouldn't surprise me if the entire gift was meant to throw us off his true intentions. Either scenario makes complete sense."

Agent Reese goes on to explain the inner workings of twisted minds. He describes killers he has taken down in the past. I can feel what little bit of color I have in my face drain away. Tiny beads of sweat grow in my hairline and on the tip of my nose. The walls of my office creep in closer, leaving me suffocated, I'm drowning in my own imagination. He is painting a clear picture of the extreme measures' stalkers have taken to inflict pain and fear on their victims. *Me... He is talking about me, I am the victim.*

He explains that this psycho could watch me for weeks, months, or even years before striking again. Or, on the other hand, his last kill may have initiated some sort of torture spree. This would explain why he left the message on my car the morning after. This massive agent has seen each outcome. Because of the level of violence displayed in the murders, he is leaning toward the spree. Based on his experience and observation, the agent thinks that by communicating with me through the locket and the picture, he has graduated from an onlooker to a full-on serial killer.

He will now stop at nothing. According to Agent Reese, killers of this caliber see the world differently. I've heard of dangerous social disorders before, but only on television shows. This is real and I'm having a hard time wrapping my mind around it.

"We are in his world now, and will be playing his game." Agent Reese says. "It's like chess for the insane, and you have the next move. I'm here to help guide you on what piece to put where. We have to throw him off. You can't play the part he's expecting you to play. If your actions confuse him, then it might buy us time between murders."

"Might?"

"Yes, ma'am. Might. As I said before, he hasn't left enough evidence to point us in a clearer direction."

My body heats. He just had to say the word, murders. Plural, as it will happen again... multiple times. The word leaves a restricting feel in the back of my throat. *Air, I need air.* Without another word, I rise from my chair and rush to the window. I shove it open and stick my head out. Deep breaths of fresh air fill my lungs and a fraction of life is returned to me. I savor the crisp night as I run the agent's logic through my head. It takes me a few minutes to catch my breath. Detective Sharpe and Agent Reese must have seen the conflict inside me between vomit and losing consciousness. They give me the space I need, quietly waiting.

I scan the large, overstuffed parking lot from my second story window and try to regain composure. There's a small group of teenagers almost in hearing range. They snuck out of the theater to have an illegal smoke or drink, no doubt. Huddled together, they puff away and laugh at each other's jokes. A ping of jealousy hits me, and a sudden yearning for Beth sinks in the pit of my belly. *It just isn't fair.* These young fools are only yards away from me, yet we live in completely different worlds.

My vision slowly clears, and my body rids itself of the prickly lightheaded feeling. I continue to look around the parking lot. In the furthest corner, I notice a lone male figure leaning against a sedan. I can't quite make out the details of his face, but he seems to be looking in my direction. I squint tightly trying to get a closer look.

"Phil, someone is out there." I announce. "I think he's watching me in the window."

Chapter Six

Agent Reese remains seated calmly. Detective Sharpe swiftly closes the distance between us. Just as he reaches my side, the figure moves. A hand is lifted out from inside his pocket, and he waves. It's a familiar wave, one I have seen before. The distinct motion I had witnessed at *Frenchie*'s is being repeated. The intense grin I had seen on Vincent's face flashes in my memory. The notion is like a still frame picture of him slapping me in the face. A shockwave hits me, igniting my bones.

"It's Vincent," I tell the detective.

"How can you tell?"

"I know that wave."

Just as the words leave my mouth, Vincent reaches in his pocket to pull something out. The detective carefully places a hand on the pistol that is holstered under his jacket. He's ready to quick draw if necessary. I freeze in fear. Vincent pulls out a black square, points at it, and then puts it up to his face.

"It's just a phone." Sharpe sighs in relief.

A loud ring sounds from my cell phone sitting on the desk. I glance back and forth between the two lawmen and out the window at Vincent. He is leaning against his car casually with the phone to his ear, awaiting my answer. My feet are concrete, unable to carry me across the room. I stand in place, petrified. Vincent has been all but cleared. There is a gargantuan FBI agent just a few feet away. But, I am still scared shitless to answer my phone.

"It's probably best you answer." The deep voice sounds from across the room, bashing my eardrums. "Will you put it on speaker, please?"

At least he is polite about it. I clear my dry throat.

"Um, yeah." I answer before the call goes to voicemail. "Hello?" I croak, after pressing the answer and speaker buttons simultaneously.

"I was starting to wonder if you were going to pick up." Vincent is calm and confident.

He sounds the same as he had during our date the other night, confident... cute. The wide range of his voice somewhat turns me on, yet leaves me unbelievably irritated, all at the same time. *How can such a strange man have this kind of power over my emotions?* Butterflies flutter, and blood boils. Being this confused pisses me off.

"Um. Yeah. Sorry about that. You caught me at a bad time."

I want to burst out at him. I want to ask what the hell he's doing here, and why he's outside of my office. It takes everything I have to hold back.

"Well, I've been standing here debating on whether to come in and apologize for the other night or not. I guess now that I've been busted, I figured it best just to call."

I can tell the words are being spoken through a smile. Agent Reese mouths to me in silence. He tells me what to say.

"What do you have to apologize for?" I ask, repeating the coached side of my conversation.

"Well," he pauses, "I saw the news, and then the police came to talk to me. I'm just sorry that it has taken me this long to check up on you." His confidence remains strong and fully intact. "Trish told me everything. She knows about your neighbor. She's pretty shaken up, especially since you didn't want to talk to her. She's worried. Are you okay?"

My chest sinks at the thought of Beth's mom. Although I know cutting contact with her was the best move, it still pains me. I imagine she is reliving Beth's murder just the same as I am.

"I... Um..." Again, the Agent clearly mouths an intended statement. He wants me to invite Vincent up.

"Can you give me just one second?" I ask Vincent.

"Yes."

I press the mute button on my small white phone as it sits on the desk, taunting me.

"Hell no!" I shout at the agent.

I can't invite him up, I don't know how to act or what to say. I'm scared of everyone and everything. If he comes up here right now, I'll lose my shit. The sweat on my hairline has graduated from small forming beads, to a dripping perspiration. I grasp at the front of my loose blue t-shirt and fan the collar. Agent Reese can clearly see my panic. He reluctantly agrees to let me finish out this little interaction over the phone.

"Just tell him it's a bad time and ask if you can get back to him. Let him know you'll be okay." His eyes lock onto mine firmly and he warns, "it will be very beneficial for everyone," he enunciates the word through clenched teeth, "if you see him again. I'll explain to you why after you finish the call."

He has become very pushy. *So much for the previous courtesy.* I nod and hold back tears. As much as I want to disagree and cry, I understand that I have to cooperate. If that means another awkward date with a possible killer, so be it.

I touch the mute icon again and allow my voice to be heard. "Sorry about that, you just caught me at a bad time." I force the instructed statement without taking my clouded eyes off Agent Reese.

"I completely understand."

"Um. Is there a good time I can call you back?"

Though I am teetering on the edge of a meltdown, I'm still able to fight the waterworks, at least while I talk to Vincent. I have to finish this call and do whatever else is needed of me, for Beth. The faces of my loved ones from that tainted photograph haunt me   I need to protect them.

"Yes, any time really." He is too enthusiastic for comfort. "Whatever I'm doing can be put on hold for you."

I can't tell if he is excited, or just that confident in general. Naturally, I'm scared, but I'm also irritated. If he isn't responsible for my best friend's death, then who does he think he is? I've been out with him one time, and he shows up at my work uninvited. He's also willing to put his life on hold for me. On a normal day I'd be pushing him away for fear of him being too clingy. I can't handle needy men, which is probably why I'm still single, but that's beside the point.

"Okay." Agent Reese continues to mouth words to me. I repeat, aloud, to Vincent. "If you'll be up for a while I can call you tonight when I get home from work."

"Yes, absolutely." He sounds eager and it feels wrong.

"Okay then," I hesitate. "I'll talk to you in an hour or two." *I can't believe I'm agreeing to this.*

"I'll be waiting." His tone has changed from excited and eager, to slow and sensual.

"Bye." I rush an end to the conversation, then click the off button before Vincent can voice his farewell in return.

Chapter Seven

I collapse into my seat and allow my legs to relax. My arms dangle at my sides. A few tears overflow, leaving my cheeks damp. I let them fall to my shirt, not bothering to wipe my face. Detective Sharpe makes a quick call to a nearby officer, instructing him to tail Vincent for the night. Without asking any questions, I listen intently to the agent and my tears continue to fall.

He explains to me that staying at work or home all the time could easily cause my stalker to act out. Apparently, the creep wants to see me. If he's unable to do so, he'll do awful things in effort to draw me out into the open, or so they tell me. Again, I'm reminded that these are all their professional opinions, and we cannot be certain of anything at this point.

Agent Reese explains that the more active I stay, the more they can keep an eye on the people around me in a crowd. He tells me that the killer would likely stay close but not too close. He'll be in busy places, and follow me from a distance so that he feels safe and he won't be noticed by anyone – especially me. In addition to the local law enforcement, there will be undercover FBI agents watching me.

When he tells me to try not to worry, I feel like laughing in his face. *How the hell am I supposed to not worry? I have a killer stalking me, picking off my loved ones one at a time! This can't be real.* It feels like I'm stuck in a bad dream, like I'm being suffocated by a pillow in my sleep. *Why does this have to happen?* My life was practically perfect before I lost Beth. When she was alive, we were carefree and living the dream. *Who is this bastard, and what does he want from me?*

Agent Reese moves on to discuss Vincent. The chance of him being my stalker is possible, but the fact that he has an alibi has nearly cleared him completely. He tells me that by going out with him, they can watch his demeanor and they can learn more about him firsthand.

He says that if Vincent isn't my stalker, then it would very likely draw the actual stalker out in some other way. Dating Vincent is a bold move, and it is one that I don't have much choice but to take. Being strong willed and moving on with my life will throw him off.

I'm also instructed to go out with friends as soon as I can. A night out to a club or bar will be huge – scary, but huge nonetheless. It will be bait that my stalker won't be able to resist. Not only am I not allowed to grieve or dwell on my recently reopened past, but I'm going to be paraded around, dangled in front of a brutal murderer. I'm bait on a hook.

Our last topic of conversation involves Brock and his big mouth. I'm instructed to keep my head down and to look away from any cameras when I get home. There will be a press conference held in the morning by the FBI agents on the case. They'll explain only details that are beneficial for the public to know. Agent Reese promises to squash any attention toward me, and to veer the vultures away. He even promises that each news anchor and their crew will be approached personally after the conference. They'll be asked to pack their shit and leave.

This is the only comforting news yet. Apparently, they have the right to come and go as they please, they cannot be forced out, but Agent

Reese is confident that most reporters and paparazzi will back down if they are told that their presence could easily attribute to more deaths, especially if they are warned that they are likely to be next.

"Gets them every time. A brave few may linger, but for the most part they'll move along." The agent declares proudly.

Detective Sharpe encourages me to stay strong, and reminds me of the backup that is always close by. Yet again, the words do nothing for the churning in my bowels or the wrenching in my chest. We finish our conversation, and they prepare to leave. Detective Sharpe asks for a moment with me alone. Agent Reese kindly abides by his request, and then turns for the door. I watch as he ducks his head to get through the doorway. *My God, he is big.* I try to collect my thoughts from all the information this giant of a man left me with. It doesn't take long for Detective Sharpe to clear his throat. I refocus and jerk my head back in his direction.

"Sorry." I mutter.

"Look," he hesitates. "I know asking if you're okay is a bit of a cliché right now. But I can't help myself. You don't look like you're holding yourself together very well."

No shit! I want to shout at him. "Sorry I cried." I apologize instead, it seems like the adult thing to do.

"It's not just that, Markie. You look... I don't know." He hesitates again. The man obviously doesn't dare say exactly what is on his mind. "You don't look healthy." He finishes.

"Healthy?" I ask.

People around me are being killed, and he's worried about my eating habits and hygiene? I don't know whether to be angry, embarrassed, or flattered. I think I am a little bit of everything.

"Well, maybe if you were to take a few hours for yourself, you know? Maybe you could clean up, eat a home cooked meal, and watch an old movie you love or something."

This, too, catches me off guard. Maybe Kam's right and he does like me. What kind of grown man gives such simple, yet completely insightful advice anyway?

"Thanks for your concern." I mumble, looking down at the floor. *Yep, it's embarrassment.* Embarrassment takes the cake, more so than anger or flattery.

I'm serious, Markie. Promise me that you'll take care of yourself through this whole process. You don't deserve this." Sharpe says.

Unable to say anything back, I burst into tears again. I let him wrap his arms around me in a long, tight embrace. It changes nothing, I still have no romantic feelings for him, but the warmth of his body is comforting. He has broad shoulders and strong arms. For the first time in days, if only for a few brief moments, I feel safe. I don't want him to let me go, but he's got to, at some point. His grip loosens, and we slowly break contact. He takes a profound look into my eyes, drinking me in. Without another word, he turns for the door. I'm left standing alone, again.

"What the hell am I supposed to do now?" I whisper to myself through snot and tears.

I sit back down, contemplating my 'chess moves,' or so Agent Reese called them. I decide to find Tiffany before the two most popular movies playing come to an end. I need to let her plan a damn girl's night. Then I must get out of here, fast. I need to leave before a crowd forms. I don't want to be here when they push their way out of this theater.

Being in crowded places may have been advised, but for tonight, it's one hundred percent out of the question. The need to be home and to check on Kam suddenly consumes me. I rise to my feet and brush my fingers across my face for a quick freshening up. The remaining half of my fountain Pepsi is chugged, and my back and shoulders are straightened.

"Here goes." I say before making my way to the door. I'm off to face reality, to play my part in this shitty game of outsmarting a murderous lunatic. "You can do this." I whisper these words of self-encouragement through tight lips. As I leave my office to find Tiffany, an entirely new, overwhelmingly strong fear catches me. Like a predator's trap, it snatches me up and won't let me go – I know deep down that my journey with this freak is only beginning.

I march down the stairs and toward the main entrance. Muffled sounds from each movie escape out into the halls. There are a few impatient looking women waiting in line for a turn in the restroom. I make it a point to speed past them without looking up. I can feel their eyes taking aim and their thoughts pulling the trigger in my direction. There is no way to tell if all the angry stares are from their knowledge of my part in the local murders, or if I am just paranoid and imagining their judgment. Either way, it feels like every person I pass is glaring at me. There are two sets of stairs in the building. One main set of stairs leads to the balcony of each individual theater. The second is a lone, private set leading only to my personal office.

I've always thought it nice to be separated, allowing peace and quiet. At this moment it's coming off as nothing but an inconvenience, forcing me past everybody that's out and about, not to mention how awkward the officer tailing me makes me feel. He reminds me of a loyal dog, Dingo, I had as a small child. The officers switch off a couple times a day, giving me no reason to make friends, or small talk. I do my best to ignore them, as instructed.

I notice our janitor, Jared. He's cleaning the short hallway to movie house one. He is a quiet man in his early fifties. He's worked at the multiplex even longer than I have, yet we've never had a real conversation. Jared is a lanky man, with hair just past his shoulders and a short, scruffy beard. He is a bit odd and seems lonely, but he's always courteous to everyone.

Jared has maintained this same appearance since I've known him. He does his job and keeps to himself. He always has, and I imagine he always will. I picture him living alone by choice. He's content to work at the same place, mopping the same floors, and washing the same windows for the majority of his life. For most people, his lifestyle would be boring and sad, but for Jared it just seems to fit.

It's nearing 8:30 P.M. and there is still some light outside. Leaving so early feels strange, I'm in no way used to it. I'm usually among the last to go after closing time. There are only a few employees I trust to lock up the building, and fewer that I trust alone with the night's income. Good help is hard to find these days, so I make sure to treat the ones I do have well. I take my turn in their rotations, and work with their hours as much as possible.

Luckily, it's a Friday. There are two closing employees on rotation, Tiffany and Brad. Brad is a young college student. He's kind, outgoing, and dependable. He's also very big, so I've never had to worry about the place when he's alone here at night. I'm sure he can handle himself well. The movies are due to end within the next twenty minutes, so I must find Tiffany quickly.

"Jared," I lightly speak down the hall toward him.

He glances up from his mop and bucket. He makes clear eye contact and waits for me to speak. There is obviously no need for a response until I address my question. I have his full attention.

"Do you know where I can find Tiffany?" I'm quiet and direct.

"I just saw her in the locker room." His scratchy voice carries back to me an octave above a whisper.

Jared's attention returns directly back to the task at hand. His head tilts down toward the floor as quickly as he had looked up from it. He continues the light cleaning motions. Back and forth his arms sway, with shoulders hardly moving. The job is nearly done, the halls are shining. He has little left to finish before his break between crowds.

At that point the second round of movie watchers will move in, and the next round of shows will start. That's when he will begin again. From one end of the building to the next, picking up garbage, sanitizing bathrooms and handrails, and once again mopping the floors. I feel a little bad for Jared, what a crappy job. Though, he doesn't seem to mind the monotony.

I think about the list of strange people and possible suspects I had given to the detective. I make a mental note to add Jared to the list. Although he's never given me any reason to suspect him of being a violent or vindictive sort of guy, he *is* still strange. I suppose that qualifies him as a candidate on my growing list.

I watch him for a moment and shudder. A vicious picture of him ramming a knife over and over into my best friend repeats in mind. The thought makes me choke on my spit, drawing his attention. Jared's head jerks up in an instant. Without missing a beat, the glower he shoots me is menacing and mean. He scowls straight at me. The whites of his eyes are not white at all, but dark. They're bloodshot red. Without a word, I look down at my feet and walk away.

What the hell was that all about? Maybe he's mad at me for staring at him. Or, maybe he heard about the picture, and blames me for the murders, too. I run all possible scenarios through my head as I practically sprint to the locker room. I have never seen such an evil look in Jared's usually kind eyes. I stop at a tall wooden door and stare at the handle. My God, everyone I see I'm afraid of. *I'm losing it!* Even the janitor, whom I've been around almost every day for nearly fifteen years just gave me the chills.

"Pull your shit together," I whisper as I reach for the door.

The locker room is a small average 'Employees only' type of space. One wall contains a few tall metal lockers, a fridge, and a bulletin board. In the center of the room there are two small round tables with comfortably padded chairs around them. Sitting on a couple of those chairs are Tiffany and Brad. They appear to be kicked back, enjoying their break before the next crowd floods in. While munching on popcorn and churros, their eyes widen upon my entrance. My unexpected appearance is obviously a shock. Both sit speechless, holding their breath.

"Glad to see you left your cave," Tiffany finally blurts. Her mouth quickly closes, and an embarrassed shade of pink clouds her ears.

"Yeah, well, I guess you were right. I can't stay in there forever."

My puppy dog officer stands in the doorway. Brad shifts and shuffles around on his seat, looking at the cop from the corner of his eye. The police officer is clearly making him nervous. He looks like a kid trying to hold his bladder. Oddly enough, I don't find it strange or frightening in the slightest. I've expected this reaction from most people and I'm a little surprised it's taken so long. Brad throws a large handful of popcorn in his mouth, and chews at an abnormal speed. He must be a nervous eater. I resist the urge to roll my eyes, as I wonder if he is stoned.

I imagine him to be the type of kid who gets searched every time he gets pulled over, just because he can't help but to act strange and guilty around authority. What an amateur. And to think, I had put so much stock in him being a tough guy. *It's time to put my personal intu-*

ition and judgment of character in check. I take a seat next to them, strategically placing myself between Brad and the officer. I try to block the clear view they have of one another, hoping to ease Brad's growing tension. The last thing I want to do right now is talk to a nervous, overgrown boy.

"So, I was thinking about what you said, and maybe I do need to get out." I tell Tiffany. "Do you want to get a drink in a few days or something?"

I'm not going to go into detail about my strict instructions from monstrous Agent Reese, and I'm especially not telling her about my intended chess moves. All that Tiffany needs to know is that I want her around. I feel guilty for using her, but I'll do what I need to. She nearly jumps out of her seat.

"Really?" She beams. "I'm so glad you want to do this, Markie. A night out is exactly what you need." She is completely fearless. "Of course, I want to! What about tomorrow night after I close up?"

It seems as if she doesn't know anything about the murders at all. I don't understand how anyone can be so trusting and unguarded around me. Had the shoe been on the other foot, I wouldn't be caught within a hundred yards of her.

Confused by her excitement, I hesitate. "Well, I, um…"

"No, you're right." She interrupts my stammering and tripping around, "You need a day or two off first. I'm open for Monday night, if that's better? Then the bars will be a little less crowded. We could go earlier, and it may be more comfortable for you."

Finally, a little common sense. I knew she had it in her somewhere. The fear I have for her, and for myself, is pushed down into a dark corner of my mind.

"Monday would be okay."

"Perfect!" She says.

She reminds me of an eager, middle school aged girl, anxious but still excited for a first date.

"One more thing," I change the subject. Getting back on top of my responsibilities was also a topic recently discussed. My whole life I have been a strong, confident girl. It's time I regain some of my strength and self-worth. Or at least appear to do so on the outside, anyway. So, I hold my head high.

"Do me a favor, both of you, if you wouldn't mind." I look back and forth between them. "Send out a group text to every employee. Type up and make copies of a notification to put in here, and under the ticket window so everyone knows. We need to have a mandatory meeting before the weekend is over.

"Yeah, sure." Tiffany agrees.

A silent, wide-eyed nod, is all Brad can muster. Then he peeks his eyes around me at the listening officer. His head quickly darts back behind my body's shield. He straightens his back and twiddles his thumbs.

"The elephant in the room will be addressed, and I will honestly answer everyone's questions. There'll be no more talking behind my back, and there'll be no more rumors started. I'm the manager here, and I'm going to put an end to the unnecessary chatting before it gets any worse."

A silent agreement is displayed with short nods. Brad's eyes begin to cloud over as he refuses to blink. Tiffany's mouth opens ever so slightly, revealing a fraction of her big, perfectly white teeth.

I continue. "I'll be taking tomorrow night off. The two of you are still on schedule, so I trust you'll handle the Saturday night rush okay. I'm guessing there will be less people out than usual due to the recent," I pause, thinking of the right word to use. "Events. Our meeting will be Sunday afternoon at five. That should give everyone enough time between the matinee and regular shifts. Does that sound okay with you guys?"

An understood, "yeah," quietly sounds in unison.

I conclude the bitchy boss persona, only to have that annoying ping of guilt return. I hate using Tiffany like a pawn.

"Tiff, please let me know you've made it home safely tonight, okay? You have my number, just text me or something."

I can't help but speak softly, almost under my breath. I know my stalker could in no way tell I had made plans with her, yet, but I'm still scared for her life. I can't help but assume that anyone I talk to could easily be found dead, brutally attacked and bled out like an animal taken to slaughter. Just then, the sound of voices come from down the hall. I panic.

"I have to go!"

I race for the door. The show in movie house three has ended, and the crowd is slowly pushing their way toward the exit. They're like a wave of zombies – wiping and rubbing their eyes as they adjust to the light. Some of the older people walk with stiff legs, stretching and arching their backs. Luckily, that particular movie had been played in the furthest theater from where I am. I make it outside and to my car ahead of the rushed mass. An overwhelming smell of urine hits me like a brick as I rip the door open.

"Oh my god!" I startle at the scent and cover my face with my forearm.

It isn't a simple possibility that it might be pee. It's a sturdy, unmistakably powerful smell, the kind that could gag the strongest stomached man. My car is radiating with a scent you could only experience from a public bathroom full of dehydrated morning pee – piss that has sat for hours without being cleaned or flushed down the toilets. My stomach churns as my head shoots back and forth between my putrid smelling car, and the wall of humans swarming toward me. Couples stare and whisper to each other. A mother parked next to me glares, grabs her child's hand, and jerks him away. It's as if I carry a plague. *I've got to get out of here!* I hold my breath and jump in.

It takes a mere matter of moments before my jeans are soaked through. I puke in my mouth. The regurgitated Pepsi and nacho cheese are gulped slowly back down my throat – one big troubled slug, and it's gone. With my head down to avoid the forming crowd of onlookers, I turn the key. My not-so-trusty Tahoe screams to life, I slam on the gas pedal and speed away before anyone has a chance to approach me.

Looking in the rear-view mirror, I'm glad to see my police tail can keep up. He follows at a comfortable car length behind me. He stays close enough so as not to let anyone between us, yet he gives me just the right amount of distance that I don't feel overcrowded. I pull out my phone, press call on Detective Sharpe's number, put it on speaker, and then set my phone on the dry passenger seat.

"Hello?" It only takes one ring.

"Can you get a DNA sample from pee?" I demand, as I hold back a second round of barf.

"Pee?"

"Yeah! You know, like piss?"

I lean my head toward the open window, desperately scrambling for fresh air. The urine I'm sitting in has soaked my pants from belt loop to knees. The cushion sloshes as I wiggle in disgust.

"The bastard peed in my car!"

"Oh my God." His voice lowers in revulsion. "Where are you now?" He asks.

"Just leaving work. I'm about ten minutes from home, and I'm sitting in it!"

"If you want to pull over I can have someone pick it up. You could ride back home with your tailing officer."

This is an offer I can't refuse. Again, I am grateful for the help. "Deal." I gag, and then exit on the first off ramp I come to.

The remainder of the ride home feels like a lifetime. I sit on a towel on the passenger seat of my loyal tailing officer. He's angry at me for almost losing him on the drive, and for stinking up his cruiser. His strong tan hands grip the steering wheel, his knuckles are white. I can tell by the bulging jawbone protruding from his face that his teeth are clenched so tightly he could easily break one.

The towel placed between me and the car's seat is surely soaked through. I kind of hope it is, this guy is a dick. Out the corner of my eye, I notice him crack his window. He blatantly yanks the white cotton tee from underneath the collar of his uniform to pull over his nose. My eyes roll, and my brows lower in anger. Seems like innocent motions that anyone would take given the situation, but the look on his face indicates otherwise. He huffs to himself, shakes his head in disapproval, and looks down at me in anger out the corner of his eye. Typical guys guy, blame it all on the helpless girl to be such a victim. *What a douche.*

If not for the nasty wet reminder on my ass that this pee is touching me, I may have been glad to stink up this man's car. His name tag reads Smith. Officer Smith. So far, he has been my least favorite of the loyal followers. At least most of the others have been courteous. They say hello and goodbye, one of them even paid for my coffee. This uppity Smith character hasn't so much as made eye contact with me his whole shift. I wiggle my hips just a little bit to help push the wetness of my sitting towel through to his seat. It sloshes on my thighs and the nasty scent is stirred into the air.

Officer Smith has left the radio off. It allows me to listen only to the wheels on the pavement and the thoughts in my head. After wiping away my last tears for the night, I let myself feel the hatred and anger I have towards Beth's killer, rather than my fear of him. I detest him with a burning passion. I loathe him. He is an abomination in my previously perfect life, an incurable disease. A spark ignites inside me. It's one that I have never had the need to ignite, and now it's a burning inferno. I'm deciding to use this hate to overcome my fears. *I'm not playing your game, fucker.* I repeat the thought over and over.

I have a whole new feeling. A heavy weight of burning hatred presses down on my chest. Its boiling my blood from the core out. A new Markie is emerging, and I can feel it with every fiber of my being. I may have been strong and independent before, but now I will have to be smart and calculated. I'll have to harness this loathing and cage it down deep – it's to hide in a place where I can pull it out one bit at a time. The new Markie will be as cold and ruthless as the man making my life a living hell.

I no longer want for him to be stopped – I want him dead. I want to look into the empty eyes of his blood stained, lifeless face. I want to see pools of crimson flowing over a freshly mopped floor. I want to see his clothing ripped to shreds, just like Beth and Breanna's. I imagine the meaty fat from his flesh exposed. If it even is man, my conversation with Detective Sharpe the other morning still has me confused at the possibilities. The imaginings of revenge makes me smirk. I temporarily forget the piss as it continues to soak its way further and further into my jeans.

Darkened windows and an empty driveway somehow make my house look cramped and lonely. Kam must be out with dipshit Brock. *Just wait till I get my hands on that piece of shit.* A variety of news crews are spaced out on the block. I'm guessing that they haven't all heard the big news of my "gift" yet. *Thank God.* A lone van is parked right next to the base of my driveway. Fuck, I hope they don't know anything. A woman in a classy dress suit with perfect blonde hair and a tiny waist steps out. *A Barbie doll reporter, how wonderfully cliché.*

"Marketta!" She shouts as I step out of the cruiser.

Doing my best to ignore her, I put my head down as instructed and book it toward my front door. All I want to do is shed the rank layer of ruined clothing from my legs. Officer Smith remains seated in his car. He's gazing directly ahead with anger, refusing to look over at me. Normally he, or any other officer, would have jumped out of the car before I did. He should be walking me to the door, then searching through my house to make sure it is safe before I enter. Apparently, this man is too set back by the scent of my stalker's urine to do anything but sit in the smell and pout.

"Marketta, please stop!" Again, reporter Barbie's voice echoes.

My blood boils. The newfound hatred bubbles and pops inside me. It's all I can do not to explode into a thousand fuming pieces. And that's when she says it.

"Please Marketta, Tell me about the photograph! Do you know who he is going to kill next?"

Just like that. A simple sentence that to her means nothing more than part of a narrative – a fictional story to be told through her perfectly painted pink lips and thickly shadowed eyes. A story to share with her audience of ignorant television viewers, most of whom have never experienced a real loss of their own. *Who does this princess think she is?* She's using myself, Beth, and Breanna, as some sort of tall tale characters, to get herself a pay raise or promotion. I reach my key toward to door to unlock it. She repeats herself, as if I hadn't heard her the first time.

"Markie, did you have anything to do with these murders?"

I turn on my heels, and scream. "You stupid bitch!"

The rage explodes out of me. While stomping toward her like an angry bull, I continue to shout and point a shaking finger in her face.

"You stay the fuck away from me and my family."

Slowly, she backs up. She's like a kindergarten girl being pushed into the corner by a shouting bully. Only a light squeak escapes her plump shiny lips. I cut her off before any words can slip through her ever-widening crack of a mouth.

"I don't know where you're getting your information, or who the fuck you think you are, but if you don't get off my property you're fucking dead!"

I said it. I said a word that means so much more in my life than just an empty threat. A word that to her, in this very moment, is as real as the salad she ate for lunch. *Dead.* And I meant it.

My tailing officer snaps out of his pointless hissy fit just in time to witness the event. The overwhelming scent of piss has, I'm sure, set up residence in his cruiser. That is a fact that he'll have to deal with. He jumps out in panic, and rushes to my side. A hand is held on his hip ready to draw. Blondie is backed up all the way to her van and leaning against the passenger door.

Her driver is asleep against his window, a string of slobber dangles to his shoulder. Her eyes dart back and forth between him, me, and the officer who only adds to the anxiety of the moment. He takes a few steps closer, this time a little slower, and much more prepared. With knees bent slightly, one hand in the air and the other on his pistol, and a core as straight as an arrow, he awkwardly closes the gap between us.

Harness it, I think. *Control it. You need to use this anger, but not here and not now.* I take one step closer, so our faces are inches apart. Her breath is shallow, and cheeks pale.

"Don't come back." I warn.

I'm in sniffing distance of her face. The rush of my outburst is intense, and to be honest, it's strangely compelling. A thrill dashes through my veins. My chest pumps with a surge of excitement. I study her frightened face, her giant blue eyes. With one quick nod of her head, she pulls on the handle to her van door. I back up a few steps, giving her the space she needs to escape. The deep hatred boils up from my belly and shoots from my eyes. Staring her down from the sidewalk, I watch her closely. The driver returns to consciousness and speeds away.

Wet pants slosh between my thighs. Even in the fresh night air, the smell of urine fills my nostrils. The van disappears far into the distance, and I retire into my empty house. Finally, I am properly accompanied by my distracted officer.

Every room of the house is swept through before his replacement shows up for the night. I
set quickly to the bathroom to strip down and
clean up. I rid myself of my disgusting soaked
pants, and the smell they carry. As soon as the
door closes behind me I violently strip them off
and throw them in the trash.

Chapter Eight

Steamy hot water fills the tub. The mirror in front of me returns hateful, bloodshot eyes. *What does he want with you?* I pick up my phone to call Kam and Detective Sharpe before I take his advice and relax in a long hot bath. As odd as I feel taking a bath with a strange policeman sitting outside the door, I've decided it is the closest thing to relaxing I can manage with the circumstances. I press call on the phone and listen to the soft hum of a ring on the other end. Kam chimes in loud and clear.

"Markie, are you okay?" It's an octave above her regular tone.

"I'm fine. That motherfucker peed in my car today!" I vent. "What's up with your voice? And, where are you? I thought you'd be home. You're not with Brock, are you? I have some things to say to that piece of shit!" I can't help but rant. Every part of me is fuming. My skin crawls with adrenaline and anger, not to mention my nude

legs are cool and sticky from the lingering dampness of urine.

"No, I'm at Mom's house."

"Why?"

She gains my confused, yet still very distracted attention. Kam refuses to spend quality
time with our mom, she always has.

"Well, don't panic or anything, but she sort
of..." Silence reaches my ear as she searches for
the words. "She had a bit of an incident."

"Kam, what the hell are you talking about?"

"She's insisting on keeping it a secret, Markie."
Her voice plunges to a whisper.

I can barely hear her on the other end. I'm un-
sure if Kam is hiding her conversation from any
law enforcement, or from our crazy mother herself. I close off my free ear and listen closer.

"Honestly, I can't tell if she's trying to get our
attention or if it's a real thing, but she's kind of
freaking me out," Kam whispers. "You know that
she doesn't keep anything a secret. As weird as
she's acting, I can't help but believe her."

Annoyed at the suspense, I ask again. "Please
just tell me what is going on. I really don't have
the time or energy for Mom's shit right now."

"She said she was drugged. She took her medication this morning just like any other day. The next thing she knew, she woke up and it was late afternoon. She doesn't remember anything all day long. And she's really sick."

"Why doesn't she want to tell the cops?" I demand.

My impatience continues to build. My bath water is nearly full. I've had enough nonsense for one day, and I'm ready to relax. I've got to try to put today behind me – not to mention calm my nerves before calling Vincent.

"If she's being secretive, then obviously she's lying."

While holding the phone to my ear tightly, I take a hot washcloth and scrub my legs. I'm not about to share my bath with the leftover piss on my skin.

"Apparently she keeps poison in her medicine cupboard." Kam explains.

The moment of shock is short lived. "What do you mean, 'poison!?'" Now I'm enraged. I throw the dirtied washcloth into the garbage on top of my jeans.

"Why the hell would our crazy ass mom need poison?"

"She said it's for the birds, but she's acting really weird about it. She thinks that's why she's so sick. She's ranting about being drugged and poisoned. She's insisting that it'll only kill you if you have a lot of it, or if you keep taking it over a long period of time, but if you only have a little your body will puke it out." Kam pauses. "How she would know that information is beyond me." Silence again fills the line. *What do I make of it all?* Kam continues. "She is insisting that someone messed with it, drugged her, and then stole it."

"Do you actually believe her? It kind of seems like she's acting crazy and paranoid for the attention, as usual."

"That's what I thought when she first called me. But now I don't know."

"What if it's real? What if it's him?" I wonder aloud, more so to myself than Kam. My heart descends to the pit of my stomach.

"She's thrown up three times in the last two hours. I tried talking her into letting me take her to the hospital, or the police station. She insists that she is starting to feel better, and she doesn't want anyone to know she keeps poison in with her medication. She said that she'd rather die than let anyone see her so sick."

"Typical." I roll my eyes. "Of course, she's more worried about how she looks than her health."

"Yeah, I know." Kam's voice is airy with exhaustion.

I can't recall ever hearing my sister sound so drained. I realize in this moment just how selfish I've been over the past three days. I've been so worried about myself and completely engulfed in my own fears that I haven't even stopped to think about how this has affected anyone else. Kam interrupts my guilty thoughts to continue about our sickly mother.

"She's probably just waiting to make a big deal of it when she feels better and isn't afraid to stand in front of a camera."

"Oh my God, I hope not! Are you going to stay there, do you want me to come over, too?"

Please say no, please say no. God, I don't want to go to my mother's house right now, even if she has been poisoned, and even if it was by my psycho stalker.

"Yeah, I think I'm just going to stay here. I might have Brock come and stay with us."

"Yeah, because he'll be loads of help if anyone shows up."

"Will you please cut him some slack?" Kam asks.

"Hell no! He told everyone I work with about the photograph!"

"Ugh. Maybe I should just come home and make mom come with me, then we can all be together. I don't want to leave mom alone, but I don't think you should be home by yourself, either. Did you say someone peed in your car?"

"Yes! I don't really want to talk about it right now. Just come home, okay?"

I'm worn out. As much as I don't want to deal with my mom, I'm still worried about her. It's strange, the mixed emotion you get when it comes to family.

"I'm going to take a bath, and I have more phone calls to make, so I have to go."

"Okay," Kam whispers hesitantly. "I love you, Markie."

"I love you, too." Choked up, I force, "please be safe."

Our conversation turns quiet as Kam disconnects her end. I'm not certain what to make of it all. I squeeze the phone tightly in my hand and slowly release a lungful of air.

The smell of urine is still in the air. I'm sure it'll take some time to get it out of my nostrils. I dump a handful of potent lavender bath salt into the steam, then scan down my contact list looking for Detective Sharpe's number. I try to wrap my head around Kam's news of our mother. The ability to focus my vision on the numbers is nearly impossible. Names blur together, and I stand naked staring at the screen.

The last time I talked to Detective Sharpe, he promised to send someone to pick up my car. I'd set the keys on the dry passenger seat and left it on side the road in front of a busy gas station. I'm not worried about my car, obviously no one would come within 50 yards of it, not with the awful scent of piss spewing out the windows.

The news of my mother is another overwhelming addition to my day. **Detective Phillip Sharpe**, his name screams at me in bold black letters. *Do I tell him about Mom?* The question lingers, as does my finger over the call button. I make the decision to wait to tell the detective, at least until I talk to my mom. Seeing her out of my own eyes, outweighs the gut instinct to turn her in. The pad of my pointer finger finally presses down. No answer. I'll have to try back.

I slide into the bath, toes first. The warmth of the water stings my legs as I lower myself in. Wet heat makes its way up my thighs, to my torso, and finally reaching my tense shoulders. Soon my hair smooths out as it soaks on top of the popping bubbles. Lavender permeates the air; the scent floats up from the ceramic tub and fills my nostrils. The heat, steam, and relaxing scent is much needed, and more than welcome. Finally, my muscles loosen, and I can breathe easier.

I close my eyes tightly, trying to make sense of the events leading up to this moment. Again, hatred fills my core. *What am I going to do now?* I push the revulsion down deep and the shove anxiety aside. I decide to use this head clearing moment to focus on what may be smart, useful, and necessary. I think about Agent Reese, his giant hands, white teeth, and menacing words. He was right. I have to call Vincent. I was hoping to talk to Detective Sharpe first, but who knows how long it will take him to call me back.

For some reason, the thought of Vincent's voice and the bright alluring shade of his eyes while I'm completely naked is arousing. I dry my jittery hands on a fluffy gray towel and reach for my phone. A deep breath fills my lungs. My heart leaps at the sound of his sultry voice.

"Hello, Markie."

His words are confident and obviously spoken through a sexy smile. I fail to gather composure and form words.

"Are you there?" He asks.

"I... Um, yeah." I stutter.

"I was just thinking about you."

The pulse of my heartbeat pounds from ear to ear. "You too." I confess shyly. I feel like I'm walking on a tight wire of adrenaline, fear, and wonder. "Is this a bad time?" I hesitate, "I can try back later."

"No!" He stops me. I jolt in the water with excited fear. "I mean, now is a great time." He recovers quickly. "Are you okay?" He sounds genuinely concerned.

I want to scream at the top of my lungs, but instead, I quietly lie. "Yeah, I'm alright."

If he keeps up the caring questions, I may either break down into tears, or freak out yelling like a raving lunatic. "I was actually wondering if you want to get together. Like, maybe tomorrow?"

There, I did it. How could a man in question of being a brutal killer make me feel this way? I do want to see him. I can't even talk to him without the butterflies in my stomach going wild. I imagine my legs wrapped tightly around his fit waist.

"I was hoping you'd let me see you again. Dinner?" I can almost hear him beaming through the phone.

I shake nervously from the inside out. *What the hell am I doing? Use your head, Markie! You're playing a chess game – A game that you have no choice but to win.* My brain feels like it's running in circles in my head. Then it hits me. I feel like a warm blanket of reassurance, a deep-rooted confidence wraps around me. I pull the power from the pit of my belly.

"I was thinking more like in the morning. Do you drink coffee?" *Smart move.*

"Well, yes. Of course, I drink coffee, who doesn't?" He teases, easing the tense air around me. "That doesn't feel much like a date, though. Are you bumping me to the friend zone?"

I can't help but let out a small chuckle. A much-needed splutter pushes out of my lips. It's a humor I haven't had the luxury of experiencing for nearly a week. "The friend zone?" I ask.

"Yeah, you know. I'm just that guy who you want to hang out with and talk to, but would never take home after dark."

Strange choice of words, I think. Though I am a little more relaxed, this still leaves me unnerved. I am so confused. *Focus, Markie, think fast.* I retort without missing a beat.

"What if I told you I want coffee because I don't want to wait any longer than that to see you?" I flirt. It's a frightened and awkward flirt, but it feels amazing.

"Well, then I would have to say, I could come to see you tonight, and make your wait even shorter." *Shit!* Not the reaction I was going for.

"Really though, Markie, I'm thrilled that you finally decided to talk to me. The other night didn't quite go how I would have liked it to."

"Me either." I honestly reply. "I should probably go. There's a small coffee shop on the corner of 9th, Strong Bean, it's down the block from my theater. Can you meet me there at nine?"

A proud smile spreads across my face as I try to veer the conversation to an end. Rather than the yes and goodbye I was shooting for, he comes back with an inevitable question.

"Yeah, I know the place. Where are you anyway? Your voice is echoing."

He had to ask me that!

"In the bath." I almost shout my answer.

I quickly bury my face into the towel I had dried my hands on. The rest of my body remains parked in the steaming water. I can't believe I actually told him. I just confessed to being completely and utterly nude. I've never been shy around a man before, yet for some reason the small sexual gesture of calling Vincent from the bath has left me mortified. A slight choke on the other end rings through before Vincent lets out a bellowing laugh.

"What's so funny?"

"You're making this too easy."

His voice is dark. No longer am I confused, aroused, or even embarrassed. My emotions have changed at the drop of a dime to sheer terror. *Making what too easy?* The question lingers in my mind, but I can't find the courage to ask.

"I really have to go." I say, and quickly hang up the phone.

With eyes wide, and face frozen in place, I stare at the wall across from me. The sound of his sensual voice repeats over and over in my mind. *You're making this too easy. You're making this too easy. You're making this too easy.* The ricochet of words in my mind leaves me paralyzed. Unable to wrap myself around the gesture, I just can't decide if he meant being with me in general, or if he meant something different. I can't help but suspiciously fear the latter. There is something dark and menacing about him. Something unnerving, yet undeniably sexy.

With eyes closed tightly, I draw in a deep breath and slip under the water. Now that I am completely submerged in steamy, soapy lavender, I do what has been needed for days. From under the water I scream. Knowing my voice is somewhat masked, I let it out. Every one of my toes curl, and my fists tighten. Every muscle in my body is clenched. I push through my wide-open mouth the longest, loudest scream I can. Breaking down the anxiety with my voice, I tremble in the sloshy heat. It doesn't take long for my air supply to run out. I pull myself upward until my head bobs.

Again, I force my body to relax. One muscle at a time, I focus on letting go. Vincent, Detective Sharpe, Brock, the reporter, and even my mom is pushed from my mind. My meditation is deep and excruciatingly necessary. I relax my eyelids, though they stay closed, allowing my face to loosen up as well.

By taking in deep breaths, I fill my body with refreshing new focus. As I exhale, I release my fears, anxiety, and anger. One part of my body at a time, I allow myself to melt away. My mind syncs with my breath. From my calves, to my abs, to my head, and every single part in between. I take my time in the bath, wishing to never have to get out at all.

Chapter Nine

The clock on the microwave screams at me, we're probably going to be late. My head pounds, and the anxiety in my chest is unbearable. I stand against the kitchen counter, tapping my foot. Kam and Brock insist on joining me on my coffee date with Vincent. Though I'd never admit it aloud, I'm grateful for their embarrassing intrusion. I wait impatiently for Kam while Vincent's words play on a loop in my head. *You're making this too easy.* My body wants to pace the floors like a caged lion, yet somehow, I'm able to plant my feet firmly on the kitchen tile.

The press conference Agent Reese had promised took place an hour ago. A replay of the entire thing is blaring from the TV in the other room. It had been conducted by none other than Agent Reese himself. I picture the stern, straight face he maintained as I listen to his words for a second time. He explains the rumors of a picture and note as a "hoax" and asks the public to "refrain from gossip and lies."

He asks the city to kindly go about their lives with caution, and to show the victim's family the respect and privacy they deserve.

He even added in a respectful gesture to Beth's family, asking the public to include them in their prayers along with the Snyders. I want to talk to them so badly it aches, but I can't. I'll just have to keep avoiding them until everything is settled and smoothed over. I haven't gone this long without talking to Beth's mom in years, since long before she died. I can't put them in any more danger than they're already in.

I'm assuming Agent Reese even kept to his promise to speak with the reporters after the conference about leaving our neighborhood alone. Not one news crew, van, or camera is outside this morning. *What a relief!*

I glance across the bar at Brock. His fingers are hard at work playing some ridiculously childish game on his lime green covered phone. A half smirk sits on his face, while his eyes shoot back and forth. We have already gotten past the hashing it out over his big mouth, yet it takes all my strength not to reach over and slap him across the face.

Our mom is still in bed sleeping off her night of vomiting, and fever finally breaking. I felt so bad for her last night, I even let her take over my room. My bed is the most comfortable, so hopefully it offered her some rest and rejuvenation.

Kam strolls into the kitchen looking like a supermodel, as usual. Her hair is swept up in a fresh wavy ponytail. A casual yet sleek black V-neck hugs her curves. Her jeans are tight, showing off her long legs. I look down at the black skirt and pink silky blouse clinging to my body. Kam had the dressy choice laying on a chair next to my closet this morning. Although I feel inferior in every way, I suck it up and hold my head high.

"Well, I guess we better get going." Kam mumbles with a reluctant look on her face.

"Yep." Brock hops off the bar stool and tucks his phone into his sky blue golf shorts.

I glare at him from the tops of my eyes and stand my ground. He gawks innocently back at me. *I hate that 'pity me' face.* Having such a soft touch at life in general truly makes me question his manhood.

"Look, I said I'm sorry. Are you going to hate me forever?" He whines.

I don't hate him any more or less, than I had before. How does he not understand that? I let out a sigh and grab Kam's keys from her outstretched fingertips. My car is still at the station having tests run on the urine. Kam knows I'll insist on driving, so she gives up the keys to her own car without hesitation.

"Whatever," I snap at Brock. "Let's get this over with." The drive is short and quiet. Strong Bean is packed, as usual. It isn't a big surprise that we have to park in the farthest corner of the lot. I spot Vincent's sedan a few cars down from us, but he is nowhere in sight. I check out our surroundings nervously.

The building is small, and it stands alone with a well-manicured grass patch on each side. A couple picnic tables fill the space on the vibrant green lawn. One side is shaded well with a tall bushy tree. The other is bare, allowing the sun to beat down in full force. The line inside is forming all the way back to the door.

The hustle and bustle of people rushing in and out multiplies my anxiety level. On a normal day, I find the chaos comforting. Knowing I'm one with a crowd of so many is surprisingly hum-bling. Today, that is not the case. I search frantically for familiar faces. I look for Vincent and anyone else I would know. I can't help but fear someone here could possibly be Mr. Evil himself. One face stands out.

"What the hell is Jared doing here?" I ask.

"Who's Jared?" Brock responds from the back seat, high pitched and confused.

"The janitor at my Multiplex."

Kam jumps in. "There's a ton of people here, Markie, chances are you're bound to know one of them."

"You're right. He's probably getting coffee, too." My heart races. I can feel sweat forming above my lip.

"Do you see him?" She asks.

"Not yet."

"Look at you!" She sounds pleasant. "You like him, don't you?"

"I don't know what you're talking about."

"You. Like. Him." The dramatic repetition is inevitable.

I swivel to the side, just enough to face her, and glare. No words are necessary.

"You're all jittery and cute." Kam's eyes glow with excitement. "He isn't weird at all, is he? You were just saying he was weird because you actually like him, and it freaks you out!"

My sister is relentless.

"Yes, Kam." In as sarcastic of a voice as I can manage, I admit. "I want him. Oh, baby." I can't control the upturn of my lips corner.

"This is ridiculous!" Brock declares from the backseat. He exits the car and stomps towards the building.

"Wow." I say. "Who put sand in his vagina?"

"He's been a little snappy since last night." Kam confides. "I think he's as worried as the rest of us. He just expresses himself differently."

"Maybe he's on his period."

"My God, Markie. It's always has to be the feminine jokes, doesn't it?"

"Well, if the shoe fits."

"You say that, but you don't know how good he is in bed. Trust me, he's all man!"

We giggle and watch Brock disappear into the crowd, just inside the door. He stomps his feet, head down and hands in pockets. He throws hissy fits like a teenage girl.

"I kind of want to see this Vincent guy before we go in, just so I have an idea about what you're all googly-eyed over. Do you see him yet?"

"No, not yet."

It feels nice to laugh and joke with my baby sister. For the first time in days, I feel like a normal human being again. Though the moment is short lived, I feel a fraction of myself coming back to me. I wish things could return to normal with Beth, as well, but they can't. She's gone forever. The realization is of my life's trauma is overwhelming. Our grins are replaced with anxious frowns the second our conversation is over. Just like that, reality has returned.

Chapter Ten

BROCK

That stupid bitch! She's laughing, joking around, and *dating*. What the hell!? Has nothing I've done affected her at all? I'm going to have to do something drastic to put a stop to this. There's no backing out now. Kam knows she's going to spend eternity with me. Whether she wants to admit it or not, she must know it. Even if she does get scared when I tell her my secret, she'll forgive me.

We'll always love each other. It's that stupid bitch sister of hers that's always gotten in our way. If it wasn't for Markie, Kam would never have broken up with me in the first place. That whore doesn't know who she's dealing with!

Chaos of the morning coffee crowd swarms me. Standing in the middle, hidden amongst the detached group, I stew. While my thoughts shoot back and forth in plotting with blood and revenge, my face remains a stone. Handsome, cold, soft stone. Like a sleek sheet of perfect, unreadable granite. So what if I like the theatre? It's done nothing but teach me, in detail, how to be exactly what people expect.

Acting is the only thing that's gotten me from day to day, and I must admit I am phenomenal at it. Not a soul has ever been able to read my mind, I'm like a vault. And who fucking cares if I like pink and have a classy wardrobe. Can a guy not express himself? Who is *she* to judge *me*?

It's a good thing I have so much practice in the acting department. Ever since my mom and sister got "sick" when I was little, pretending comes naturally to me. Serves them right, too. It's been sixteen years – I'm still glad they are gone. My mom was always more supportive of my sister than me. How very cliché that her name was Beth. I like to refer to her as My First Beth.

A little boy holding his mother's hand stands only inches before of me. A chubby pointer finger is shoved into his dirt-covered right nostril. Long, matted hair clumps on top of his obviously unwashed head. The mother is well dressed, clean, hair carefully styled, and makeup perfected. At least I assume she is his mother. They share the same slope in the bridge of their nose, as well as an identical abnormally high forehead. She clutches the poor kid's hand so tight that her knuckles whiten. She yaps loudly on her cell phone. She cackles and gossips to the not-so-lucky recipient on the other end.

Oh, little boy, if you only knew how deeply I can relate to you. I want to take the hopeless kid under my wing and show him how to get revenge on that failure of a parent. Though my sister's death was quick and fairly painless, my mom suffered for weeks before I finished her off. At fourteen years old, I finished my childhood with nothing but a drunken, grief-stricken father, who willingly granted me all the freedom I wanted.

I toy with the thought of slipping a few drops of the poison from my pocket into the woman's coffee. My imagination fills with the thought of her with a pale, sickly, vomit covered face. Ideally, it would be a satisfying scenario and much deserved, I'm certain. A true tempt, but I have more important plans for the toxin. In order to execute my plot, I need it all. Every last drop is imperative. I examine the little boy's filthy shirt and worn sandals, and I remember all too well the similar pair I sported as a youngster.

I feel like I'm gazing into a mirror image of myself at his age. He smiles a full, gap-toothed grin, before pulling the finger from his nose to give me a wave. I smile and wave back as we fulfill the purpose of the imaginary mirror between us. The careless mother yanks him a few steps forward as the line moves.

A familiar, small set of fingers slip into my hand, they intertwine comfortably with my own.

"I love how sweet you are with kids." Kam whispers into my ear.

"I'm practicing for when we have our own." I whisper back.

Her face flattens, and she drops my hand. *Perhaps the mention of kids and our future was too much. Markie will rot in hell for veering Kam away from me.* The last couple days have been a nice change, as Kam has shown me at least some affection. I'll take it. The confusion of this "stalker" has only drawn Kam closer to me. It is an unexpected convenience on my part. This assures me that what I'm doing is the right thing for us and our future. Kam's body is only inches from my own, allowing me to take in the heat and scent of her.

It's been months since she's let me fuck her. It's all from the advice of her nosy sister, no doubt. I struggle to recall the taste of her, and I hate Markie for that. I can see it's all about to change. Kam's confusion is making her vulnerable. It's an easy opportunity for myself to become just as vulnerable in her eyes. It's such a simple act, I could do it in my sleep. Everything is playing out exactly how I've planned.

I let the fall of her hand roll off like a careless drop of water. I show no reaction to it. If Kam wants me to be her friend only, then that's exactly what I'll be – for now, that is. If nothing else I'm a patient man. Markie approaches the other side of me. Just wait until she sees what I have in store for her today! I watch her out of the corner of my eye while I pretend. I pretend to be a caring family friend who wants to assist her on a fake date with a 'possible killer,' that's a laugh. This poor schmuck picked the wrong bitch. If he stands her up, it will most definitely be beneficial to him.

"There he is." Her voice is screechy and nervous, like nails on a chalkboard.

I cringe on the inside, and grin on the out – it's too easy for me. The bitch nods her head in his direction. It isn't hard to catch who she is gesturing to. The man lights up from the inside out when they make eye contact. *Fool.* They're practically eye fucking each other from across the room. The twinkle in his cornea may as well be blinding. Disgusting.

I do like the color fade in his jeans though, and his shoes are fantastic. At least the idiot has a good sense of style, I'll give him that much. I'll have to try and make time to ask him where he does his shopping while he still can form words.

"He's handsome," I note.

My shoulder gives the bitch a playful nudge. Kam lowers her voice just right and leans into me so only I can hear.

"He actually looks nice. Do you think it's *him*?" She asks Markie, emphasizing her curiosity.

"I don't know." She answers.

Without taking their lustful eyes off each other, he pushes his way through the crowd toward us. We continue to babble as he bobs and weaves through the people. I can't help but think about the watermelon gloss on Kam's lips, and how badly I want to lick it from them.

"Well, I don't think it is," Kam continues. "He looks innocent to me."

"The worst ones always do." I jump in.

"How would you know, Brock? You're as soft as a wet noodle." Markie says.

"I can only imagine." I lie perfectly.

"Oh, you mean you can imagine more in life than rainbows and butterflies?"

"Markie, please. That's enough for today." Kam says.

My sweet, perfect, angel. She always knows to put a stop to Markie's insults. I don't even have to flatten my innocent looking smile. It's too bad her boundaries to my defense are limited and temporary. If only she could shut Markie up for good, then I wouldn't need to do it myself. *A real shame.*

On the other hand, then I wouldn't get the pleasure of seeing the life slowly drain out of the people she cares about. There's just something about watching a human's life force slip away, it's magical. Most will never have the pleasure of feeling the divinity of a kill. It's a raw power. Gets me hard every time.

Vincent is clearly a confident man, because he approaches us with his head held high. He looks like a show horse being pranced around an admiring crowd. A slight shadow of a beard blankets his face, it's just enough to give him a perfect blend of rustic and groomed. Closing the gap, he smiles at Markie. His unintentional grin shouts, "hey, look at me everybody! I'm handsome, clean cut, and in love." *What a fucking tool.* Florida seems to be full of his type.

The small vial in my pocket wants to jump out at him. I hold it tightly with a firm fist. After a moment, I loosen my grip and leave it behind, allowing my hand to exit my pocket empty. Before saying a word to anyone else, he reaches out toward me and introduces himself. He's a typical man's man, respectable, establishing dominance. He makes his place known with the other gentleman in the picture.

Gently, I place my hand into his, it's an immediate response. Without shaking back, I merely allow him to squeeze my palm and complete the gesture himself. I return his dominant eye contact with a secretive twinkle. If he only knew he's touching a hand that only seconds ago gripped his near fate. The introductions are short, an exchange of names and that's all. Once his attention is turned to Markie, there is no more acknowledgement of myself or Kam.

The line has quickly risen from a comfortably crowded chaos, into an awkward suffocation. Kam and I stand side by side and listen to the disgusting lovebirds next to us. I notice Markie's body language. Her feet are turned in his direction, allowing her torso to tilt toward him. Jittery fingers fiddle with the buttons on her blouse. Her chest fails to rise and fall with each breath, and her voice responds to him in fragments of chopped words.

Kam leans into me, and after closing the gap, she points an alert ear in their direction. We eavesdrop as a team. Her curiosity is sexy. I want to bend her over right here and now. The urge to fuck her in front of everyone at Strong Bean is insatiable, but I put instantly in check. I shake off the delusional fantasy.

"You look absolutely stunning." Vincent says, oozing confidence.

"Thanks, you're not so bad yourself." The bitch stammers. She must be embarrassed.

"I didn't know we were having company."

"Yeah, I'm sorry about that." She looks at the slatted wood floor as her face darkens.

"No, I'm glad." *Fucking liar.* "You have more reason than anyone else in this city to travel with company."

"I'm sure you are."

She rolls those ugly, bland eyes of hers. There is that infamous sarcasm, I was starting to wonder when it would come out.

"It just reminds me of how smart you are. I have a thing for brainy women."

She is already beaming. *This is going to be epic!* Killing this idiot is going to be my best move yet. Markie looks over her shoulder nervously. Her fingers begin to twiddle like an anxious child. The giant FBI Agent I saw with that nosy detective last night, and on the TV this morning stands only two people behind us in line. She clearly knows he's here. A man like him doesn't go unnoticed. She looks again in his direction, then shifts attention back to her toes almost instantly. He must be making himself known, but it doesn't intimidate me in the slightest.

They're all fucking imbeciles. Boisterous, arrogant douchebags, every one of them. This one must be brave, though, to test the waters like he is. Most of them sit back and watch from a distance. They attempt to hide. I can always sniff out law enforcement. Each one has too many tells – the way they're constantly looking out of the corners of their eyes is usually the first giveaway. Then, of course, there's the body language; each one keeps a shooter hand close to their side at all times. Hell, even the way they hold their shoulders makes them stick out like a sore thumb – stiff as a board.

Agent Reese is unlike any officer I have seen – he is smart and bold. I'll have to be extra careful with this one. I'm going to have to make it a priority to somehow have a conversation with him. I'll make him know me for the Brock I want him to see. I can't go out of my way to introduce myself, though, that might be too much. Before he suspects me to be anything different, I'll have to get into his head.

We move a few steps forward in line. I continue to stew and brainstorm. The bitch attempts conversation at my left side, and Kam continues to eavesdrop at my right. I'm tempted to wrap my arm around her perfect waistline as she leans into my side. I resist the urge. Today's challenge is going to be a little more complicated than the flowers and picture on Markie's Tahoe. Even the piss was a simple task. I can't wait until the results come back from that genius surprise!

I just hope I'm around to see the look on Markie's face when she finds out the urine belonged to none other than Breanna herself. I had told her I needed to "pass a drug test" and paid her to pee in a jar. Teenage innocence, and greed, weighed the scales in my favor. Naïve little whore even swore to God not to tell a soul. She honestly believed how ashamed I was of my addiction. She didn't want anyone to know about my struggles.

Breanna's murder was a debate in my head for some time, but it's one that paid off immensely in the end. Seeing her little boyfriend sneaking in and out of the house late at night ultimately proved that the brat wasn't as perfect and innocent as she seemed. It also told me that she could keep a secret. My classic puppy dog eyes won her over in minutes. She even told me exactly when she would be alone to pick up the pee. She informed me where to hide my car in the alley behind her house, and the best way to get over the fence in her backyard so that no one would see me there.

That stupid slut practically made the decision for me. So far, she's been my favorite. She was easy, and she played her part perfectly. Dragging her into the entryway to kill her was a brilliant confusion tactic. Plus, the scarlet color of her blood was beautiful. Her struggle for life was a lovely event. I'll never forget the airy squeak in the slice of her throat, or the last little quiver of her tits as her body twitched in its final movements.

The shitty parent in front of us finally tucks her phone into her bra and orders a spiced latte. Kam wraps her hand around my arm, just above the elbow, It mirrors the gesture that Markic and her date are engaged in. I glance in Kam's direction and give her a quick, friendly wink. It's a look that she has told me on numerous occasions "just melts" her.

She flashes me that gorgeous grin, then nods her head in her siter's direction. Her eyebrows raise in excitement. I lift mine back, hold my chest out with an obviously big drawn in breath, and then lift my shoulders intensely. A thrilling moment is shared between us. Then I mouth to her, so that no one else can see the silent words, "I know, right?" She tilts her head back and pretends to let out a squeal. I love everything about her, and I always will.

Kam then pulls her bottom lip down at the corner, exposing her nervously clenched teeth. She looks over my shoulder, again with eyebrows raised, quite obviously pointing with them. My attention is drawn to the agent. I purse my lips, and I furrow my brows. It's the best concerned face I have ever pulled. Proud of myself on the inside, I portray nothing but a frightened youngster outwardly. I love that we can have a complete conversation without even saying a word. Kam loves theatrics almost as much as I do. She sucks at acting, but the attempt is always adorable. Kam fits perfectly into my life's plan.

Vincent orders his coffee black. I glance around myself in every direction. I take note of all law enforcement, memorizing exactly where and how they stand. You can never be too aware, or too cautious. Markie and Kam order next. A young girl with long dark hair gazes over a tall counter, locking eyes with me. She has giant, beautiful, nearly black eyes, and a toothy grin.

"What can I get for you, sir?"

"I'll take a small decaf cappuccino." I kindly request. "Oh, and your bracelet is to die for!"

"Thank you," she blushes.

"Go ahead and put the three orders in front of mine on my ticket as well, if you don't mind."

"Sure!" She squeaks, and then turns to start making our orders.

"I can't possibly let you pay." Vincent interjects.

"Yeah, what gives?" Markie stands with her arms folded, and head tilted to the side. Her eyes are piercing with an annoyed, bitchy glare that I've seen far too many times. Her brows gather in the middle, and mouth pulls down to one side.

"Seeing you blush and flutter is cause to celebrate!" I shuffle my shoulders like an excited child. *These fucking idiots will fall for anything.*

Kam grins from ear to ear. "Thanks, Babe!" She grabs Markie and Vincent, each by an elbow, and pushes herself between them. She makes it impossible for Vincent to protest further.

"One of the tables outside is open, we'll be there." She flashes me a loving wink and pulls them away. *My God, she's amazing.*

Chapter Eleven

I find the perfect spot to wait, and I watch an older Latino couple who were directly behind me take their turn ordering a beverage. Following them is none other than gargantuan himself. His voice carries like a deep echo down an empty tunnel. It's a sound that instantly draws the attention of everyone standing close, as if his size isn't enough. He must be used to the lingering eyes, because he doesn't even flinch at the attention. His coffee is also ordered black. What is it with these manly men? It's like they have to prove something. I don't get it.

It's easy enough to impress and deceive, I don't understand why people try so hard to look tough. *Oh well,* I think, *if that is their preferred lie then so be it, at least I have the balls to go all the way.* There's nothing more manly or empowering than to take a life. I'll earn my gratification the right way. All these so-called "tough guys" can run around like a clump of ants on the same hill, crawling all over each other with no purpose.

My hands are steady, and my breath is calm. The terrible mother still grips her dirty child with one hand. She pays for her latte with the other and walks away. The dark-haired beauty behind the counter hustles to prepare our drinks. The Latino couple stands at my side, also waiting patiently. Agent Reese drags his giant feet in my direction. I purposefully and obviously lean around the cozy couple to make very clear, unmistakable eye contact.

I melt my face kindly, and I raise my eyebrows just enough to look nice as a greeting. This gives him no choice but to acknowledge me. There's no need to calm my breath or ease my nerves. I feel the same around him as I do every other second in every other day. I am emotionless, and completely unfazed.

"You must be Agent Reese." I look straight up at him as he closes the gap between us.

He walks directly around the couple and stands at my other side. He's very close, leaning in my direction. His voice is a little quieter than before, to keep a lower profile than he did when ordering his drink, no doubt. The close crowd includes the strange janitor from Markie's work, who just so happens to be sitting at a table just next to the door. Yet another convenience to be used at my leisure.

"And you are Brock."

The agent's body bends slightly at the middle as he greets me. No handshake or smile is offered. His face is enormous and stone cold. He is standing purposefully too close for comfort, with his chest only inches from my face. This must be some sort of intimidation tactic. He's testing me, just as he's testing everyone else here. He wants to see how we react to him. I'm not afraid. It takes merely a matter of seconds to assess the situation. *This is a cakewalk.*

How would someone else in my shoes act in this very moment? I must be somewhat affected by him, of course, but I also have to appear to be a scared, innocent boy who fears a killer on the loose. Pulling this off will be a breeze. In fact, I'm grateful for the opportunity. Finally, I have a chance to use my acting skills in a situation that requires my full potential.

"Yes," I place my hand on my chest, and pull my brows together. "Look, I am so sorry about telling the girls at Markie's work about that photograph." I sigh, "I just get so nervous. I don't handle being questioned well."

"This isn't the time, nor the place to talk about that." If it were possible for the man's voice to deepen, it would have. *He is scolding me, a helpless bystander. What a fucking dick!*

"I'm sorry, I'm sorry. You're right." *My skills at their finest.* "Markie yelled at me all morning. I don't know how to handle all of this. I'm just glad you're here." I squeak quietly in effort to appear nervous.

I look down and shake my head lightly. "I just can't wait for this creep to be behind bars and this whole mess to be over with."

I focus my eyes back on him apologetically, I and soften them at the corners. I can feel the success of our interaction rising. The agent's face softens in reaction to my stress and pity. *I knew it would work. Dipshit.* A boost of confidence weaves itself into my guts.

He reassures me, "that makes two of us."

As soon as his eyes are averted, I strategically place my left toe on top of the loose shoelace on my right foot. There's only one camera in the room, and it happens to be in the corner behind us. *This is perfect,* I'll use it to my advantage as well. As the Latino man pays, his jacket reaches over the top of a cup that is clearly marked BLACK.

This makes him the second person the camera will catch coming in close enough contact with Vincent's drink, the first being the pretty girl who prepared it. Just as the man reaches for his change, my own order is called. I take a step forward with my right foot first. This allows my left to hold the shoe lace in place. My laces untie with ease, leaving no one around me the wiser.

I pay for our beverages and compliment the girl a second time on her cheap bracelet. She blushes again, looks at her feet, and hands over my change. I'm the third to encounter the drink. I grab the cardboard holder that contains all four of our coffees. I offer a short respectful nod in Agent Reese's direction as I pass. This is my final little gesture of courtesy toward him. I'm not worried about the camera catching me with Vincent's cup.

Thanks to my dad's ironclad alibi the night of Breanna's murder, I've officially been written off the list of suspects. I told the police I was there all night visiting him. The drunken slob I call a father would rather tell a bold-faced lie than admit to passing out drunk in the middle of dinner. I was there when he blacked out and when he woke up. To him, that's as good as spending an entire evening. It's all the same thing in his eyes. *Chump.*

Markie's old janitor remains seated by the door. He is at a tall, single person bar style table, with a lone stool next to it. He occupies the space wearing the same brown jacket, and the same worn out jeans that I've seen him in a dozen times before. *He'll play his part well.* The crowded nature of the shop adds to the chaos of it all.

I walk slowly and listen intently for Agent Reese's drink to be called. I need him to be distracted when I make my move. I'm confident that he's the only one here with a useful talent of observation. I'm not at all worried about any of the other fools. The obvious undercover officer standing by the main entrance is completely worthless to their case. He spent more time staring at Kam's ass when she walked in than anyone else in the room. Even now, he's distracted by an old, chubby woman flaunting her cleavage. *Useless.*

"Large coffee, black." A cute voice calls.

Just in time. The place is packed, person to person. I push through the crowd with our drinks in hand. I make as much effort as possible to block our drinks from the camera's view. The more possible people passing by me in close enough range to touch our drinks, the better. *Isn't that nice?* The magic number could be raised without even any effort on my part. I near the door.

"Excuse me," I speak directly to Markie's hopeless janitor. He sits inches from where I stand. "Do you mind?" I ask.

Without waiting for an answer, I set the drinks down on his small table. The cardboard slides across, touching his own drink. The gesture forces him to reach up and grab it with his free hand. His body is strategically placed between the camera and Vincent's coffee. He's now my fourth. While I bend down to tie my shoe, I reach into my pocket and slide the toxin into my jacket sleeve, concealing it just right. Then I tie my shoe at record speed.

I click open the lid with my thumb and pinky finger as I rise to a stand. It's a move that I have practiced dozens of times. Carefully, I make sure no drop is spilled. My time window is tight, and my aim must be precise. The hole on the coffee's lid is tiny. I grab up the tray with my empty hand. The toxin is held carefully with the other, it remains hidden.

"Sorry about that," I flash him my friendliest smile, "I almost tripped on my laces."

"No problem." He huffs.

Jared's attention is quickly returned, spacing blankly into the crowd. He continues to sip his drink. The man is in no hurry, and obviously has no desire for small talk with anyone. Talk about being in the wrong place at the wrong time. I couldn't have picked a better schmuck to pin this on, had I planned it myself.

Smoothly, I continue to move through the crowd. My timing is precise and calculated. In the time it takes me to pass through the door's frame, and away from the camera's view, I have a mere amount of seconds to dump the toxin. If it takes any longer than that, I may be noticed by my small awaiting group. In one steady motion,

I reach for my own beverage. My readied hand passes over Vincent's cup on the way. I smoothly dump the poison, using two fingers only. It's easy to keep the small bottle hidden by my sleeve.

With a flick of my wrist, the toxin is dumped. And, with what has appeared to be one quick pull of my own cup from its cardboard restraints, the deed is done. The entire bottle of poison has been emptied into Vincent's drink. There are now three other suspects to pin it on, one of which has obviously rubbed Markie the wrong way before. Jared, I think she said his name was. She seemed unnerved when she spotted him here. *He's a perfect mark.* Evidence provided by the security camera would pass in a court of law any day.

Chapter Twelve

"Oh, this spot is nice." I beam, as I set the tainted coffee on the picnic table in front of its soon to be doomed consumer. "This tree gives perfect shade." I'm sleek and casual, as always.

"It is, isn't it?" Kam grins.

I set my own drink in the perfect spot right in front of my chair, slide both hands in my pockets, and kick back. A proud sensation of accomplishment washes through me. My body slumps back with relaxation. Vincent is distracted, his eyes glued on Markie. Her voice carries to him in awkward, choppy waves. He is smitten, and it's disgusting. The emptied poison bottle lingers in my pocket. I'm calm. I patiently wait for his coffee to cool enough for him to taste. The upper half of his body leans across the table in Markie's direction. I'm going to have to ditch this bottle before the effects of its emptied content take action.

On and on, Markie rambles uncomfortably about work. She shifts around in her seat, and she spills her guts about a girl's night. That stupid blonde friend of hers from the theater is planning it. I think I'll give her and Kam space for that annoying little event. Maybe I'll plan a dinner with my drunken father. I'll eat burnt spaghetti and watch reruns of some tasteless sitcom. He will pass out in his recliner. He may even piss himself, if it's a real good night. Either way, it still sounds better than watching Markie sip on martinis and dry hump the air to some repugnant blend of techno and pop.

Vincent watches her close and listens intently. He's like a smitten dog watching a bitch in heat. I imagine him waiting for the chance to pin her down and fuck her brains out. My beautiful Kam grins from ear to ear. She clearly likes him. She'll be shocked as well, but that's fine. I can use her dismay to my favor later tonight. Or even tomorrow. Or both! The excitement of all rises in my chest.

Anticipation is eating at my guts and pushing my heart up to my throat. My hands remain calm in my lap. There are several garbage bins spread out within the building, including one giant blue one that sits only inches from Jared, the strange janitor. Losing the evidence won't be a difficult task.

An undercover officer makes himself comfortable at the table next to us. He sits at a perfect angle to eavesdrop. Sticking out like a sore thumb, he picks up a newspaper and pretends to read the classifieds. He's as obvious as a whore in church. Even his concealed weapon leans out of his jacket, defeating the whole purpose of concealment. *Amateur.*

"So, are you sure you want to go out like that?" Vincent asks, with a concerned pull in the corner of his upper lip.

"No, not really." It's a surprisingly honest response. "I... I... I think it will be a good thing though." I can't tell if she means it or not. "I could use a fun night out."

Well played, bitch. You're cleaned up. You're flirting. And you're going out with friends. Obviously, this little meeting with FBI yesterday is the reason for the confidence boost. *Touché, Mr. Reese, you just wait.* The excitement and anticipation continue to build. Here comes my big début. This will be my first public kill. I can't wait!

"I'll be with you the whole time." Kam chimes in. "I think with all the cops around, and if we stick together, it'll be okay."

"I don't think it's a good idea."

I look Kam straight in the eyes. Her hand is casually resting on the table. I take the opportunity to place my palm over hers tenderly and continue.

"When you're not by my side, I get sick with worry."

"I'll be okay." Her kind eyes are pouring unspoken reassurance. "I promise."

"I don't feel good about this." I whine.

Vincent pipes up, "I agree." *Of course, he is on my side.* "I mean, don't you think it's best to stay in for a while? At least until the police have more time to look for this guy?"

You're a real knight in shining armor. No wonder Markie thought he was weird. Or, no wonder she pretended to be weirded out by him. A real man's man, this one is. Not for long, though, it's a shame I'm going to have to walk away for the best part. It wouldn't be right if I didn't, though. This entire coffee event must play out just right. *It has to.*

Markie jumps in before anyone else has a chance to protest. "Look!" She's easily irritated, as usual. "I don't think it really matters if it's a good idea or not. It's what we all need. And besides that, who knows if they will ever even catch this creep? I mean, really, are we supposed to hide from him forever?"

I purposefully keep my stone-faced gaze on Markie. My brows pull to the middle, leaving a puppy dog shape to my eyes. I hope she's picking up on the worry I'm trying my best to portray. I give Kam's hand a loving little squeeze. She returns the affection. Out of the corner of my eye, I can see Vincent bring the cooled cup of coffee to his lips. *That is my cue, I had better get moving.*

"I guess if you think it's best. I just hope you will consider letting Vincent and I come with you. You know, to keep an eye out." I turn my whole attention to him. The cup lowers after a few long gulps are swallowed. "You don't mind, do you?"

He lets out a small, uncomfortable cough. "No, not at all." He reaches up giving the base of his throat a light touch.

Markie rolls her eyes dramatically but doesn't say a word.

I rotate in my seat, turning back to Kam. After picking up her hand and kissing the palm of it, I go on. "We don't need to decide anything right now. Just consider it, okay?"

"Okay." She promises, humbly ignoring her sister.

I'm not worried about the outcome, because I know Markie will have her way. She always does. They won't ask, nor will they expect me to come. Especially after what is about to happen to Vincent, the wanting dog at my side. He begins to shift in his seat.

"I have to tinkle." I announce, before standing to excuse myself.

Kam again smiles that adoring little half grin, and she watches me as I rise from my seat. The cop next to us doesn't even look up at me as I move away from our table. Of course not. He has dismissed me as the weak, useless boyfriend, as has everyone else. I reach into my pocket and grab the container. I quickly wipe it down with the sleeve of my jacket. The large pockets of my shorts are serving their purpose of concealment well. I reach the garbage by the door. The café is crowded.

The people standing between myself and the security camera in the corner are shoulder to shoulder. No one notices as I drop the container, which is wiped clean of fingerprints, into the tin. The strange janitor is gone. Again, I'm filled with a sense of accomplishment. The feeling of completion and self-admiration pools in the pit of my belly. I'm moving toward the bathroom at a normal pace. There's no need to hurry. I know I have a few more minutes before Vincent is consumed by it.

Just as I am washing my hands – and any incriminating residue – after using the bathroom, it happens. The screams are blood curdling. Kam's in particular stands out amongst the rest. My heart wrenches for her, but it is worth it. I dry my hands quickly and dart for the door. Amongst the crowd, I move with the wave of coffee addicts.

I'm one with the rest of an innocent and confused people. As we grow closer to the center of chaos, I push my way to the front and rush to Kam's side. As the loving, frightened boyfriend that I am, I wrap my arms around her and shield her face. I block her view, and I protect her from the sight of Vincent's convulsing body.

The foam spilling from Vincent's lips isn't quite white, but it isn't brown either. A foul mix of fresh bubbling saliva, yellow bile, black coffee remnants, and scarlet blood droplets are all swirling together. A small breeze pushes past the frigid chaotic crowd, and it sends a light waft of the vomit scent straight to my nostrils. I squeeze my eyes shut, and I pretend to be too frightened to open them. As my face is bunched together, I take a deep whiff of the scent.

It smells like death. I pull it in, secretly relishing the rotten, sour, nastiness of it all. I love the smell of death. A fraction of shit and rust infiltrates its way into the growing acidic smell. It's beautifully disgusting. I continue to hold Kam's shaking body tightly. She clings to me. I place a hand on the back of her neck and squeeze, the way I do when we fuck. She loves that. My other hand wraps tightly around her waist. I pull her in, close enough to feel the warmth of her thighs as I harden.

"Everybody stand back!" Demands the undercover officer who was sitting at the table next to us. He waves the crowd back with open arms. "Please, is there a doctor?"

The beautiful event doesn't last long. No one can to step forward and help him in time. Even if there had been a courageous hero around, they would be of no help anyhow. Vincent had too much, and he doesn't stand a chance, I made sure of that. A small Asian woman pushes her way through the tight circle of shocked onlookers.

She shouts, "I'm a nurse, let me through!"

Vincent's shoulders give one last twitch. I stare into his eyes as the life drains away. God, I love that part. It's hard to enjoy the moment with so many people, but the rush of it is phenomenal! There is so much chaos, confusion, and fear filling the air around me. There is a distinct thrill amidst it all, one that I've never felt before. *This is amazing.*

Of all my kills, this is definitely one for the books. The woman drops to his side, but she's too late. She kneels next to him, and she places her fingers over his carotid artery. Her head drops to her chest and she shakes it slowly in disappointment. She places her hand on the inside of her shirt, then uses the cloth to scoop the foam and vomit from his lifeless mouth. Then she begins CPR. It's pointless, I know that, and she knows that, but I suppose for the crowd's sake it's necessary.

Chapter Thirteen

Our space is small and crowded. A thick taste of sweat in the air makes me nauseous. I sit next to Kam on an uncomfortable metal bench. Our legs are pressed tightly together and my hand rests between her thighs to comfort her. My fingers are squished firmly in the middle of her crossed legs, about three inches above her knees. Rather than protesting the gesture, she accepts it and leans into me in a way that I've sorely missed.

It's been a long morning at the police station. Each of us have been questioned repeatedly, first by a nurse asking if any of us have experienced any symptoms such as hot or cold flashes, any vomiting or diarrhea. She checked us for raised blood pressure, dilation of eyes, and then drew a few vials of blood. Of course, we all passed. I was able to play along. I asked the most concerned questions – my act was flawless.

After that ridiculous fiasco, the real questioning began. I'm not worried in the slightest, I nailed my answers like a pro. Markie, Kam, and I have each been pulled into the questioning room one at a time by three different men. Agent Reese was the second. Not only did he refrain from obvious suspicion, but he apologized to me for my personal trauma. I'm glad I had spoken to him at Strong Bean. I think the initial innocence of our previous introduction helped to ease our interaction here at the station.

Morning drags into early afternoon. They still won't release us, so we sit patiently and wait while they review the cameras from Strong Bean for the hundredth time. I know what they will find, so my confidence remains intact. I'm a little bit disappointed that they haven't found the empty poison container from the garbage. *Incompetent imbeciles, they'll never be able to prove anything.* Kam has been quiet. We all have been, but her more so than the rest. Her gorgeous face has remained stiff and unreadable.

Her eyes look dry and her demeanor is stony. This isn't exactly the reaction I expected from Kam, but I can still find a way to bend her emotions in my favor. I can only dream that I won't need to push her, and that she will progress to my level on her own. *Wouldn't that be per-*

fect? Perhaps this strange reaction is a sign of strength. One way or another, she'll be mine again very soon, I can feel it.

I know the thought of their mother must have crossed her mind, Markie's too. Yet, for some reason, neither of them mentioned her. Unless she'd been brought up during personal questioning, and they aren't telling each other about it. I have a comforting feeling that crazy woman hasn't been discussed. She may be nuts, but she's smarter than they give her credit for.

She was even able to hide her illness from the prying officers. She knows better than to give away her own little secret. Catching her using that poison a few months back was a blessing for me. I know her secrets, and it scares the hell out of her. Although, I have had to watch my back around her. You never know what that kind of crazy can get away with.

The little warning I gave her with the poison before dipping into her stash was necessary. It still doesn't change the fact that I feel strangely at home when she's around. Since the incident, she acts as more of a mother to me than my own ever did. Kam and Markie struggle to get along with her, but she is different with me than she is with them. It is as if she can read me as a mother should. She hides her true self from the world, just like I do.

We're on a different level from the rest of society, Evelyn and me. Our bubble is outside and above everyone else. There's a connection there. It's another reassurance that I am meant to be with Kam. We are family. There's no need for Markie, and I know that their father will never show his face again. Soon we'll be able to live a carefree life together, one that we deserve. As soon as I feel Markie has had the proper punishment for her attempt to dismantle everything that holds meaning in my life, I'll finish this game.

Kam's eyes remain blank as she stares across the room at her sister. I follow her gaze and join her in the watch. Markie looks like she's been hit by a truck and it's left her hunched over in the middle. Her shoulders slump forward, and she grips her stomach tightly with both arms. Her skin looks cold and pasty. Not only is her color gone, but there seems to be a film of something nasty growing on her top lip. A yellow tinted sweat lingers on her face.

Stupid, stuck up little whore. It's about time she showed some sort of reaction. After all I have had to risk, and all the trouble I have went through. I should've known that it would take killing someone right in front of her before she realized what I'm capable of.

Detective Sharpe's jacket hangs loosely over Markie's shoulders. Even in the growing heat of this waiting room, she shivers. She's in shock. I bask in the moment. He sits on a metal chair next to hers. Sharpe has been hovering over her on and off since we arrived. He paces around Markie like a protective mama bear, then he sits next to her and places a hand either over the top of hers or on her shoulder. I don't understand the attraction these men have to her. She has pretty eyes and a decent shape, but she is absolutely nothing compared to Kam. Markie's an eight, and Kam's a ten plus. I suppose that does make the bitch more approachable.

My Kam is intimidatingly beautiful. All our friends tease that she is out of my league, but I don't care. She's practically out of anyone's league. Most men struggle to maintain eye contact while talking to her. I don't really care about social labeling or status, her beauty doesn't intimidate me at all. We're drawn together on a much deeper level than just looks. Aside from all that, she loves being treated the same as everyone else. She hates it when people act differently around her because she's pretty. She knows how attractive she is, yet she underplays it. She's humble, and I love that about her.

A short, chubby man trots into the room. It's the same man that had called on each of us at the request of our interrogators. His shiny name badge reads Jason Laws. He looks to be in his early forties. He has an upbeat bounce to his step and an overly kind, yet unclean smile. I highly doubt he's a daily brusher. There's a thin brown layer growing over his front teeth. Despite the crappy job, and obvious lack of hygiene, he doesn't fall short of confidence. We all look up at him upon his entrance, eager to hear good news, or any news for that matter. A break in this tiring process would be appreciated.

"Well, it looks like they are almost ready to let you get to your homes. I've just got to ask you all to come with me." He bounces just a little, rocking back and forth from his heels to toes. "All together this time. The questioning is over for now, but Agent Reese would like you to look at the videos with him and possibly identify a face or two."

We shuffle out of the room. All at once, we push our way past each other through the small door. While making our way down a narrow hall, Kam grazes her hand down my arm and into my own. I wrap my fingers around hers, pressing our palms together. She gives me a squeeze. Her facial expression remains unchanged as she stares ahead, wide eyed. Jason stops in front of a door that is only three down from where we've been waiting, the journey was brief. As he reaches for the handle, Detective Sharpe turns to prepare Markie before going in. They're standing only inches in front of Kam and I, allowing me to hear every word. Again, I'm regarded as harmless.

"Markie, please don't panic when you see this."

"Why? Do you know who it is?" She instantly assumes.

"Not exactly. But you're not going to like what you see."

"What is it?" Her voice is starting to raise, as is the panic in his eyes.

The detective glances over his shoulders in every direction to ensure no one noticed her short outburst. "I'm not allowed to share any critical or confidential information with you, Markie. Please keep your voice down. I assure you we don't know who's doing this. I haven't lied to you. But there was someone at the coffee shop this morning. I'm only telling you this now because I need you to prepare yourself and focus."

She nods but says nothing.

"I need you to tell me that you can focus. You can be strong."

"I can." Her timid whisper isn't at all convincing.

Jason opens the door. He stands on the outside, holding it respectfully for us all to enter before himself. Once we've shuffled in, he stands tall by the door. His stomach pushes out past his feet, and again he rocks his body from heel to toe. The room is simple. There are no decorations and only a few chairs opposite a square-shaped desk with a flat screen mounted on the wall above it. A uniformed officer sits at the desk controlling the TV's functions by an old keyboard. Agent Reese stands behind him, prepared to bark orders. Detective Sharpe places a reassuring hand on the small of Markie's back. Again, Kam gives my own hand a squeeze.

Chapter Fourteen

"There are two surveillance cameras at the Strong Bean on 9th Street." Agent Reese jumps right to the point, wasting no time, and focusing only on the flat screen before him. "There's one in the parking lot which shows the front door in case there is a break-in after hours. The other is designed to point at the register. Luckily, it's able to capture most of the room."

The entire time he's filling us in, the officer sitting at the desk gawks at Kam. *She's mine, fucker.* I force myself to look away and show no reaction to it – a master performance, as usual. With all this practice, it's no wonder I'm great at it. If this officer were any closer, he'd be drooling all over her. Kam's used to this reaction from men.

I'm used to pretending I don't notice. Agent Reese instructs him to fast forward the tape to when Vincent entered the Strong Bean. I glance at Markie from the corner of my eye. I consciously put on a sad face at the sight of Vincent on the screen – it's like watching a ghost.

The memory is gripping as we relive the moment. *It's too bad we won't be seeing the best part, I'd love to see that again.* For the second time, I notice Vincent's stylish jeans and shoes. Shit, I'd been too worried about myself to ask him where he did his shopping. Maybe if Markie hadn't been rambling on about her life, as usual, I may have been able to squeeze it in. Oh well, it's too late now.

Shockingly, Agent Reese's voice seems to deepen. It catches the attention of the officer who had slipped right back into his infatuated stare at Kam. He quickly returns to position.

"As you can see, there are no hands that come in direct contact with his mouth, including his own. The crowd is tight, but there isn't a moment where he consumed anything."

We watch closely, confirming the agent's observations.

"Pause it." He examines our faces as we take in the paused screen. "Look closer. Do you see anyone or anything out of the ordinary?"

I scan the faces and positions of everyone on the paused screen. Markie, Kam, and I are visible, but only from behind. I look closely at my hand placement and pockets and I see nothing. *Phew!* There is nothing in this shot that could possibly trace the murder back to me. Kam shakes her head slightly; she can't see anything either. Markie takes a step forward and squints her eyes at the TV screen.

"Oh my God." She whispers.

"What is it?" Kam asks. This is the first thing she's said in the last hour.

"Right there."

Markie points her finger at the top right corner of the screen. There's a man that I've never seen before. He's reaching a right hand into a container that sits on the tall counter of ingredients next to a large cappuccino machine. I didn't notice this man while we were there this morning. Even now, I'm certain that I've never seen him before. He's a fit looking Hispanic man. He's wearing the same Strong Bean uniform as the rest of the employees. Another unexpected convenience for me. Today just gets better and better. I can't wait until I get to leave with Kam. I hope she finally lets me back inside her.

"Do you know that man?" Detective Sharpe asks her. He lifts a brow and cocks his head to the side. I can tell he already knows the answer.

"I dated him." Markie chokes, her bloodshot eyes widening.

"Who is it?" Kam asks again. "I don't remember you ever dating anyone who looks like that."

It's a nice way of saying she doesn't ever remember Markie dating a Hispanic man. I'm surprised she didn't just say it outright. Kam usually doesn't sugarcoat anything. Perhaps having Agent Reese stand so close is persuading her to stay on her best behavior. She stares at her sister impatiently with lowered eyes.

"It was a few years ago." Markie explains. "Do you remember that Roberto guy Beth dated?"

Kam offers a nod, nothing more.

"She talked me into going out with his brother a few times. His name is Hector. I don't remember his last name. It was different from Roberto's, and I could hardly pronounce it."

Kam seems slightly unsatisfied with the answer but refuses to respond to Markie, or at all for that matter. She turns her attention back to the TV and takes a closer look.

"I actually put his name on the list." Markie mumbles to Detective Sharpe.

Agent Reese again takes control. "We suspected you may know him. We contacted the owner of Strong Bean and spoke with them directly about him. He's only been employed there for a few months. His name matched one on your list, but we couldn't be certain it was the same Hector. Watch closely as the video continues."

The officer presses play, and the film resumes. Hector is only in the video for the few seconds it takes to place his hand into the coffee, then he walks away.

"Now keep your eyes on the container." Agent Reese instructs us.

I watch the video closely, as does everyone else in the room. Like zombies, our attention is unwavering – we all stare wide-eyed, our bodies leaning forward, arms to our sides. I don't watch the container as much as myself, the visible officers, and Agent Reese. Even the woman that had been in front of us with her dirty child and the old couple directly behind us are in perfectly clear view. We move forward in line. I watch myself slip a hand into my pocket – it didn't look out of the ordinary in any way. *Damn, I am good.*

The container Hector had reached into remains untouched until after we all order. I watch my beautiful Kam pull Markie and Vincent outside. I watch myself waiting for our drinks. Just then, the cute woman behind the counter mixing our drinks reaches into *the* container. Her hand swirls around for a moment before she tips the container to its side. She is very clearly scooping the very last ration of coffee out of the container. She dumps the scoop into a small single cup machine, presses a button, then she proceeds to refill the container.

"Pause it." Agent Reese says. The officer obeys, and the screen stops in place. *This is classic!* "As you can see, this is the one and only cup of coffee made with that very scoop." *What are the odds?* "Hector had placed his hand in the container, walked away, and then this young woman used the contents for one cup of coffee only. Now, watch that cup."

The officer presses play again, and we watch intently. The Strong Bean girl filled a much bigger coffee machine, the kind that is normally used to mix dozens of drinks at once. Then she returned to the single cup that had been made with the last, possibly tainted coffee from the container. She writes one word on the side of the cup with a marker then places it in a four-drink holder sitting on the counter.

"Zoom in." Reese commands. As the picture closes in, the word comes into focus. BLACK is printed very clearly on the side of the cup. "Zoom back out." The screen returns to normal. We continue to watch closely.

"Oh my God." Markie whispers.

I join in the shocked moment. I place my free hand on my chest, squeeze Kam's palm with the other, then I draw in a very deep breath. I let the air out slowly and obviously. Looking spineless and in shock always is imperative, especially around Agent Reese. The video rolls on. The cardboard drink holder is filled. I watch myself on the TV walk up, pay, and then grab that very holder.

"Pause it again." The screen freezes at Agent Reese's command.

"I don't get it." Kam says. "I mean, why use that last scoop of coffee to fill just one cup? Why didn't she just refill the container and get the big normal machine working? It doesn't make any sense." She looks over at Agent Reese, confused. "Does it?"

"The only sense we can make of it is that it would have taken too much time had she waited for the bigger machine. By preparing one cup first, it prepares in moments, and it gives time to refill everything else."

Kam nods in agreement.

Markie is starting to sway in place. It's not a big movement, but if she doesn't unlock her knees, she might pass out. *That would be perfect! My efforts are finally paying off.* She shifts her body weight onto one leg and bends the other at the knee. *Damn it!* Her silence remains.

Agent Reese goes on to explain. "Hector, as you can see, is our first person of interest in light of this morning's events."

"Wait." Markie springs back to life. "First? Are there more?" Her chest rises and falls in short, panicked breath.

"Yes. Now that the drinks are in Brock's hands, watch them closely." Reese instructs.

The video resumes, and I hone in to watch myself. Our morning continues to repeat itself before our eyes. It's hard to see the drinks every second as I walk through the crowd, I weave in and out of view perfectly – still seeming innocent. The cardboard holder is visible for one second, and then hidden the next. Shoulders, heads, and elbows all mix together in chaos, making it impossible to watch the drinks only. Then I stop and place the drink holder down on a table. The view is perfect, exactly how I had imagined it to be.

"Right here, pay attention," the agent jumps in.

The footage rolls on. The back of Markie's janitor is in full view before our eyes. We all look closer, witnessing the events. It plays out just as I had meant it to. I had bent over to tie my shoe and Jared's hands lifted towards the drinks on the table, yet the exact placement of them is blocked. The angle is perfect, as I suspected. There was a short gap of people passing between the camera and myself. My heart drops, and I look even closer. *Thank God.* The view of my hands confirms the fact that I was tying my shoe. There is no way to see into my sleeve. The poison bottle remains unexposed. *That was too close for comfort.*

I can feel Agent Reese staring at me as I watch the video. His eyes are burning a hole into the side of my face. I'm not surprised. He's a smart man, and he's watching my reaction to the video, no doubt. I'm the only other one who handled the drinks, so his caution makes sense. *Well played, sir. Well played.* It's a good thing my poker face is perfected. I haven't even flinched. I'm unreadable, completely untouchable. Little does he know they helped the killer rather than hurting him.

Now that I know exactly what the video shows, my confidence is secured. It's confirmed, they have nothing against me. I'm a step ahead and assured in my proof of innocence. They can't even play any sort of connection or coincidence in Vincent's murder with the death of my own family members. My mother's and sister's deaths were ruled as "natural causes" with no foul play suspected. As far as Agent Reese, or any other intruding FBI fool knows, I'm a broken young man who lost his beloved family to an incurable illness at a tragically young age. I have the incompetence of our local Coroner's office to thank for that. Markie pipes up as soon as the video shows me walk out the Strong Bean door and out of sight.

"That motherfucker." She mumbles.

"Do you know who that was?" Detective Sharpe asks. "We've been trying to identify to him, but he didn't look up into the camera even once all morning."

"His name is Jared, he's the janitor at my theater."

"Are you sure it's him?" Agent Reese asks.

"Yes." She rasps, with a sickly dry throat. "He wears that exact jacket every day, and I saw him when we first got there."

Kam butts in. "You can't actually see his hands though, isn't it more likely it was that Hector guy?"

"We have to consider all options." Agent Reese answers quickly. "The question is, Markie, would you be able to confirm the identity of either of these men in court?"

"Yes." The word catches in in her mouth and she chokes on her spit.

Chapter Fifteen

My car glides perfectly into a tight slanted space in front of my apartment. It's the same spot I've parked every day since I moved in years ago.

"You think it's okay that I left Markie to come with you?" Kam struggles with her words.

I can hear the dryness in her throat. This is the first I've heard her voice since we left the station. I turn in my seat to give her my full attention, then I grab her hand and place it gently into mine.

I assure her, "yes, Detective Sharpe promised to stay with her for the rest of the day. Markie will be fine."

"It's not Markie I'm worried about." Her face is flat as she stares out the windshield. That awkward unreadable gaze she had at the station has returned.

"Kam?" I give her hand a gentle squeeze. There's no response. I cup her jawline in the palm of my hand, and softly turn her face toward mine. "I'll never let anything happen to you, I promise."

She gapes into my eyes with her own wide and burning. There isn't a hint of fear. It feels like she's warning me in some way, but she can't find the words. Her brows pull down angrily in the middle and her lips are pursed – so tightly that they're tinted white around the edges.

"Can we just go in?" She finally mumbles angrily.

"Yes." I whisper back.

We sluggishly move up the short walkway, hand in hand. A police cruiser parks directly across the street. I know he's only there to keep an eye on things. They haven't followed Kam quite as closely as Markie, but they still *have* been following her nonetheless. The officer doesn't step out, he only watches. My key turns in the lock with a small click, and we step inside.

Immediately after the door closes behind us, Kam shoves me against the wall. No words are spoken as she forces her body against mine. Our lips press tightly together. The kiss is deep, passionate, and violent. Her tongue moves roughly. My hands feel their way around her perfect body. They start at the base of her neck and move slowly down. Her back is warm. I grip my hands around her hips as they press against me. Reaching up her shirt, my fingers melt at the warmth of her skin. I pull my mouth away and search her face. I've got to know if this is what she really wants. I examine her eyes intensely, she doesn't blink. Her tits press against my chest, allowing me to feel her wanting breath.

"I need you inside me." She breathes inches from my mouth.

I grab her around the waist and return the affection. This time my kiss is just as rough. I shove my tongue against hers, drinking in every drop of her. My shirt is ripped from my body and I return the favor in one swift motion. The hooks on her bra snap under the pressure, allowing her breasts to escape. The pink tint of her hardened nipples is perfect.

Her back feels hot and smooth under my fingertips. She bites my lip. I can taste a small tinge of rust as the blood is drawn. *Oh my God, this is happening – it's finally happening.* I'm hard as a rock. Her body pushes against mine. Heat radiates from her body and fills the room, her warmth surrounds me.

I grab hold of her pants and pull them open at the button. My hand glides down her center, squeezing its way in. She is wet and hot. With half of my fingers in and half out, I make a fist, then lift. I pick her up by the middle, spin her around, and slam myself against her body. We switch places, putting me in complete control. Kam lets out a lustful moan as her back crashes against the wall. One of her legs lifts to my side, wrapping around my waist. Her stomach clenches to my touch. I pull out my hand and drop to my knees. To savor the moment, I slow things down. I take in every inch of her body. My eyes gaze up at her and I peel off what's left of her clothing.

Perfection stands before me. She leans against my wall, panting, waiting for my cock. *How did I get so lucky?* My hands feel up her legs and around the back of her as I begin to taste. She likes it when I bite, that's one thing I could never leave out. To start things off, I give a soft nibble and her knees buckle.

This is much better than Joyce, although, I don't think I'll quit her, not yet. Joyce has done her part in keeping us a secret, and I may need to use her in some way or another.

Kam's hands reach down to grab the skin on my shoulders and her back arches harder against the wall. The flavor of her is to die for, I'd never stop killing for this.

Breanna's dying face flashes in thought as my tongue continues pulse against Kam. I also think of Beth – her scent was similar to Kam's. It's an amazing blend of sweet and salty. I had to have a taste as Beth passed, I couldn't help myself. As Kam crumbles before me, I go back in memory to the day I took Beth's life. Just as Beth was slipping away, I had reached inside her, and then I let her watch me as I sucked the wetness from my bloodied gloves. The terror in her face had been identical to that of Vincent's this morning. The thought of all the empty lifeless faces sends a surge of adrenaline down my spine.

The pace of Kam's breath and the squeeze of her fingers on my shoulders let me know that she's getting ready to climax. I stop. I'm not ready for her to cum just yet – I want to go with her. I want to make sure that her reaction to me today will be remembered. I'm going to punish her, let her body build up the tension, then relax before she can finish. I'll do it all day if I must. I want this to be our best sex yet. By taking a life this morning, I started my day out right.

I'm going to finish it exactly how I've dreamed for a long time. I stand slowly while she catches her breath. Her chest rises and falls. Her mouth is open just a crack. I lick her bottom lip and drop my jeans to the floor.

I press against her, trapping her between myself and the wall. I lift her arms far above her head by the wrists and caress them. Very slowly I skim, letting my hands stop as they caress her ribs, just beneath the breast. I move them inward, just enough to allow my palms to take hold of her tits – only the outer edges, the meaty part, my favorite part. Kam gasps as I force my hard cock between her wet thighs. I don't push it inside her, I just rub her against it getting myself hot and slippery. I tease her. She knows I'm big, and I'm ready, but I make her wait.

"Is this what you want?" I whisper seductively in her ear.

"Yes." She gasps.

"Tell me."

"I want you."

"You want me to what?"

"To fuck me." She manages to say.

"How?"

"Hard."

"How hard do you want me to fuck you?"

Kam shoves me away with one quick push. Her eyes are burning with anger.

"I want to feel every inch of you. I want you to fuck me harder than you ever have before." She demands.

Kam takes a step toward me, and she pushes me again. The couch stops my body from being shoved any further, the leather arm reaching mid-thigh.

"Tell me again." I insist.

I love to hear the words – to watch her mouth as she says it. Again, she presses her hot body against mine. Her voice is lowered, and her eyes are piercing.

"Fuck me now."

As soon as the words escape her mouth, I grab her. My hands squeeze tightly around her waist, our faces only an inch away from one another. Her eyes bore into mine. This feels different, more intense than ever before. It's the realest moment we've ever had. She's reading me like book. I feel like she's looking into my soul for the first time. Adrenaline surges through my veins. She knows me, and she's not afraid. She wants it, and I'm going to give it to her. She'll take in every inch of me, just as she's asking for.

I kiss her softly, but only for an instant. Then I grab her by the hips and in a flash, I throw her body forward over the couch. Her back end is exposed, allowing me to slam my cock inside her. As hard as I can, I thrust in and out. Her squeal is muffled by the cushions of the couch. I hold her upper body down with my forearm, relinquishing control of her ass and legs to me. Switching the angle, I bend at the knees and push.

She clenches, and her right thigh gives an involuntary jolt. I lift my arm from her back and allow her to come up for air. As she inhales deeply, I grab her ponytail by the base and jerk back. I pull her to a standing position violently by the hair. She moans with pleasure in reaction. She likes it rough and I love that about her.

Her hands form into tight fists grabbing hold of the couch. She takes me in, arching her back. I fuck her as hard as I can. She moans each time I enter her and tightens her grip on the couch. One of her hands reaches back and she wraps her fingers around the back of my neck. I feel around her waist, up her chest, and between the tits. They bounce with each pump. I grasp one and squeeze tightly.

After a few minutes, Kam pulls away from me. She turns so we can face each other. She reaches her hand down to put me back inside her. I'm not going to give it to her. It's her turn now, and I'll make her work for it. I guide her to my room by her hair. She's exactly where I want her, and I know she'll do anything. She finally wants me.

"Get on the bed." I order.

Kam climbs onto the bed and lies flat on her back.

"Do it."

She knows I like to watch. My bed is tall, it reaches just below the waist. I grab her by the ankles and pull her to the edge as she touches herself. Her hands are hard at work and her eyes are wide open as she watches my face. After a moment of pleasure, she closes her eyes and drops her head back on the mattress. As softly as possible, I tickle the inside of her thighs.

My eyes are glued on her. Her chest rises and falls. She has let me watch before, but she was more self-conscious. This time she holds nothing back. My head tilts to the side. I imagine Breanna and Beth. Had I not been dressed head to toe in a plastic suit, I may have allowed my body to feel their warmth drift away.

Kam's breath is getting heavier. I pull her down the mattress closer to me until her legs hang over the edge. She lifts them up and wraps them around me. I watch closely as I ease inside. I allow myself only a few pumps before I grab her around the middle and toss her further back onto the bed. I climb atop her, delicately tuck a loose hair behind her ear, and kiss her passionately. Her cheeks are hot and flushed. Our bodies move in sync, pushing and pulling each other from one end of the bed to the other. I take her at every angle.

Kam is amazing in bed. I've missed this. I will never let her get away again. I would rather her be dead than out of my bed. She climbs on top to climax. Her hips rock and sway. She leans back, giving me a full view. I'm ready, I let myself go as I feel her tighten around me. Her head falls back, and she lets out a squeal. The heat and nerves of my entire body pull to the middle and my stomach flutters. Veins surge, and a powerful shockwave takes over. I sit up and wrap my sweaty arms around her damp waist. I push and twitch as the last of me surges into her.

We collapse next to each other on the bed, momentarily paralyzed. Every muscle in my body is relaxed. I struggle to catch my breath. *This is the best day of my life.* Fuck Markie and fuck those stupid bitches I had to take out. Kam is worth it. This moment is worth it. Kam would never have come with me this intensely if she hadn't seen me kill Vincent this morning, I know it. After a few minutes of holding each other close, Kam finally lets me in on her thoughts.

"Do you remember a few years ago when we were playing around and arguing over who loved the other more?" She continues before I have a chance to answer, "I asked you if you would die for me, and you asked if I would kill for you?"

I sit silently, I'm not sure how to respond, exactly. I continue to rub and tickle her back without a flinch.

"I would." She whispers flatly.

"You seem different." I say, secretly digging for more. I'm not ready to tell her yet. She might be talking like she's ready, but she isn't. She's smart, but I won't let her trick me into confessing anything.

She sits up to look at me. Her face is blank, and her eyes have an intense, almost confused pull at the outer corners. "Is it weird that I was glad when Beth died?" She asks.

"No." I answer honestly.

I stare back into her face and try to understand what she is getting at. She's completely unreadable. She waits for a more detailed response. I hold back. She's clearly not ready yet. Hopefully soon, though, very soon. Kam lies back down at my side. Her head rests in a comfortable slump between my shoulder and chest.

"I haven't been scared. I've been confused, sad, and even sick, but not scared."

"You'll always be safe with me." I comfort her.

"I enjoyed watching Vincent die today." She lets out a deep breath. "That's what scares me."

I can't tell if it's the truth or a lie. Her statement seems forced, as if she is rummaging for something. I can't help but get a feeling like she's testing me, *and after such unbelievably amazing sex. How dare she?*

Chapter Sixteen

KAM

A warm swig of whiskey sloshes around a shot glass between my fingers. I stare at the rank liquid, knowing that it's going to taste awful.

"Are you sure you want to do this?" I ask Markie. It's been exactly two weeks since Vincent was killed.

"Yes!" She barks. "We've already canceled and rescheduled it enough. You heard Agent Reese, it's necessary."

"Last time he was wrong."

"You think I don't know that?"

The color in my sister's face has changed. Not just today, but slowly over the last few weeks. The dark rings under her eyes are prominent, and the rosy hue of her lips has faded into a sickly cream color.

"I'm just saying, Markie, it's been two weeks since you quit working. Nothing's happened while you've stayed home. Maybe it's best to give it a little more time."

"Exactly." Her voice is shrill. "Nothing. No leads, no arrests, not even a person of interest. Nothing." She says matter-of-factly.

"That's not exactly true. They are still watching Jared."

Markie rolls her eyes and lifts the shot glass sitting directly across from my own.

"Fuck Jared." She mutters.

Our glasses clink together. My throat burns in reaction to the rampant liquid and it heats my chest. I wash it down with iced soda, then pour us each another. Vincent's murder changed my sister in a completely different way than Beth's had. She has developed a weird sort of anxiety that comes and goes almost hourly.

It's as if she's slipped into a permanent state of shock. When she isn't pacing around itching her skin and grumbling at everyone, she becomes a blank slate. Physically she is present, but inside she is gone. A manic state seems to take over, and she fades away.

It's a good thing the owner of her theater let her take a leave of absence. I'm quite certain she wouldn't be able to work like this. She can't even function around the house like a normal person. I've had to carry her weight in practically every way. I don't mind the cooking, shopping, or the cleaning. I even had to shampoo the couch and carpet in the living room. There was a hint of urine that was starting to get to me.

I know that I should have turned it into Detective Sharpe, especially since the whole incident with Breanna's pee in Markie's car. I couldn't do it, though. I'm still too undecided about what to make of Brock.

It's too much to risk. I've seen him pee on far too many friends' houses and people's cars after they've upset him. Once I asked him why, and his response was,

"I can't think of anything nastier or more degrading than being pissed on."

I know how badly he hates Markie, so I cleaned it up – along with the rest of the carpet in the house, to make it seem like a normal thing to do. I even told Agent Reese that I was trying to do something nice to cheer Markie up – I'm pretty sure he bought it.

I love Brock. I'm glad we're back together, too, but at the same time I'm confused. I don't want it to be him, but something is off. I know him better than anyone. He's hiding something, I can tell, yet somehow the deaths are drawing me closer to him. It's unnerving and stressful, but I'm determined to figure it out. I even pretend to be vindictive, just to see if I can lure any kind of confession from him. Though he does make a good point about Markie, she really is a selfish bitch. She doesn't care about me, and never has. I've tried my entire life to put her first, right along with everyone else.

I may talk a big game, but inside I'm just as big a wimp as the next person. Who would have thought that I'd be the one holding everything together and trying to get to the bottom of things? Markie and I have fun together, for the most part. We can talk to each other freely and openly, we're even comfortable enough to play practical jokes, but she holds back, I can feel it. I'm just not Beth.

I will never measure up to her best friend, therefore she'll never let herself open up completely. *It kills me.* Every time I try to tell her how I feel, she clams up. She turns away from me and shuts down. She always has, too, even as little kids. Markie has never trusted me, and never loved me.

If Brock does have a sadistic side, if he really is a killer, then *I think* I can get past it. Even after watching Vincent die. I love Brock, and he loves me. I can help him. *Right?* The more I consider it, the more certain I am that he'll let me help him. I don't want anyone else to die, but I don't want to lose him either. He's worth it. *Isn't he? God, I wish I wasn't such an indecisive fool!* It's a curse to be so understanding. I get where he is coming from, I really do. I even understand the thrill of death, I've felt it myself.

I take a profound look at Markie. She sits across from me and glares blankly into space. It's a look I've grown accustomed to. The only person she seems to normal up for is Detective Sharpe, or Phil, I should say. I don't think he's going anywhere, so I might as well get used to it. She even calls him by his first name, and it's much more irritating than I want to admit. The simple truth of their strange connection is exasperating. It makes my helping Brock very complicated.

Then again, it also pulls Brock closer to me. He needs me that much more. Detective Sharpe's little infatuation with Markie is a distraction, and that's good, but I think he's starting to suspect Brock. He's been questioning him a little more. Brock handles it okay, but I know him too well. He's second guessing himself and stumbling over his words more and more often. Markie lets out a long sigh as she relaxes her head into the palm of her hand. Her elbow is supporting the weight of her head entirely. I guess its time to address the issue before Brock shows up to give us a ride.

"I don't understand why they completely stopped watching Hector." I point out.

I slide my sister's refilled shot glass back into her fingertips. She sits up straight, lifts her brows awkwardly, and raises her cup as the words come out. She's clearly mocking Agent Reese, as she pulls her chin to chest and lowers her voice.

"Clearing that coffee bin of any sign of poison is enough." She mocks, then lets her shoulders slump back to the previous, 'I couldn't care less about life' position. "Fuck him, too." She declares just before gulping her second shot.

I hang on to my own shot, not quite ready to drink it.

"Who all is coming tonight?" I ask.

"I'm not sure. I left it all up to Tiffany."

"You haven't called anyone yourself?"

"No." Her response if flat. She doesn't seem to really care. That, or she doesn't want to talk at all.

"Well, I think it's too soon, but..." I stand up straight and take the shot. My shoulders shudder as it goes down, then I finish my statement. "I'm going to try and have fun anyway. I can't take all of this depressed shit."

"Yeah." She mumbles, then reassumes her palm to chin position.

"Brock should be here any minute. Do you want another one before we go?"

Markie takes a glance at her empty glass. One lingering drop of leftover whiskey taunts her from the bottom, so she shrugs.

"Sure, I guess. Might as well save a couple bucks. No sense in spending too much at the club."

"Yeah." I agree.

I stopped on my way home to pick up this bottle of whiskey, knowing full well the reason Markie would want to drink before the club. I used to sit back and watch quietly as her and Beth would repeat the ritual time and time again. I was never invited, and never included. I'd listen from a distance while they laughed and joked about only spending twenty dollars on a bottle and then letting other people pay for their drinks at the bar. They'd compliment each other's outfits and hair, catch a buzz, then leave.

I'd be left alone at home, hoping Brock would show up. He always did, too. Even when I took Markie's advice and tried to blow him off, he was still there for me. It's strange how my body now can feel that same vulnerability it had then, just from the memory of it. A thin, steady stream of liquid escapes the bottle in my hand. The exact same whiskey *they* used to drink fills *our* glasses. Despite my efforts, Markie doesn't seem to notice or care. Yet another day of pissing into the wind with her. It's pointless, I know.

"Have you tried calling Dad since all of this has been happening?"

I already know the answer, but I ask anyway. Neither of us have spoken with our father for God knows how long. Years. I bring him up now for conversation's sake only. He's been heavy on my mind, and I can't place why. I'm glad I met Brock before our father left us. He was the only help I had in getting past the abandonment.

"I haven't tried." Markie downs her drink without even looking up from the table. "Why would I? It's been years. We probably don't even have the right number anymore."

"I don't know, just thought I would ask." I sigh and swallow my drink. No "cheers" or clinking of glasses. *It's going to be a long night.* "Well, I tried calling a few times. It goes straight to some automated voicemail." I make effort to keep conversation flowing. It's an utter fail.

"Fuck him, too."

Her short declaration of carelessness says so much more than three short words ever should. She stands slowly, and then drags her feet across the floor to exit.

I look down at the loose, sparkly gold top that hangs elegantly from my body. My back is completely exposed. It's a top I've owned for a couple years but have only worn on one other occasion. I usually like to stay modest, but tonight is different. Brock is going to drive us, and I want to give him something to think about. Maybe if I can make him weak at the knees he'll cave in and finally confess. The more time rolls on, the less I think about Vincent. Even the image of Breanna's bloodied body passes through my head less and less. I feel safe with Brock. This little game we're playing is wrong, I know, but it's exhilarating.

There's something delightful about the risk of it all. An unspoken secret is passed back and forth between us. Not only is the not knowing an adventure, but the sex is unbelievable. Brock seems so different lately, like a wild animal. He's caged in public, and I get to release him at night. I even have a couple bite marks to support my theory. My hand reaches up and rubs a sore, swollen spot on my ribs, just below my right breast.

A ring of the doorbell catches the air in my chest. It can't be Brock, he doesn't knock. I hurry to pour and swallow another shot. A second ring echoes through the house. Markie obviously isn't going to answer the door. I roll my eyes and sigh, as if someone can see the notion. *Of course, she's not going to answer.* I hurry to the door anxiously. I'm readying myself for anything that tonight might bring. Agent Reese fills the doorway completely.

"Kambriella." With an outreached hand, he addresses me formally.

"Sir." I accept his engulfing handshake with a friendly smile.

Detective Sharpe stands to his side. Over his shoulder I can see a uniformed officer parked in the usual spot, as well as an undercover man in a black pickup a block down. He is ready to follow us to the club, no doubt. I step aside and hold my arm out, allowing them in. The routine never gets old. They come over regularly and it's the same thing – formal and kind. They're getting nowhere, and they're making no progress.

The agent's eyes scour my body as he brushes past. *Yes! The outfit is a hit already.* This is going to be great. I can't wait to see the look on Brock's face when he gets here. Markie is sitting on the couch. Her face lights up at the sight of the detective. He's like a switch, waking her brain.

"Markie." He acknowledges her, and makes himself comfortable on the couch, close enough for their legs to brush, but not too close to consider it a cuddle.

"Hi, Phil." A light, airy breath escapes her as she gives him a short greeting.

"Can I get you guys anything?" I offer. "A drink. Water, maybe?"

"No, thank you." Agent Reese declines loudly. "We're only here to go over a few things before you go to the club. Your boyfriend was right behind us. We can wait until he comes in."

Brock barrels through the door before I even have a chance to sit. The agent wasn't kidding when he said, 'right behind.' Brock must have hurried when he saw them pull in, so he wouldn't miss anything. It's odd that I didn't see him when I glanced down the road. Detective Sharpe rolls his eyes, very obviously, at the sight of him. It's clear that he's not a fan of Brock. It makes no difference to me.

Brock stops in the entryway. Wide eyed, he gawks in my direction with an open mouth and flushed cheeks. I return his stare with a confident beam. He's frozen in place with no notice of

235

our audience. It's an uncomfortable moment of silence for everyone else in the room. I couldn't care less either. It doesn't take long for Agent Reese to clear his throat. Irritated and loudly, he draws our attention.

"I... Um... Hi..." Brock stutters into the agent's direction, but his gawk at me is unwavering.

I chuckle and look down at my outfit. "You like it?" I ask.

"Yes." Brock's response is fast and eager. He grins from ear to ear, still unable to look away.

Brock moves to my side, slow and devious like a fox. He grabs me by the hand and pulls me down onto his lap. We sit in the chair across from our guests. Our backs are turned slightly and only the front of our bodies are visible to them. A chill rushes over my skin as his fingers instantly feel their way up my exposed back. I shift on his lap. I can feel the heat of his legs through my skirt.

"We've already spoken to Tiffany and Meagan. We actually just left Tiffany's apartment."

Agent Reese jumps right into the business at hand. No pleasantries. No fooling around. Aside from the slight distraction of the sexy hidden back rub and the forming lump under my lap, he has our attention.

"I just want to go over a few reminders." He continues.

Markie finally looks away from the void of nothing she's been lost in. Her careless attention meets the agent's face.

"We'll have a few men inside and outside the club. There's enough of us to focus on each of you, always. No one will be left unattended, but naturally we want to make sure that you take your own precautions as well."

"What about Joyce?" Markie asks.

"We spoke with Meagan over the phone this morning. According to Tiffany, Joyce isn't planning to make it. We tried to call her just in case, but we were unable to get through. We left her a very detailed message."

"Maybe we should stop in on our way there and see if she is home." I suggest to Markie, trying to get her attention. "Maybe she'll change her mind."

Brock shifts uncomfortably underneath me.

"I'm pretty sure she's home." He says. "I've been at my dad's house all day. Her car was in the driveway when I left to come here."

Brock's father lives right next to Joyce. The houses are close enough that you could jump out of a window from one house and land inside a window of the other. They were very close friends as kids, Joyce and Brock. Her parents moved to some hoity-toity neighborhood a few years back and gave her the house she grew up in. They travel the world, and she enjoys a carefree lifestyle. It's a life that's been handed to her on a silver platter. I kind of think she's the one who planted the whole 'Brock is probably gay' notion into Markie's head before she even met him.

"I don't want to stop," Markie jumps in heavily. "It's best she doesn't come anyway – the less people around me, the better." She looks at her toes. Agent Reese resumes his lecture, paying no attention to our Joyce notion.

"Stay together. At the bar, when you're dancing, even in the bathrooms. Never be alone."

"No shit." Markie mumbles.

238

She's lost all respect and regard for everyone but Detective Sharpe. She's outright careless. Sometimes I wonder if she wishes it was her that had been attacked, rather than the others. Other times I think she couldn't care less either way. Agent Reese shoots her a look to kill. He glares beneath his brows.

"As I was saying…" He turns his direction to me and talks at me, rather than to me. His voice drops in warning. "Don't put your drinks down. No matter the reason. Retrieve them each yourself from the bartender, at the bar only. No waitresses. No passing through crowds. No buying drinks for each other. Even if you must go to the bathroom, take them with you. Do not let your drink leave your hand for any reason. I'm not saying don't have fun. I'm saying be cautious."

He scowls at me for a few moments to make sure I understand completely. I give him one sharp nod. He nods back and then turns his attention to Brock.

"Brock, what arc your intentions for the evening?" The question is direct, with much authority.

"I plan to drive, sir." Brock chirps. No one in the room is the wiser as to what is going on in his pants below me. I remain in place to cover his growing secret.

"Are you going to stay there the entire time, or just come back to pick the girls up when they're ready to leave?"

"Well," he pauses, looks me over, and pulls my top half closer into his arms. A warm hand reaches around the front of me under the loose part of my top. "I had planned on leaving and coming back, but now I'm not so sure." He grins.

"Oh my God!" Markie yells. Detective Sharpe cringes in reaction to her outburst. "Just because we need a sober driver doesn't mean you're fucking invited! You two are disgusting."

Brock doesn't even flinch at her statement. The gaze we hold is unwavering. I give him a quick little peck on the tip of his nose and confide quietly.

"I'll save you a dance for when you pick us up."

"Deal." He says before breaking the moment. "So, there you have it." He says to Agent Reese with a smile. "Looks like I'm just dropping them off. I suppose I'll go back to my dad's until I get the call. He was bragging about some new pasta recipe, maybe I'll let him cook me something."

I know full well that Brock's father will not be cooking anything. He was probably passed out before Brock even left the house. Brock will eat leftover spaghetti or cereal while his father saws logs, sprawled out in the recliner in a raggedy old shirt and underwear. He might even piss himself, but that's only if it's a really good night. I don't say a word. Instead, I take it a step further and play along. Brock loves it when I join in in his little acting games.

"Have him make extra," I beam. "Your dad is an amazing cook. I might want to try some after the club."

"Perfect." Brock says. "Maybe you can just come home with me, and we'll feast."

"I can't wait." My smile is uncontrollable. I'm growing to love the pleasure of the act.

Chapter Seventeen

Time is rolling up on 8:45. Agent Reese and Detective Sharpe excuse themselves, allowing us the space we need to make the most of our night. We pick up Tiffany before making way to Meagan's, then the club.

Meagan lives about fifteen minutes out of the way, but I don't mind the drive. A short open road gives me a small opportunity to eavesdrop on Markie and her work friend. The look on Brock's face tells me that he's taking advantage just the same. Tiffany is bubbly and excited. I like her well enough, so I should be able to get along with her tonight. Although, she couldn't be more of an ass-kisser if she tried.

The girl practically lives in Markie's rectum. I'm shocked that she can breathe through all the shit. Most of the time she even mirrors Markie's appearance. An annoying adoption of the plain dress style, or no style at all I should say, has taken place. Ordinary graphic-less teenage boy shirts and old jeans make up the majority of

Tiffany's attire. Most of the time her hair is casually swept up in a plain messy bun, identical to Markie's signature look. No matter how hard I try to help Markie dress up, she eventually goes back to her same tired old stuff.

I'm surprised to see that for tonight, Tiffany has stepped out of the box a bit. She seems genuinely excited about the night. Her flowing blonde hair is down and curled. A flashy zebra striped pencil skirt accents her shapely hips. Tiffany isn't afraid or nervous to be around Markie at all. Nothing but confidence and excitement radiates from her. Fearlessness is an ample reflection on her stupidity. *Oh well, though. Fuck it.* If Markie wants to choose such a dumbass for a friend, then so be it. She'll probably even put her first, before me, just like she did Beth.

I wriggle in my seat at the thought of it while listening intently to the two of them chatter in the back seat. Markie lightens up, pulling herself momentarily out of the dark slump she's slid into. She even giggles a little at some awkward attempt at a joke from Tiffany. My body heats a little. I can't tell if it is from jealousy, or all the whiskey shots. *It must be the whiskey,* I convince

243

myself. It really is nice to see Markie smile for once.

An old house constructed solely of red brick sits on the edge of a quaint tree line on the outer edge of town. Meagan steps onto the porch the second Brock rolls up the driveway. She must have been watching and awaiting our arrival. There isn't a slightest hint of smile on her face. She glides slowly down the walkway and across the lawn toward the car.

Her eyes are fixated on her feet as if she's counting those steps, one by one anticipating her doom. Even though she's greeted with a hello from each passenger, she offers nothing in return aside from a fake smile and a nod. Bunched up creases around her eyes leave her looking scared and uncomfortable in her own skin. *Who can blame her?*

The rest of the ride is quiet. Markie and Tiffany have fallen short of words. An unfriendly weight of stress has been packed into the car with us in the form of Meagan. After what seems like a lifetime, Brock's car glides slowly into a parking space, as does his hand on my thigh.

"You look amazing." Brock says with a lustful twinkle to his sly grin.

It's a much repeated, yet welcome compliment. His warm fingertips linger just beneath the edge of my skirt.

"I can't wait to see you later tonight."

He assumes I'm spending the night with him. Why wouldn't he? I mean, after the little display of his semi-erection and my playing along with his lie, our sleepover is inevitable. I snicker under my breath at the thought of it.

"We'll see." I tease.

I escape the grip on my leg and slide smoothly out of the car.

It's a small dance club with loud bumping music. The air is muggy, it smells of sweat and vodka. Strangers grind their damp bodies together. Had it been a normal night before Beth died, she and Markie would have jumped into the crowd without a hint of hesitation. Tonight, that's not the case. The four of us linger shyly in a corner by the doorway. Our vibe is tainted with death. The pain of the last few weeks fills the air around Markie so thick, I could cut through it with a chainsaw.

"Maybe we should start at the bar?" I yell over the music.

"Okay." Tiffany hollers back.

Markie offers a mere nod, and nothing more. Meagan follows us with her head down. At the corner of a small rounded bar we huddle and sip on our drinks. Mine is a tall strawberry blend that a nice brunette man carefully mixed. Undoubtedly, he skimmed on the vodka. You would think with all the attention he put into making it, that he could have added a little more alcohol. The taste is fantastic, but it will do nothing to maintain the buzz I've already acquired from all that whiskey.

The back of my throat cools as giant gulps slides down it. I can feel a brain freeze forming, but I don't care. Something is off, and I am determined to be completely hammered to deal with it. No sooner than my empty glass hits the table, my admiring bartender is ready to mix me a new one. Honey whiskey on the rocks is my next choice. There will be no more fooling around with fruity mistakes tonight.

It could be everything that's happened all piled together that's causing this new paranoia, but I really don't think so. I feel like there is something more going on. There is a different feeling tugging at me, and it's burning a hole in the pit of my stomach. I just know deep down everything that's happened is only leading to something bigger. I wish Brock would just confess already so that I can talk him out of whatever it is he is plotting. Tiffany intrudes my thoughts, and she puts an abrupt end to my contemplation zone.

"Our drinks are all almost gone!" She shouts with a voice that struggles to carry over the loud music. "I think we should dance before we get another one!" An excited beam consumes her face. *And she's back. Finally, the possibility of fun!*

I'm glad the music volume has blocked us from any sort of real conversation. Markie and I both nod and smile back in agreement. A pulsating tingle is making its way up my legs causing a wet noodle effect as I move – it feels amazing. The occasional drink I enjoy with Brock before sex hasn't been enough for me. I've been in some serious need of a drunken release. I'm not sure why, but my body has been craving it. An excess of alcohol isn't normally in my nature, but as of late, I itch for it.

This feeling started the day Vincent died. Something changed inside me when I witnessed his death. It was frightening at first, but as the life drained out of him, so did my fear. The memory floats around my head while I let my body enjoy the beat of the music. A recollection of every detail of the event swims around. Brock had tried to cover my eyes to protect me, but he sucked at it. Little does he know, I could see everything through the inviting spaces between his slightly spread fingers. It was an electrifying event, as was the connection between Brock and I afterward.

I can't help but notice that Meagan's flat face still hasn't lifted. There's been no emotion since we picked her up. Even in dancing, her body is stiff. She must really care about Markie to suffer through her fears and show this kind of support, despite the risk. Brock is the only person on this planet who I've ever been or will ever be that close to. I'll forgive him – we can move past this. My decision is made, and that's final. My body is relaxing more and more as the alcohol does its job.

A stranger rubs up behind me. Glancing over my shoulder, all I can see are his foul brown teeth. I cringe and move as far from him as I can get. The notion of it all makes Markie and Tiffany giggle. The tension melts away, and the intended girl's night out is finally starting to be a success. Even Meagan can't help but to show a little enjoyment at my expense.

Time is passing quicker than intended. My cute tipsiness has graduated from a beginner's experiment into a full-on drunken extravaganza. So much so that it's hard to make out Detective Sharpe's face from across the dance floor. A wave of skin blends with the color of his yellow tie. Even his suit looks to have two lines of buttons rather than one. I giggle at the thought and reach over to place my hand on Markie's shoulder.

I miss completely and nearly crash to the floor. Luckily, Meagan is there to catch my fall. She laughs freely. I'm glad the alcohol has loosened her up, she has a pretty laugh. I almost want to kiss her. Almost. Instead I shout as loud as I can with a childlike slur.

"Hey Markie. What the fuck is your boyfriend doing here?"

Markie's eyes cross at the middle in drunken confusion, "What?!" She strains to hear me, tilting her head in my direction.

"Your boyfriend!" I force even louder. I depend on the forearms of Meagan and Tiffany at each of my sides to hold me upright. "Phil! Phil! It's fucking Phil!" I laugh uncontrollably at the sound of my own words.

"I know!" She yells back. "Isn't he hot?"

Now I know Markie is just as drunk as I am. We have been here for a couple hours and her eyes are practically crossing. She'd never soberly admit her attraction to Detective Sharpe, especially after what happened with Vincent. The four of us giggle at her stupidity and continue to dance. It takes me a minute to remember what I had asked her in the first place. I stumble a little trying to gain my footing and hold my body steady.

Why is he here? Detective Sharpe was supposed to stay away and leave tonight solely up to the undercover guys. Focusing all the way across the room is proving to be a struggle. *Was it even him, or someone that looked like him? That's it, Kam, you've had enough!* My head twitches to shove the confusion out before I get back to my confident dance moves. Just as the song playing belts its final note, he appears like a ninja. I didn't even see him coming.

Loud and clear through the silence between songs Detective Sharpe addresses our drunken party. "Ladies," he has the same serious, yet very curiously sympathetic look in his eyes that he had the night Breanna died, "please, come with me."

"Wow!" Meagan yells. "Where the shit did you come from?"

"I told ya' he wassss hot." Markie slurs awkwardly.

She leans against him, then belches under her breath only inches from his face. A fit of laughter escapes me. It rolls in parallel waves with Tiffany's matching reaction to the completely inappropriate moment.

"Something has happened. I need you to come with me now." He repeats.

Just like that, the fun's over. The laughter stops, the smiles fade, and hunched posture is replaced by tall, straight, rapidly sobering bodies. Despite the fun we were having, and the unhealthy amount of alcohol surging through our veins, the seriousness of the moment takes hold. Everyone around seems to be staring directly at Markie, including myself. Her head shakes violently from side to side, and her eyes are wide enough they could likely escape her head.

"Not another one. Oh, God. Please not another one." She pleads.

Chapter Eighteen

"Yes," I choke, "that's him."

Markie nods and mirrors response, "Yes."

Her voice is hardly loud enough to carry the single word to the coroner. He must have heard it, because he nods then pulls a thick white sheet over our father's corroding face. He wheels the body away, leaving us alone in a small room constructed of windows on every side. Markie and I are completely exposed. We're forced to share the horrific experience of identifying our own father's body with no less than twenty other men and women trudging the halls that surround us. I am sick. Whiskey tainted bile forces itself up my throat. I run to a small garbage that sits in the corner of an otherwise empty room and hurl.

As I squat over the can, I wait for the next round of puke to come up, and I listen. Sounds of jumbled voices ring loudly in my ears. I strain to make them out through my body's nauseous spin. *This can't be real, not my dad.* Brock would never have done this. Everyone else makes sense, but this doesn't add up. I know how much he detests Markie, but he'd never hurt me alongside her – not like this, anyway. It couldn't have been Brock.

The knot in my stomach loosens, giving me a short moment of relief, just enough to regain a fraction of composure. I sit slowly on the cold tile and squint my eyes toward Markie and Detective Sharpe. His strong left arm is wrapped around the small of her back, the other rests to his side with a hand placed casually in his pocket. The sleeve of his button up is rolled, which allows me to see the muscular shape of his forearm. I notice for the first time what great shape the detective is in. Markie is lucky to have him by her side. He comforts her as her head bows forward in grief.

A curious wonder of Brock's whereabouts forms in my head. *Why isn't he here with me – the way Detective Sharpe is here with Markie'?* I slip off my shoes, grip the ankle strap with a firm fist, and hold onto them tightly. My legs quiver below me as I struggle to a stand. A light hand is placed on the windows surface next to me, relieving some of the weight of my unbalanced body. The room continues to spin, and I clear my throat.

"Markie?" I struggle, drawing their attention.

"Yeah." She whispers without turning to look at me.

"What are we going to do?"

Her head shakes, but no words come out of her mouth.

Agent Reese creaks the door open slowly, and steps in with caution. He asks politely that we follow him into a different room, one that offers a little more privacy. We're silently compliant. The room we're led into is small, but he was right, it's definitely more comfortable. This room doesn't have windows allowing onlookers to peer into our lives and the tragedies we're forced to withstand like the other one did. The carpet is thick and squishy beneath my bare feet, and the chairs are heavily cushioned. Markie sits close to me, reaches down, and grabs my hand. Physical contact from her is few and far between, so it feels nice.

"My condolences about your father." Agent Reese says, as he lowers himself into a seat directly across from us.

"Thank you." I manage. Markie offers nothing.

"He was found in the wooded area behind the subdivision your mother lives in." Detective Sharpe says.

Markie and I snap out of our trances and face each other. She shakes her head back and forth in denial. Her mouth opens a crack to talk, but no words come out, only an awkward croak and stammer. I turn back to the agent and speak in her place.

"Where is she?"

"Your mother?" Agent Reese asks.

"No, *your* fucking mother!" Markie barks at him.

Detective Sharpe jumps in the conversation. His voice is lowered with authority. This is the first time I have heard him speak at Markie in a scornful manner.

"Be respectful." He warns. "We're still trying to find her. You need to keep yourself in check, Markie. You've been through more than anyone should, we understand that. But taking it out on those who are trying to help you is counterproductive and completely unnecessary."

He holds a wide-eyed gaze into her face as he waits for her to acknowledge his warning. *Finally he has grown a pair, I am impressed.*

"Okay." She mumbles, before bowing her head back to her chest.

"What do you mean you haven't found her?" I ask, trying not to slur my words. The chair feels unstable under my swaying drunken body.

"Your mother's car is home, but she is not picking up the phone." Agent Reese explains. "We're unable to go into the house without a warrant. We contacted Brock and he offered to go inside and look for her. He said he has his own garage opener, and that the door in it is always unlocked." Agent Reese is unfazed by Markie's outburst as he fills us in on the situation. "He arrived there a few minutes ago, about the same time you were identifying your father. We're still waiting for an officer to call with any news."

I suppose that does give Brock a good reason not to be here with me. He is forgiven. Although, I don't remember ever giving him an opener to my mother's garage. *It must have slipped my mind.* I can't make sense of it all, especially the memory of my mother's sickness, and the poison she had admitted to having in her house. *It doesn't make sense,* I think. I should be fearing for my mother's life right now, but for some strange reason I'm not.

I know deep down that she is okay, I also know there has got to be a reason she can't be reached. The death of our father would normally give her all the ammunition she could possibly need to make herself known. Why isn't she here, throwing herself around dramatically with a fake display of grief? Markie must be thinking the same thoughts, because she blurts out without hesitation.

"She has poison."

"What?" Agent Reese all but shouts. "Markie, what are you talking about?"

"My mom keeps poison in her house. She told us a couple weeks ago. She said somebody fed some to her, and then stole it."

"When exactly was this? And why didn't you say something?" The detective demands.

Just as Markie opens her mouth to continue, I cut her off. "Was he poisoned?" I shout over them.

The detective holds up his hand towards me, attempting to shush my words. "Markie, answer the question." He says.

"No, Markie, don't say a word!" I command.

My right knee buckles as I stand to my feet, it's a struggle to find balance. The thought of Brock in my mother's home at this very moment awakens something inside me. Who cares if I'm still drunk? I can't allow this conversation to go on any further. Markie isn't in her right mind. I've got to protect Brock, and I have to protect our mother.

"Was our father poisoned or not?" I demand. "We have the right to know, and we don't have to tell you anything else about our mother unless it's relevant."

I stand tall and pull Markie to her feet by the hand. The look of surprise on her face is undeniable. It's slightly reassuring to see life in those usually blank eyes of hers. She squeezes my hand and straightens her shoulders.

"My sister is right." She agrees. "How did he die?"

"We can't be sure until a full autopsy is conducted." Agent Reese answers. He also rises to his feet, towering over us. "Did she admit to keeping a toxin before or after Vincent was killed?" He asks.

My hand clutches tighter and tighter around Markie's. The air is thick and catches in my throat. My knuckles whiten with a constricting grip causing her to wince. *Please don't say anything stupid. Please don't say anything stupid. Please don't say anything stupid.* God, I wish she could read my mind. Markie takes in a breath, then speaks with caution.

"With all the events that have taken place, it's hard to be sure." She lies. "Now, if you gentlemen don't mind, my sister and I would like to call a cab, so we can get home and grieve the death of our father properly."

Yes! There's the strong, independent, and very intelligent sister that I have looked up to all my life. I knew she was still in there somewhere. Markie and I can get through this together, I know we can. I'm just going to have help keep her head in the game. For now, we need to find our crazy mother, and get to Brock. We stand strong, shoulder to shoulder and look up at the agent with attitude. He frowns down at us, his impatience burns through his hunched shoulders.

"There is no need for a cab." Detective Sharpe offers. "I can take you."

"No." Markie interrupts the kind gesture before he's able to stand completely.

"Excuse me?" He asks with pain in his eyes.

Her face softens at the sight of him, but only a little. "I'll call you later, okay?" She explains kindly. "Right now, I just want to be alone with my sister."

"Okay." He slumps with understood defeat, and he sits back in his chair. His glare could burn a hole in the floor.

Agent Reese's face remains unchanged. He's clearly full of impatience and anger. "Follow me, then. I'll show you out." He snaps.

We walk hand in hand behind our storming escort. I imagine him to be a kettle with its top completely off by now. I even have a drunk buzz in my ears to help complete the fantasy. For the first time since this entire ordeal started, I feel like I have my sister back, the one who used to hug me to sleep as a toddler because I was afraid of the dark. The sister that I knew before Brock ever came along.

We were inseparable as children. Our friends and the divorce of our parents pulled us apart, but now she is back – even if it only lasts this short moment as we exit a building that has brought us death and trauma. I hold her hand tightly and relish the moment, because we can never tell what the future holds for us. I'll take what I can get from her before it's gone.

Agent Reese holds the door wide open for us, anger searing through his eyes in our direction. We duck past him into the fresh night air. A uniformed officer stands next to his cruiser. He and the agent nod to each other, an obvious unspoken gesture. The man is there awaiting our exit. He will follow us and "watch" as usual. What felt before like a necessary and welcome safety precaution, now feels like an invasive suffocation. We cannot escape them. They haven't helped anything or saved anyone.

It feels like the police are homing in, they have us right where they want us, just in case. *Sneaky.* Markie and I take a seat on a small bench just outside the main entrance. A crisp breeze feels nice against my flushed face. It reduces my nausea – I inhale deeply. Before I have a chance to call a cab, my phone rings loudly. I pull it from the black purse hanging at my side. It's Brock, thank God.

"Where are you?"

"Just leaving your mom's house. Are you okay?"

"No." I croak, holding back tears.

"I didn't think so. Where are you?"

"At the morgue. I was just going to call a cab."

"Well, don't. I'm on my way to get you."

"I think Markie wants to be home with me, alone." I inform him as I look in her direction. She nods but doesn't make eye contact with me, or say a word.

"No." He demands with a stressed urgent tone. "You guys have to come with me."

"Why?" I hesitate.

"Because I'm hiding your mom in the trunk."

Click.

Chapter Nineteen

MARKIE

"We can't get a cab." Kam mutters, stone faced.

"Why?"

"I can't say. Brock is on his way."

I glance up at the officer leaning casually against his car. Of course, it must be none other than Mr. Smith. The same douchebag that gave me a ride when I was covered in Breanna's pee. I hope his car still stinks. A casual smirk sits on his smug face as he stares at us, waiting to protect and serve. I feel like they're wasting their time. They've been following us around watching, yet somehow everyone I care about is still dying. My loved ones are being picked off one at a time then discarded like rotten apples.

I can handle most of the law enforcement on the case, but there are a choice few who seriously rub me the wrong way. Officer Smith is at the top of the list. I even asked Phil if he would pull some strings and keep this man away from me.

He blew off the request as if it were nothing at all. I suppose he was right, there are bigger fish to fry obviously, but it's still irritating. I can tell there's a reason for Kam's lack of explanation, and I respect that.

"'Kay," I agree, and relinquish my desire for a cab.

There must be an important issue at hand. Something bigger than a mere want of her stupid boyfriend, because her hand is gripped so tightly around mine that I'm losing the feeling in my fingertips. It must be something more than the obvious. *What does she know?* We sit in silence and wait. My stomach churns as I think of the dead, mostly my dad. He was barely recognizable.

His body was past the stiff, bloating point. I've seen that several times on dead animals while watching Discovery Channel. My dad was emaciated and rotten. Had it not been for his wide-open eyes, I may have questioned whether it was even him. They were dirty and sunken in, but definitely his, nonetheless. My mind circles around his shriveled lips that were stretched thin over an open mouth. His prominent cheekbones and strong jawline were forced to stand out. My nightmares will be inevitable.

I shut my eyes tightly, trying to block the memory of that face, but all that replaces it is everyone else's. Vincent's bloody vomit, Beth's meaty flesh, even the steady drip of scarlet that escaped down Breanna's hand into a pool on the floor. The images form and rotate in my head like a snapshot photo album. Our father is one more face to be added into the growing book.

Brock rolls up, and Kam finally releases the breath she has been holding since their phone call. His car is left running, and he steps out to comfort her. She drops my hand the second she sees him. I remain seated and watch my little sister closely as she steps into Brock's open arms. Her shoulders shake with sobs. I witness the event of her finally letting go of the suppressed emotions.

After a few moments of comfort, he holds her up straight by the shoulders, only inches from his face. Once their eye contact is unbreakable, he cups her jawline to speak to her. His voice is too quiet to hear. I strain to listen and watch his mouth closely. It does no good, I can't make out a word of it.

I actually feel somewhat bad about my attitude and behavior toward Brock. He's stuck with my little sister for years. He's always there to support her, and to make her feel loved. I suppose its time for me to ease up a little, and cut him some slack. *The fucking idiot anyway.* It'll be hard, but I'll try my best. *It all depends on what he knows exactly.* Phil and I have talked about it several times. Brock has been acting strange and is most definitely hiding something. As a matter of fact, that's the only thing Phil and Agent Reese agree on.

Getting close to the detective leaves me privilege to information that I wouldn't normally have access to. I know it's wrong to use him this way, but it's got to be done. Although he and Agent Reese butt heads when no one else is around, they both think Brock is far too weak an individual to be a killer, but it's agreed he *is* somehow involved.

Phil has been watching Brock closely, much closer that he or Kam realize. They still haven't been able to link anything directly to him, but they're trying their hardest. I'm on the fence, completely undecided about Brock's behavior. Even though I don't like Brock in the slightest, I just don't see it. I don't think he's emotionally capable, or smart enough, to pull off anything more than a bad hair day.

I glance back and forth between Brock and Officer Smith, who is still leaning against his cruiser waiting. My alcohol weighted feet carry me slowly past them all and into Brock's car. I know that Agent Reese or Phil will be coming out to speak with him in regard to anything he may have come across in my mother's house.

I really don't want to deal with any more conversation about my mother, poison, the drive, a cab, or anything else for that matter. I'm exhausted and heartbroken. Very slowly, I creep into the backseat unnoticed, and wait. Tears refuse to form, I'm all cried out. There is nothing left of me but an empty shell.

Out the corner of my eye, I watch Brock. Agent Reese comes out of the building rather than Phil. The detective must be pouting over my rejection of him. *Oh well*, I think, *he'll get over it soon enough, I can't handle the stress of him right now.*

Brock nods his head yes and then shakes it no, his hands move around as he speaks. His body language is irritating, he talks with his hands like a preteen. Agent Reese towers over them and glares inquisitively. Again, I'm unable to make out the questions asked, or Brock's answers. I really suck at this whole lip-reading attempt.

After a few more questions, Agent Reese shakes Brock's hand and gives Kam a stern nod. He turns on his heels and storms back into the building, clearly frustrated. I'm assuming that their conversation didn't make a sliver of progress. Brock and Kam join me in the car. No words are spoken until we are out of the parking lot, and well enough down the road to escape any peering eyes or listening ears. This includes Officer Smith, who is a good three car lengths behind us in the dark. Kam turns in her seat to face Brock and all hell breaks loose.

"What the fuck is going on?!" She demands, after wiping the tears from her soaked face.

"We have to stay calm, Kam." Brock says in a perfectly still voice. "We'll explain everything. But we have to figure this all out together." Confident and steady, he's in complete control.

"Wait, wait, wait… Who is we?" I ask curiously.

"I'm going to tell you, Markie, but you have to promise to stay calm as well. Okay?"

"Jesus fuck, Brock!" Kam interrupts. "How are we supposed to stay calm? Just keep your eyes on the road. I'm going get to the bottom of this bullshit!"

Kam slides her seat forward as far as it will go, then she climbs over the console and into the back with me.

"We have to get off of the seat." She informs me angrily.

She slides onto the floor, squishing herself behind the driver's seat. I gaze at her questioningly, then follow her lead. She refuses to say a word. The adrenaline she has is rubbing off on me. My hands shake, mirroring hers. From my spot on the floor I have a clear view of Brock's face. He holds the same flat look as he would on a regular day, and his hands remain steady on the steering wheel. He isn't nervous at all, quite the opposite.

There's a happy twinkle of excitement and confidence in his eye. It's a completely different look than what he had only moments ago while talking to the agent. I've never seen this switch in him before. The realization of his acting skills around Phil and Agent Reese is completely unnerving. For the first time ever, I'm frightened of my little sister's soft touched boyfriend.

I'm forced to avert my attention away from Brock to assist Kam. Her nervous fingers fumble with a short strap that latches the back of the seat. We work together and pull the latch free. The backrest of the seat falls heavily. I'm far from ready to deal with what Brock's trunk has to offer.

Chapter Twenty

There she is, peeking out at us through the open gap into the trunk. Mascara smudges and streaks down her face. Her over-sprayed hair is matted to the side she has been laying on. Her body trembles with fear. Her breaths are panicked, short and shallow, lifting her chest and shaking her chin.

"Mom?" I ask. "Are you okay?"

"Yes." She forces. "I don't do well in small spaces."

Brock hollers back to her. "Climb out, Evelyn, but stay down." His once uppity voice is replaced with a deep command. "Markie and Kam, you're going to have to sit back in your seats, and fast. That officer is passing cars to catch back up to us. He's going to be able to see into the car with his headlights."

We move quickly. I know I should be fighting the situation. I should be climbing over the seat causing Brock to swerve, or to grabbing at the headlight switch to cause a commotion. I should be doing anything that will get the attention of Officer Smith, but I don't. Something inside me is frozen at the sight of my frightened mother.

I have to know what she is doing in Brock's trunk. I have to hear, from her own mouth, what actually happened to my dad. I already know without a shadow of a doubt that she will lie and cover her tracks if the police are involved. So, with the obvious in mind, I'm compliant to Brock's orders.

Without another word, we pull her out of the trunk. The car's interior is put back into place, I take my seat, and Kam climbs back into her own spot at record speed. Our mom continues to shake. She curls up on the seat next to me, hugging her knees, and ducking from the view of outside headlights. Brock reaches over and grabs Kam's hand. I'm surprised to see her accept the notion causally. *Strange*, I think. Kam pipes up, her voice is serious and irritated, yet her body doesn't move, and her fingers intertwine comfortably around his.

"Somebody better start explaining." She says quietly.

I want to join in, scream at them both, pop off with a series of interrogating questions, but I can't. Words refuse to form. Instead, they stick in the back of my throat and close it off from any sort of passage, including oxygen. This has been happening to me a lot, I freeze and go blank. I can't help it, and I have to put myself in check often. It's my new way of coping. I'm not proud, but it seems to be the only way for me to clear my head. I watch my mother's face closely. Her head shakes back and forth wildly as the tears continue to flow.

"Evelyn?" Brock asks with authority. "Would you like to tell them, or shall I? We're running out of time. So, in order to find a solution and figure out a way to hide you, we have to fill them in quickly."

My newfound fear of Brock continues to build. He sits casually in the driver's seat, maintaining speed. The edge in his voice is crisp and precise. There's no question of his authority. The form of control he has taken is demanding and confident. *Who is this strong man who I used to know as a weakling?* Kam's recent comments about him being a stallion in bed come to mind.

For the first time, I can see it, I get it. I understand what she meant by 'all man.' I'm scared for her. Brock is completely obsessed with Kam, it makes me wonder how far he'll take things with her. Our mother still refuses to speak. Though she has stopped shaking her head, the involuntary trembles continue.

"Okay then, have it your way." He continues, "a few weeks ago, I went to your mother's house looking for you, Kam. Instead of finding you, I found your father, dead."

"Oh, my God!" Kam shouts, and turns to our mother. "I knew it. I fucking knew it! What did you do to him?"

"It was an accident." She defends herself. "I didn't mean to give him that much! I swear, I was just trying to get him to leave. I didn't want him to die."

"Now, now, let us finish, shall we?" Brock again assumes authority. He kisses Kam's hand, and goes on with the controlled explanation. "I'm really sorry that I didn't tell you, love – I am, but your mother is right. It was an accident, and I couldn't bear the thought of hurting you with the news. So, I helped her hide him and we tried to move on."

"Not well enough." My mother mumbles through frightened tears. "We should have just called the police then."

"So, what about everyone else?" I finally find the courage to intervene, asking her directly. "If you are the one who killed dad, then who killed Beth?" My voice rises in anger.

"I don't know, I swear." She trembles.

"What about Vincent, and Breanna? Who did that to them?" My voice accelerates to a full-on shout.

"Shut up, Markie!" Brock commands.

I'm shocked. He takes a breath, then lets it out slowly. He relaxes himself and regains his composure. Kam remains quiet. Why doesn't she have anything to say? Why isn't she helping me get to the bottom of Beth's murder? I don't understand what's going on. I'm confused and astonished at her reaction to all of this. I'm very obviously treading deep waters with Brock. He's frightening, and I'm starting to wonder whose side the rest of my family is on.

All the questions I want to ask swirl around me. They're lost in the air, jumbled with each other, they fill our tight space completely. There's an ever-fattening elephant that's been crammed so tightly in the car with us that it's enabled me to concentrate. *Think, Markie, think.* The only way I'm going to be able to ask all the questions that I long for answers to, is if I obey him. I must be smart. I can't push him too far, not before I know everything. He's a time sensitive bomb, not to be disabled too rapidly, or he might explode. I take a deep breath, determined to handle this wisely and protect my family.

"So, what do we do?" I ask him. "How do we hide her?"

"Finally," he says, "you've decided to be constructive."

"We can take her to your dad's house." Kam offers. "She can sneak out in a few hours."

"No!" He shuts down the idea all too quickly. He's hiding something else. There is something very strange about his father, and the time he spends there, I can feel it. Even Phil has noticed.

Our mother stammers. "The... There is one place. It's a couple hours away, though. It's up the coast."

"Perfect." Brock agrees. "One problem," he looks over at Kam, "you have to come with, too, both of you. We can't risk not being together, any of us, not at this point."

"No!" I protest. "I'm not going anywhere with you."

"Markie, he's right." Kam says. "We have to go."

"They will find us, Kam! And when they do, we'll be in just as much shit as her." I point to our mother as I push the argument further. "If we go home now, then we can keep our mouths shut and just let the chips fall where they may with these two fucking idiots." I can't help myself.

"No more names, Markie, fuck!" Brock demands. "You're in this now. We all are, and it's going to play out exactly as I say, you got that? You think I'm really going to trust you to keep your big mouth shut?"

The car glides smoothly off the freeway, giving us exactly three minutes to plan. We put our heads together and agree on a plot. It's crazy enough that it just might work – of course, it's constructed solely of Brock's ideas.

"First things first." He says, "Markie, give me your phone."

"Are you serious?"

"I'm not asking."

As leery as I am, I realize I have no choice. Slowly, I hand it over to him from the back seat. He disassembles it, and then tosses the battery out the window at just the right moment. We round a turn perfectly and the most vital part of my phone is gone. The deed is done so slyly that there is no way Officer Smith was able to see. *Here we go, I am officially his hostage.*

I'm no longer skeptical of Brock, or of his capabilities. I've come to a haunting realization that he is completely and irrevocably responsible for the deaths that have circulated around me, like a plague. *Brock is my plague.* The question is no longer about the past, it's about the future. What will happen with us? Which of us will die tonight, or even tomorrow? Will it be Kam? Will it be me, or our mother? The questions are growing, and the fear is nearly unbearable.

Chapter Twenty-One

My nervous fingers fiddle and pick at my bottom lip. Smelly old shirts and tracksuits from Brock's gym bag are tossed over the top of my mother in attempt to conceal her in the back seat. Brock's a slob, so there are plenty of clothes in his car, making it no trouble to hide her. Of course, there is no dirt, just clothes.

I've always wondered about Brock's testosterone level, yet here I am being bullied and pushed around by him. I picture Beth and Breanna's violently butchered bodies. With their memories in mind, I watch his well-manicured hands closely. One of those hands is in control of the car, as he guides it into our driveway with ease. The other hand holds my sister's, gently caressing the outer edges of her knuckles with his thumb. She's content with his touch and it sickens me, especially considering the situation we find ourselves in.

"Here we are, let's not mess anything up." He commands. "That means you, Markie. You won't want to see what happens if you do anything stupid. That's a promise."

The tires of Officer Smith's cruiser roll to a slow, cautious stop on the blacktop behind us. I'm the first one out of Brock's car, and I shut the door quickly behind myself to block the officer's view inside. Brock and Kam linger, their exit is slow, as planned. I'm curious as to what they're talking about while I play my part to distract the officer.

I resist the urge to run to Officer Smith, to tell him everything I know. There was something about the serious tone of Brock's voice, his warning, I can feel the importance of it in my bones. Right now, he has my sister and mother at arm's length. I've got to protect them somehow, and if that means playing this game, then so be it. Once we're alone and my family is out of harm's way, I'll make a move.

I recall Agent Reese's description of my stalker's chess game. At least he got the "game" part right, but the major mix up is that he isn't *my* stalker, he's Kam's. This entire game isn't out of interest on my part, but revenge. All this time he's been listening, and taking it all in.

My comments, my sarcasm, my hatred of him, he has been storing it – bottling it up. Like a snake, he has slithered into place, wrapped his coils around me, and waited for the hunger to be strong enough to feast. After all these years he is indulging on people that I care about.

Brock is damn good at this "chess" game. In three minutes flat, he single-handedly plotted our devious plan of escape, down to such detail like what rooms we'll hang out in, what to pack, and how long to wait until we can get out of the house without suspicion. He gave Mother strict, and very detailed instructions as well.

He even has a stolen car hidden and waiting for us. I'm assuming it was meant to be a getaway car that he had ready for his own escape, had it come down to it, but I'm too frightened to ask. Meticulous planning like this must have been premeditated, including the stolen car. I can't quite wrap my head around it all – it's too much, he's too much. Everything is completely overwhelming and it's causing my anxiety to skyrocket.

I follow Officer Smith up the walkway and onto my porch. I unlock the door and wait in the entry for him to check my house. The sweep is getting to be very routine. He walks through the living room, the kitchen, and then makes his way up the hall. As soon as he is out of sight, I flip the porch light off and then back on quickly. That's the sign.

I've given Brock and Kam their signal to get my mother out of the car, and to help her over the fence into our neighbor's yard. The house sitting closest to our right is the only one on the block that doesn't have motion sensor lights. The yard is also very conveniently large, so she'll be able to get out of the rear gate and down the block undetected. We'll also take this route when the time is right. At that point we will meet up with her, if everything goes smoothly, that is.

A smug, accomplished grin settles on Officer Smith's face as he returns to the living room. Kam and Brock walk through the door hand in hand. I watch Brock's demeanor closely, his ability to change personalities is uncanny. Even his facial expressions are precise, and exactly what is to be expected. I'm equally as astonished as I am frightened. He assists Kam to the recliner and then offers the cop a glass of water.

What seems like a courtesy is nothing more than tactic, meant to keep the officer in the house long enough for my mom to get away and nestled into the designated hiding place. Brock is allowing her plenty of time, just in case a dog barks or she accidentally causes commotion in the dark. "We have to cover our asses, in all scenarios." He had said while plotting – yet another unnerving factor into his meticulous psyche.

Officer Smith follows Brock into the kitchen while Kam and I sit in the living room waiting tensely. Try as I may to quietly draw her attention, I'm unable. I poke at her arm and murmur her name.

"Kam," I whisper. "What are we going to do?"

Nothing. She looks past me, her bloodshot, post-cry eyes are fixated on the wall. She's ignoring me on purpose.

"Kam, snap out of it. We have to do something. What did he tell you? What else do you know?"

Still nothing.

"Kam," I continue to pester. "We have to work together and stop him. We have to get Mom and get away from him."

I stop and listen closely to the voices coming from the kitchen. I can make out bits and pieces of a lie. Brock carries on about how scary our mother's empty house seemed. He's filling Officer Smith with his falsehoods over a chilled drink. They swap stories of confusion and fake theories. The cop is soaking up Brock's deception. I listen closely and am certain that he's absorbing every word that spews from Brock's dishonest lips – like a dried-up sponge placed in a wet sink. Brock even adds in a sniffle, I can picture him wiping a fake tear with his rosey shirt sleeve.

"Kam," I push, and beg. "Please... talk to me, this could be our only chance."

My sister's mouth cracks slightly, and her sharp eyes meet mine. "I... I still love him, Markie." She whispers, then turns her head away again.

"What do you mean? He is a murderer, Kam. You've seen what he does to people."

Before she has a chance to defend him, Brock and Officer Smith join us. *Fuck.* The officer's expression changes to one of annoyance at the sight of me. The downward pull of his lips and the bunched skin under his eyes make him look much older than the mid-forties he otherwise portrays. My heart drops a few inches in my chest, I watch him pivot abruptly on his toes and walk out the door. He leaves us to our fate. The couch I'm sitting on swallows me whole, the walls close in. From bottom to top, my eyes scour Brock.

"Let's do this." He commands. "Kam, move fast, my love. Markie, get off your fat ass, let's go."

I pack quickly, as I'm told. The not knowing what happened to my father, and why my mother did it, is eating me alive. I hope she made it to the hiding spot okay, but I'll strangle the answers out of her myself if needs be. Brock stands over my shoulder and watches as I cram as many items as I possibly can into a backpack. From my closet, I throw in underwear and a few pairs of jeans and T-shirts. I grab a comfortable tank top and yoga pants to slip on for now.

"Are you going to watch?" I scowl.

"Yes."

With arms folded across his chest, Brock leans against my closet door, opening it wide. His head is cocked to the side. A creepy smile grows across his confident face. He doesn't seem to be worried or at all in a hurry. He knows things are going his way, I can see it in his eyes. I turn my back to him, and strip off my skimpy club dress as quickly as my trembling fingers allow. I've never felt so naked and exposed. The piercing of his eyes shocks me and raises bumps across my back. I feel dirty and violated.

"I just don't get it." He says as I dress.

"What do you mean?"

"I don't understand the power you have over these men. You aren't nearly as pretty as your sister. Even Beth was more attractive than you, and she was seriously flawed."

"It was you, wasn't it?" I ask quietly.

I already know the answer, and the last thing I want to do right now is set him off. But he is the one who brought it up, and I can't contain the impulse. I want to hear it. I need to hear it. His callous grin widens, and a rolling laughter escapes. He folds his arm across his stomach and his shoulders bounce. The sound of his open laugh is much different than that of his usually feminine giggle. I've never heard such a noise, and it's frightening. His face drops as fast as it had lit up, and a warning fire pours from his intense eyes.

He closes the gap between us, forcing me against the far closet wall. His breath is hot and warms my cheeks. *Clamp*, just like that, his hands are around my throat. My toes drag on the floor, barely touching. I paw violently at his fingertips trying to loosen the hold. His grip is strong and unwavering. Suddenly, I'm very physically aware of his strength. Finding air is a battle, and I'm unable to make any noise. Panic holds me by the throat, right alongside his squeezing hands. While I wriggle in the tight grasp, his toothy grin widens. A tear streaks down my face.

"If you so much as breathe Beth's name again, or Breanna, or Vincent, or even Joyce, I will gut your mother like a fish. Do you understand me?"

"J-J-J." I struggle to form her name. As soon as my vision begins to blur, Brock loosens his grip. I crash to the floor like a heap of trash being dumped from a can. My gasp is shrill.

"Joyce?"

I manage to speak only her name, but it is nothing more than a squeak. Brock's foot thrusts into my stomach. The kick takes me by surprise, again stealing my breath. I cough, gag, and sputter under pressure. The pain pulsates beneath my ribs and consumes my core. My legs curl up into the fetal position as I pant and squirm.

"I said, not a word." He warns.

I peel myself off the floor, wipe my face of tears, and limp past him into the bathroom. *Think, Markie, Think. Be smart.* The pain in my throat and stomach is excruciating, yet I manage to move my body. I rummage quickly through my things and grab everything I can fit into my bulging backpack. Brock watches me at an uncomfortable distance. He must be taking stock of every item I take. He is clearly smarter than I've given him credit for, and more ruthless than I could've ever imagined. *What has he done to Joyce?*

The second drawer down contains small travel goods such as sample soaps, lotions, and hair care product. A red zipper bag that is stashed in the back immediately grabs my attention. I throw it in my bag along with practically everything else in the drawer, trying not to make it obvious. The contents of this tiny zipper bag are sure to come in handy. How I had forgotten about it over the course of the past few weeks is beyond me.

A recollection of Beth when she slipped it in the drawer haunts me. She had bought herself an identical bag, intended for when we went on one of the many trips we had planned, but could never actually afford to go on. We spent countless hours talking and dreaming about Paris, Australia, Scotland, and yes, even that notorious cliché party spot of Cancun, Mexico. I recall the whites of her teeth as she flashed me that mischievous grin. An adorable dimple rested perfectly in the center of her right cheek. She slipped my miniature protection pack into the travel drawer of sample items that are rarely used.

I laughed at the time, and I asked if she really thought we'd ever need pepper spray, a box cutter, lighters, and a small multi-purpose utility knife all compiled together into a perfectly cute and innocent looking travel zippy.

"Why of course, my dear." She'd said with a giggle.

I never gave that bag another thought until this very moment. Like a true best friend, even in death she's helping me. The feeling of her presence is strong, as if I were to look hard enough, I'd see her, sitting on the edge of the tub, chatting up a storm about absolutely nothing.

Brock's chuckle sounds from the door, it shocks me out of my trance. I look to see Kam has joined him.

"What are you staring at?" Brock asks, with an arm draped casually over my sister's shoulder.

"She does it all the time." Kam says.

"She looks like a statue." He huffs.

"Yeah." Kam acknowledges his humor and changes the subject. "Are you ready?" She asks.

Her fingertips rest in his pants pocket casually. The only hint of practical emotion she shows is a lingering redness and puff around her eyes from the previous outburst of tears. A light cotton running suit hangs comfortably from her cleaned up body. Her face has been powdered and lips are glossed. *Lip gloss, are you fucking kidding me?*

I wonder who this woman is that has taken over my sister. Amidst my grievous haze, she has developed into his evil little stooge. I've been mentally slipping in and out of reality, and all the while my sweet, perfect sister has morphed into the sidekick of a killer. I feel like I don't know her at all. My own sister is a stranger to me, and she is knowingly in love with a heartless murderer.

Chapter Twenty-Two

It's much easier to jump the fence than I anticipated. Brock knows the one and only place to cross that allows us to land on the lawn, rather than on one of the many rose bushes that line the fence's edge. I'm forced to swallow the question of how he's privy to this information. The thought of the obvious answer sickens me. Kam doesn't seem to be fazed in the slightest.

On the contrary, he appears to be enjoying herself. The excitement of what lies ahead swirls around her – like a fluffy little cloud would the sun on a nice day. I can see joy in her eyes, and the twitch of her lip as she holds back a full grin. I guess all it took was one drunken puke, and a solid outburst of tears for her to get over our father's murder. Brock shows up and she's a changed woman, it's disgusting. I, on the other hand, am unable to shake the lingering taste of death. Even the smell of the morgue remains in my nostrils, a reminder that my father is gone.

I'm the least coordinated, so Kam goes over the fence first. Her hands are placed perfectly at the top of a white privacy slat, and she pulls her feet over with grace. She makes it look effortless. Of course she does, I wouldn't expect anything different. Brock helps me awkwardly scramble up our side, I hold on for dear life at the top, and Kam helps me not to fall on my ass when I let go. I land with a thud in the neighbor's yard. Its official, *I'm a trespasser.*

The pain in my stomach and ribs pulsates as my feet hit the ground, it's a disgusting reminder of my recent beating, as well as the nagging question of Joyce's fate. I feel like a whipped pet, sneaking around in the dark and minding her master despite his evil motives.

Brock is the last to cross the fence. As soon as he makes it over, he squats next to us. There's a distinct light in his face. When he takes in a long whiff of the crisp air, it makes me think of a predator on the hunt. We're concealed by my neighbor's elaborate landscape. Flowers, bushes, and trees surround us on every side. Even a large swing set is placed on the perfectly groomed grass.

I watch closely as Kam's eyes meet Brock's. She gives him an excited grin, raising her eyebrows and shoulders to support her expression. The moon lights up their faces, enhancing the moment. I cringe entirely to the bone. Not only is my fear of Brock growing with each passing second, but for the first time in my life I'm also afraid of my own sister. Brock shares the excitement by mirroring the gesture before he turns his attention to the house.

"All the lights are off. Let's move fast."

I follow them closely. He grabs her hand, and she grabs mine – knuckles whitening. We weave past the yard decorations and through the trees. In a matter of seconds, we reach the gate. It seems too easy. Brock is clearly an expert at sneaking in the night. It reminds me of creeping past my mother's bedroom as she slept when we were younger. Though the same rush of being caught runs through my veins, the differences between now and then are stark. The excitement of getting wasted and hiding it from my mother in the darkness is completely opposite than that of this uncomfortable growing guilt of running away with a killer.

I should be fighting harder and standing my ground. I should be stealing Kam's phone and calling Phil for help. The way I'm handling this situation is wrong, I can feel it in my gut. Although, I do try to convince myself that I'm doing the right thing. There is a vicious battle going on between my head and heart. I can't decide if I'm following him out of strength or stupidity, or even fear. Perhaps it is all three. Against my better judgment, I convince myself that I'm searching for the perfect timing. *I'll find the checkmate before you can, motherfucker.* I know that when I make my move it must count. It's got to hit hard enough to put an end to the whole damn thing.

Brock reaches for the latch on the gate. He moves it slowly in effort to keep as quiet as possible. Kam looks back at me briefly. A shape of pity consumes her eyes at the sight me, and she mouths silently.

"I'm sorry."

She squeezes my hand tightly, and for a fraction of a second, I can feel her shame. The apology is unheard by Brock, and it falls on an unaccepting ear from me. I struggle to find the truth in it. If she were sorry, why would she act this

296

way? It looks as though she is having the time of her life. Her face lights up every time he looks at or touches her. She's clearly unfazed by his realities, and in love with his false persona. I don't understand how my own sister can be so blind. The more I think of it, I'm actually pained for her. She may pity me, but little does she know I share the guilt. I've been a terrible sister and a blind human being. I return the squeeze of her hand, and I let out a sigh. *I've failed her.*

We slip through the fence undetected. The far end of our neighbor's yard has spit us out on the opposite side of the block. We take off in a jog along a thick line of hedging. The time has topped one o'clock in the morning and the streets are dead. Creepy as it may be, the light of the moon is perfect. We're masked by the dark, yet still able to see the sidewalk beneath our feet. We pass under one street light only, and my heart skips a beat from the brightness of it. A thick wave of relief washes over me when we remain undetected.

I have only walked this particular sidewalk a handful of times. There's an awkward finality in it now. I'm so close to home, yet it all seems so foreign. After the years of living here, I'm un-familiar with my own neighborhood. This may very easily be the last time I have the chance to set foot on this sidewalk. I'm already homesick.

Brock tugs on Kam's arm, veering her off the sidewalk, and pulling her onto a dirt alleyway. I follow them at arm's length. There are several of these alleyways in the area. They push halfway into every city block that lacks the average number of houses. They offer the convenience of backyard access and occasional party parking, other than that they're completely useless.

At the end of the bumpy dirt drive, a small, rundown garage comes into focus. My mom is crouched down next to it. *She made it.* An equal mix of anger and relief pools in my stomach. *Why does she have to be like this?*

The garage door is loud. It releases a grinding squeal as Brock lifts it open by hand. It is a crammed one car garage, built by hand, no doubt. Aside from the rusted over pull slide door, its constructed solely of white and tan brick. Cracks spread from bottom to top, like a rigid old tree. My mind wanders about the age of the structure. I imagine an old man with strong hands placing each brick into its proper place, then he dies, and all the love he had put into his work dies alongside him.

My distracting daydreams are interrupted abruptly by my mother pushing her way between myself and the slowly opening door. She slips inside the garage as soon as the gap is tall enough to squeeze through. Kam and I follow her lead and leave Brock outside to finish the impossible job of muffling the heavy sounds of screeching metal. It is much darker inside. We cram tightly between the wall and a covered car.

Minus detailed features, the silhouettes of my mother and Kam stand out in the darkness. They stand shoulder to shoulder, straightening out clothing and brushing fingers through their hair. They each take advantage of the moment to detangle and perfect. There are small, yet very distinct similarities in the way they move. Shoulders are squared, necks are elongated, and chins are turned up in such a way.

Strange that it has taken these many years, and a traumatic night in the dark to see how alike they are – mother and daughter, both as fake as can be. They lead secret lives with their true personalities hidden from the rest of the world. I think of all the times Kam has been so generous, yet so mouthy at the same time. I suppose both qualities fit perfectly into this freshly exposed angle of her true self.

How exactly do I fit in? A ping of guilt hits me for not trying harder to keep in touch with my dad while I still had a chance. I have a feeling that I was more like him than I'll ever know. There's a raw truth in this realization. It turns my stomach, making me nauseous. Again, the image of my father's dead face stains my memory. Like a smashed thumb, the pain throbs and swells on the inside. I let a tear fall in the dark, but only one. I won't give Brock – nor my mother, for that matter, the satisfaction of my tears, not anymore.

Chapter Twenty-Three

EVELYN

Ugh, I should've changed my outfit when I was going to, before we left. I knew that smelly trunk of his would wrinkle up these trousers. They weren't cheap, either. I shouldn't let him rush and bully me like that, I *am* his mother after all. These girls will never know about the affair, *ever*. Especially after Kambriella has been with him the way she has.

If she finds out Brock is her half-brother she'll never speak to me again, and that is beside the fact that after all these years my secret will inevitably leak to the public. I've risked too much in keeping it quiet to let it out now. None of them can ever find out. I can't afford that kind of negative attention in my life. I'll take the secret to my grave, just like Peter did. He just had to show up, my ex-husband, threatening to tell. The fool was asking for it. He even had the nerve to call me a sociopath. *Who the fuck did he think he was?*

Brock's father, Jim, was a good man before he started drinking. He was even willing to take our bastard child into his own marriage. It was the only way. Peter would have shared the secret with everyone we knew. He always did care more about being faithful than anything, and he was not about to claim a child that wasn't his. "It's because we are a team" he would say. His outlook on the matter truly was our biggest problem. The sound of his voice still rings in my ears. Over and over, he would repeat the words to me as he tried to fall asleep at night.

"A wife should be loyal. A wife should be loyal. Remind me why I'm agreeing to stay."

And so I did. Time and time again I reminded him. I gave that man everything he could ever dream of – no woman could compare. Nine months was no time at all to hide out until Brock was born. I gave birth in another state, and I signed him over. Just like that, we went back to our old lives. Marketta was too little to remember, and Kambriella wasn't born until fourteen months later. I watched my son grow up from a distance, and my real family was better off for it. That is, until Kam brought him home after a date. I look over at her in the dark and cringe at the thought of it. Only Kam would be drawn to someone who looks so much like herself. *Conceited little brat.*

Luckily, Jim has never suspected Kam to be my child. It must be because of how common our last name is. There are hundreds of Millers in the area, after all. Had Jim thought anything out of the ordinary, he would have reached out or been in contact with me in some way or another. I'm confident that even after all these years he's completely oblivious of Kam's parentage.

Peter couldn't handle watching Kam fall for Brock. He tried to tell her too many times. It was just too close, so I had to get rid of him. Divorce wasn't enough. He had to leave, and he had to cut off contact with the girls completely. Things wouldn't have worked otherwise. I remember the look on his face very distinctly when I threw his own blackmail into the mix. The pull between watching his precious baby girl fall for my bastard, and possible jail time for embezzlement hanging over his head was too much. He took off. It's a good thing, too, had it come any closer, I would've turned him over in a heartbeat.

The door to the garage is finally up completely, and the inside is lit to match the out. Brock moves quickly with a distinct air of responsibility. There isn't a hint of frightened rush, or panic. Just like Jim, Brock has a knack for taking control of a situation. No matter the circumstance, it is to be addressed in a calm, fashionable manner. Like father, like son, they share the same demeanor.

It's a shame that Jim's wife and daughter had to die the way they did, the woman did raise my son without question, after all. I used to sit in my car down the road and watch his house. It was as if the pain soaked through his walls, down the street, and into my car. Unbeknownst to him, I'd wallow in the grief alongside him. The only difference was that I was able to put the bottle away. After a few months of sharing his pain, I dumped all my alcohol down the drain and hardly touched it again. Jim could not. Drinking consumed him, and he let himself go. It's a real shame.

I suspected Brock at the time to have something to do with it. He took advantage of Jim's despair, running around with his friends like nothing happened at all. Though I was pained for his father, I still couldn't help but feel a ripple of pride for my son. I watched Brock grow into a fearless, capable being. He is strong and unstoppable, what mother wouldn't want that for their child? The way he stepped up and helped me hide Peter's body was, in my mind, nothing but proper. Even without me around, he grew into a man, and I love that about him. Obviously, he could have done a better job at hiding Peter, and it would have saved us all from this mess, but I forgive him for that. After all, anyone can make mistakes.

"Kam, grab the other end." Brock says.

She jumps to the command, and she assists him in pulling the cover off the car next to us. They move together quickly, perfectly in sync. In a matter of seconds, the weathered gray cover is removed, revealing a shiny new Bentley. His taste in vehicle fails to disappoint, just as his choice in fashion always has. At least we'll get out of this shithole neighborhood in style.

Brock presses a code on the driver's side, a small click sounds, and the rest of the doors are unlocked. I'm the first to hurry inside the car, followed by my kids. One at the time, the doors close us in. Brock pulls down the visor just above his head and a set of keys falls into his lap. There is no need to put them in the ignition, though, the engine purrs to life with a press of a button.

"Where the did you get this car?" Kam demands angrily.

"Joyce's parents have a neighbor who travels more than he's home. The gardener told Joyce that he will be in Europe for the next couple of months."

I don't need to listen any further. The two of them spat back and forth. It is a small tiff, nothing more. Kam wants to know why he has spent so much time with Joyce. She questions him on how much Joyce knows. Brock wants her to shut up so that he can concentrate on our escape. Reasonable argument on both ends, yet I find it is none of my concern. They're both distracted from questioning me, as is Marketta, and until I can work out the details of my lies, I'm grateful for their distraction.

The smooth sound of tires on pavement hums beneath our feet as we weave past the dark houses of my daughters' crowded subdivision. Markie gathers her body up like a small child and presses herself against the door, sitting as far away from me as possible. Her legs are curled on the seat and she is hunched at the middle. She grabs at her sides as if in pain and stares out the window. I may be nuts, but she seems to cringe every time the name of her sleazy friend is spoken.

Personally, I'm glad Brock is friends with Joyce, and that he stole this car from her parents' friend. I'm assuming he took it shortly after he helped me hide Peter. He must have known that I'd need his help again, a son's intuition. I don't know if he had anything to do with the other murders, and quite frankly I don't care. It doesn't concern me in any way. I have more important things on my mind than worrying about some guy Markie was hot for, or even her friend and neighbor. I must concentrate on keeping myself out of jail. That's my number one priority right now, not some fools who were too weak to defend themselves.

The tit for tat going on in the front seat is short lived. In no time at all, Brock and Kam are hand in hand, working together and supporting each other as a family should. I mull over the details of my lie. I'm confident that if I present my act perfectly, they'll have no choice but to believe the story of their father's obsession and my fear of him. *What else could there possibly be to play on?* I just hope the escape alone is enough to keep our inevitable conflict at bay for a while. At least until we get up the coast and settled under a safe roof for the night.

It's ironic that I'm taking them to the very cabins Jim and I escaped to nearly thirty years ago. I know they're still standing and just as immaculate as always, because I take the drive at least once a year. It's a very classy location, and literally the only place close that will let you stay on a cash only basis, with no need for an identification. Never in a million years would I have guessed that the place that concealed my infidelity would now be helping me to escape the law.

It's privately owned by an aging widower. He has no living family, along with no interest in local legalities or petty affairs. He cares only about privacy and escape. Taking in mostly hidden couples and battered women is his style. The place cannot be found online, and the only other person aware of it, that I know of, is Jim. There is a need-to-know basis air about the old man, and he requires no payment upfront. Receipts are never given, and in turn, there is obviously no paper trail. The place is one hundred percent off the grid. It's completely untraceable, and if we only stay for a night or two, then at least it will give us the time we need to establish a plan. I feel like I'm the star of an action movie. I straighten my back and smooth the makeup under my eyes with the tip of a well-manicured finger.

I appreciate the silence while it lasts, because it's only matter of time before I'll be attacked with questions, hateful accusations, and possibly even threats. My girls have ganged up me with their spite before. Confrontation is inevitable. Considering Kam's slight transformation in Brock's direction, I can only hope she'll take a different approach than usual.

The comforting concealment of the freeway surrounds beneath our tires as we cruise the on-ramp and join the hustle of night travelers. Finally, we're out of reach of any tailing officers or undercover FBI. We've slipped through a snug little crack completely undetected. The night has merged into a race of time. I wonder how long it'll take that stupid detective to give up on trying to reach Markie by phone and just stop by her house. Eventually, the fact that my kids are also missing will be discovered. For now, it's a matter of how far we can make it before that happens. Hopefully it'll be far enough.

"I think we should get some food." Kam suggests. "I'm still a little drunk and sick."

I sit quietly. Brock had earlier instructed Kam to request food, it's all a part of his tactic against Markie. I have to hand it to him, the ability to prepare in such profound detail is uncanny. They work well together, I'm impressed. Though Markie is my daughter, my first born, she still has no place in this crowd. I can see where Brock's hatred comes from.

"That's a great idea, babe. We should probably get enough to eat and drink for a couple days. Once they start looking for us, we won't be able to stop anywhere." Brock agrees, as planned. "But where the hell are we supposed to go at this hour?"

There are only three more exits before the freeway takes us to a long stretch of nothing but highway for over an hour. The only place we can find that's close is a twenty-four-hour drive-thru taco joint, just off an exit. There's no line of cars at the window, so we are able to make it quick. Brock doesn't bother to ask us what we want or even like.

When Markie and I try to pipe up with an order, we are very swiftly shut down. Rude, but I'm not surprised. He makes a bulk order of bean and cheese burritos, chicken tacos, and breakfast roll ups – Along with our fountain drinks for now, handfuls of bottled water and an assortment of juice for later. Then, without a word, he reaches his hand back toward me.

There's no need to ask me for the money to pay, his flattened palm says it all. He's already aware of the very large stack of cash in my clutch. He was standing over my shoulder when I took a couple thousand dollars out of a small fireproof safe that is concealed by an old family photograph in my house. It was all the cash I had on hand. Luckily, I keep it around for a rainy day. In today's case we might need it all. I turn my body to shield any view of my purse. Markie doesn't seem interested, but I still don't want her to see it.

A fat wad of cash is thumbed through, I pull out a hundred-dollar bill, and hand it over without question. Brock pays, and then shoves the change into the pocket of his faded denim skinny jeans. I'm a little surprised that he's allowed me to hang onto the money myself for as long as he has. At this point, I question the lengths he will go to to maintain authority over our situation. Not so much with me, but with my girls, and he may need the cash at some point for himself.

In anticipation of the disgusting meal to come, I watch my children. Markie is stubborn, set in her ways, and old fashioned much like Peter. *Just look at her, she even sulks like him.* Kam has an enlightened sense of emotion with practically everyone around her. She's always been able to understand the reasoning and logic behind literally everyone, no matter their actions.

She wouldn't hurt a fly. But she does, however, have a repulsive ability to look away from the evil in another. She sees past a person's insanity, into a hidden realm of decent reasoning behind it. It's an odd quality that I've spent the better portion of her life trying to decide if it's positive or negative. I'm still on the fence. Personally, I think it makes her erratic.

They think I don't notice them, but I do. It's easier, though, to remain detached from their personal lives. I only allow them to see my attention where I want them to. It's a tough world we live in, I must protect myself, too. They're grown and capable beings, they can fend for themselves. I also notice Brock.

I let my imagination wander into a different time and place that could have been. How altered my life would be, had I chosen Jim. I visit this place in the back of my mind often. We could have run away and raised our boy together. Markie could have been left with Peter, and Kam would never have been burdened to this world. It may have been nice. Brock's voice intrudes my mechanical thoughts, snapping me back to the present.

"Thanks, doll." He says with an innocent grin to the girl outside the car.

A young, chubby Spanish woman passes a third very large bag of processed tacos to Brock through a dirty sliding window. Her face lights at his compliment. She hands him our sodas first, then starts on the handfuls of water and juice. She counts them out with a thick accent and thanks him for his business before we drive off.

I watch Markie closely. It's my job to make sure she doesn't see Kam slip a tiny crushed up pill into her soda. The three of us agreed on the matter just before they helped me hop the fence. While she was distracted with the officer, we continued to plot. There can be no mistakes, not today. It isn't going to hurt her, just put her to sleep for a while. A date rape drug, Brock called it.

She's spacing out and lost in her own thoughts right now, but when she snaps out of this state she could bring about anything. Most likely she'll be full of irritability and rage. No one wants to deal with that on the drive, so we agreed it would be best for her to sleep, at least while we work out the details for tonight.

It takes no effort on my part. Markie hasn't moved from an upright fetal position or looked away from the window even once. I'm glad that I don't need to distract her. In her regular frame of mind, she is actually quite observant. Brock must have put a whole new level of fear into her. The Markie sitting on the seat next to me seems much more distracted than the alert girl who had pulled me out of the trunk. I'm sure the bitchy, egotistic Markie will resurface at full force in no time at all. She's like a ticking time bomb. You never know who you are going to get, or when she'll blow.

Markie needed to be scared, more so than what was brought about by deaths alone. Whatever he said or did to her while I was running must have done the trick. She needed a new perspective in the same way I did. Brock accomplished just that when he drugged me, too. The warning was as understood as it was necessary, I now have a completely new outlook.

It wasn't until I hunched over the toilet praying for survival that I realized what he is capable of, and that he is not to be tested. We're all better off doing as he says. I just hope the drugs kick in fast before the two of them end up getting into a brawl. Things won't end well if that happens.

Kam passes Markie's drink back to her. I reach over and nudge her shoulder to draw her attention. Her knuckles whiten around the cup and she takes a few gulps. I watch the muscles in her throat contract as the fluid is swallowed. In a matter of minutes her eyelids are drooping, and her head begins to nod. My hands instinctively reach over to grab the soda as it slips out of her rapidly relaxing grip. I help her lie slowly down on the seat next to myself, and she is out.

We're free to make the drive in silence. It's much needed to clear our minds and to make a plan without Markie's input or outbursts of rage. We're estimating her to sleep until late morning. She looks quite peaceful, really.

Although I detest the thought of a fast food joint's bean and cheese burrito, my stomach is growling with hunger. I can't help it, I indulge myself in grease and Pepsi next to my sleeping daughter. South Brooke, Florida quickly becomes a shrinking memory in the rearview.

Chapter Twenty-Four

KAM

Stepping out onto a creaky old porch, a man moves slowly with the aid of a twisted and polished wooden cane. He's very short, obviously shrunken with age, and has a back that's hunched just below the shoulders. A steady shake consumes his free hand. I watch my mom greet him with one of those awkward half hugs, half handshakes.

One would exercise the same greeting with an old lover that hasn't been seen in years, or even an estranged parent that didn't have much to do with their life. The notion brings me back to my father and the look of his dead face. If he were alive and I were greeting him right now, I would likely show the same awkward affection. It's hard to believe it has only been a few hours since I was hunched over a garbage throwing up at the morgue. It seems like a lifetime ago already, and the more I consider the untold details of his death, the less I care.

It's no shock that my mother killed him. We're all fully aware that she's crazy, so it isn't a big surprise that her narcissism got the best of her. Not that I'm excusing her reckless behavior, it's just that I understand it. Not only that, but I haven't considered Peter to be a father for years. I know I can get past the grief of his death easily. Perhaps shock is blocking me from feeling the proper emotions. Or maybe, in a way, I've already grieved over him. No matter the reason, I feel distanced, and for that I'm grateful. I need to be present and one hundred percent in the moment from here on out.

I have a delicate approach to take, in regard to my love and my sister. The club was fun, and our escape was thrilling, yet the drive has only allowed time to calm my nerves and assess the tormenting situation I find myself in. There's a stress building inside me and it isn't based on fear, or even the excitement of running.

My nerves are growing from a completely different place. I'm torn between Brock and Markie.

I don't see things ending well between them. I have a sickening, very real feeling that I may have to make a choice. I'm going to have to face Brock head to head. I need to approach him about our future before he hurts her. She may be selfish, for the most part, but she is still my sister.

It feels like Markie's the only family I have left. My father is dead, and my mother may as well be. She's crossed a line that she cannot come back from. Whether I can get past my father being dead or not is beside the point. The fact remains that she *did* kill him. I'll never be able to look her in the eye again. Markie is all that I have left, and I cannot lose her.

I take stock of Brock as we wait for my mother to wheel and deal with the lonely old man. I can tell, even from a distance, the man is very fond of her. Brock's attention toward them is unwavering. I can't quite decide what to make of the look in his face. He is completely fixated on my mother. There's a deep-rooted loss in his eyes, as if he is torn between control and approval. His jaw contracts and relaxes over and over, the corner of his bottom lip pulls down, and that adorable spot between his eyebrows and nose is slightly crinkled. I want to ask him about his own mom but refrain from it. The last time I brought her up he lost his shit.

The look reminds me of a little boy I went to kindergarten with. He spent a great amount of time sitting in the corner after throwing tantrums. He'd stare at our teacher with the very look Brock has now. Still angry yet waiting anxiously for her to give him a hug and listen to his apology. I don't recall his name, but I will never forget his demeanor. I felt so bad for him. He was always acting out. I instantly befriended him, hoping I could help ease his obvious pain in some way. He moved away before the school year ended and I never saw him again.

Brock lets out a long sigh and tilts his head toward mine. I wish I could read the mind behind those irresistible eyes. The door behind mine opens, and my mom slides back into the car. I mouth the words silently to Brock so that she is unable to hear me.

"We need to talk."

He nods in agreement, but his eyes tell a different story. His lids are buried in brow and the muscles of his neck tense. He throws the car into drive and glowers at the lightly paved road ahead.

An abundant line of trees hides the drive as it loops around the back side of the old rickety house. We follow it slowly, twisting and turning until we disappear into a thick wooded area. There are a few small yet well-manicured cabins sitting off our path. The headlights from our stolen car light them one at a time as we pass. Each is beautiful and unique. Bay windows are lined with colorful flower pots. Small porches and balconies are arranged with classy metal furniture. The doors are tall and decorated with engraved glass and classy knobs. Giant spotless windows are shaded with thick shutters and interior shades.

I don't understand why the old man would live in such squalor when his cabins for rent are clearly in much better shape than his home. Mom did mention his humility, perhaps keeping a low-key front is reason enough. One would never guess anything like this would be concealed behind a raggedy old home like his. I've got to hand it to her, even on the run, my mom knows the classiest place to go.

I'm curious to know how exactly she is privilege to this undisclosed line of cabins, but not enough to come right out and ask. She won't hear my question anyway, and even if she did there would be no explanation offered aside from lies. I have a feeling there is a whole other woman behind the face I have always known as Evelyn Miller.

"It's that one." She says. "Right there on the end. You can pull in and park behind it. Von doesn't like vehicles lined up in front of them. He can't tolerate the lane looking cluttered." She talks about him casually, as if they are old buddies.

"Von, huh?" Brock huffs. "So that's the old fart's name. Why would he care?" He asks. "I thought it was a secret and no one comes up this road anyway."

"Von walks to the end and back home every morning and evening. The beauty and solace of this place keeps him feeling young and healthy." She explains. "This is his home, and he expects certain standards from his guests. He's a very respectable man. He minds his own business and keeps his mouth shut. It's the least we can do

322

to stay out of his way, and not crowd the place up. This isn't a tourist attraction, and you never know when you may need to come back. Von is not a man you want to burn a bridge with."

A wise response. My mother rarely speaks highly of anyone. This place, and the old man in charge of it, must mean a great deal to her.

"Are there any other rules we need to know about?" Brock asks.

"Only that we refrain from loud noise, fires outside of the pits, and we're not to walk up and down the lane. There are trails behind the cabins for just that. The road is his."

"Understandable." I agree.

"Also, there are plenty of cleaning supplies along with a washer and dryer. He's too old to be cleaning up after guests. He asks that we leave the place in just as great of shape, or better, than it was when we came. He doesn't hire help, and he won't take you back otherwise. If he asks you personally for assistance with anything else while you're his guest, then do it. No matter the request."

"Of course." Brock also agrees with the old man's logic.

"Don't mistake Von's age for weakness, either." Her voice drops an octave. "This place is a sanctuary for a reason and he *will* keep it a secret. Never forget that." She warns. "There's more to these cabins, and to Von than meets the eye. Keep to yourself and stay quiet. He sees more than you know, and he'll protect his home at all costs. I've seen it firsthand."

Brock pulls the Bentley under a small tin carport that sits next to a matching utility shed. The place is welcoming and has a comforting feel of safety. I look back at Markie who is still completely engulfed in her deep aided sleep. I'm almost jealous. I don't think I've ever been so sick or so tired in my entire life. A part of me wishes we could switch places, even for an hour. Markie could worry and obsess, I could rest and rejuvenate.

We leave Markie to sleep in the car while the bags are carried in and we familiarize ourselves with the place. It's just as beautiful on the inside as it is on the out. Brock and I take claim on the larger of the two bedrooms, leaving the smaller one to be shared by my mom and Markie. The walls are tan and bare, the bedding is one solid color of sage, and the windows are giant, taking up most of the wall space. Daisies hang elegantly before the windows in black with gold laced planters leaving a fresh smell and comforting feeling.

The kitchen and living room are small, but very open with vaulted ceilings and an island bar to separate the two. Furniture is minimal. A lone painting takes up space on the largest wall. It's completely stunning, undeniably drawing me in. I close the distance and get as close as I can to admire the details. It is an abstract piece with a medley of swirls and splatters. The colors and patterns are hypnotizing, easing my mind of the anticipation of my upcoming conversation with Brock. This cabin is absolute perfection and it doesn't need any more décor than this one painting. In this case, less is more.

"It's beautiful, isn't it?" My mom's voice smashes into my eardrums. She stands next to me, practically touching shoulders, breathing heavily.

"Yes." I croak.

"Von's wife was an artist. She died almost twenty years ago. I was here when it happened.

Their love was a special kind, and he surrounds himself with her paintings. There is one in every cabin."

"What happened to her?" I ask. My curiosity of this mysterious old man grows by the minute.

"It's best that we don't talk about it." She drops her head to her chest in grief and lets out a long, dramatic sigh. "I'm going to wash up."

My mom retreats to the small bathroom at the end of the hall and leaves me to ponder on this immaculate work of art and the woman behind it. I look at the color details and imagine her. I picture a beautiful, middle aged woman in painter's suspenders and a white tank top. Her hair is swept back, and her face is at peace while she works. The image is a lovely distraction from the realities of my own life. A slam of the door brings me back, and I look over to see Brock carrying Markie's unconscious body into the cabin.

I rush to his aid and open the bedroom door for him. Markie is dumped onto a tall, beautifully hand-carved wooden bed in a heap. There isn't anything poetic about her sleep now. She looks nothing but vulnerable and helpless. No wonder it is called a 'rape drug.' I didn't have the courage to ask Brock why he was carrying such a drug in the first place. He must have planned on drugging her at some point, after all, he is always prepared. The second he pulled it out of his pocket, I took a mental note to fetch my own drinks from here on out.

Until tonight, I've remained confident that whether Brock is capable of murder or not, he would never actually hurt me. I've seen a new light of him, and I'm not so sure I can hang on to that confidence any longer. I do forgive him, though, and if he promises to put an end to all of it, then we can stay together. Even after everything he's done, and hidden, and lied to me about, I still don't want to lose him. I love him.

A small dribble of spit escapes the corner of Markie's lip, and I remind myself that the drug was for her own good. Brock leans against the frame of the doorway with his arms folded. He watches me with an annoyed twitch of his bottom lip. I adjust my helpless sister. She'll be lost, confused, and angry when she wakes up. I cannot bear for her to come into consciousness like this, not in a careless heap of such an uncomfortable, twisted mess.

I lift her shoulders and pull a strained arm from beneath her back. After, I turn her to the side, straighten her crooked neck, and pull her legs together. Her breath is steady, and her body is completely limp. I pull the loose messy pony-tail out of her hair and comb it back into a much neater tight one. The silence is paralyzing, I can't help but feel like it's the calm before the storm. *At least she'll wake up more comfortably.*

I walk straight to Brock and give him a long passionate kiss. I want nothing more than to go to bed with him, but I can't. I must talk to him about Markie and what is to become of them, and I have to do it before she wakes up and makes him angry. I recall my mom's mention of the walking trails throughout the woods behind the cabins. Although it's dark out, the sound of a walk in the fresh air sounds too inviting to pass up.

Chapter Twenty-Five

BROCK

I know what is coming by the sympathetic slump of Kam's shoulders. She feels guilty. She can't hack it like I thought she could. *Fuck!* Why can't she be more like Evelyn? *That* crazy bitch has it all figured out. I've always glorified my acting skills, but Evelyn is a true expert. She's phenomenal, on a completely different level. I have a lot to learn from that one. Now that all our truths are out in the open, I hope she'll be willing to teach me a thing or two. If nothing else, I'll have to keep her close and observe. Even if she protests, there won't be a choice.

In the meantime, I have to figure out what to do about Kam, and exactly how I want to dispose of Markie. I think I'll make it a creative death, something new and exciting. Maybe she'll hang, or perhaps I'll bleed her out. Eww, or maybe both! I haven't made up my mind on the details just yet, but I *do* know that she'll suffer. Go big or go home, I always say. We didn't come all this way for nothing. I kind of feel like Markie is my big finale. If I don't do it right, I'll regret it forever. I don't want to finish out my days with misgivings over the should haves. Markie's death must be perfect. She has to top them all or I'll feel like a failure. A decision of this size needs more time to ponder on. There's no need to rush perfection.

I tried my hardest to persuade Kam into bed. I used my best moves, yet she still insisted on a walk. I don't understand her ridiculous concept of resolve, and it's always at the dumbest times, too. There's no longer a need for urgency. I know we won't be found. There's all the time in the world, especially now that we're off the roads.

I trust Evelyn one hundred percent on this hiding place. We could stay here for weeks if need be. Now is the time to slow things down and get Kam on my side. She has to be, I won't have it any other way. It's not the time to rush into an unnecessary conversation that's bound to end in altercation, but she is unrelenting.

Kam has been pushing me a lot lately, and I sense it's a trap. The sex is unbelievable, but she's been lying, I can feel it. She is a terrible liar and an even worse actress. She pretends to be vindictive and careless to impress me. I can tell she is faking because she winces every time she says the word 'death' out loud. It's almost cute, though. She cares so much about me, and she's trying so hard to impress me, it's flattering, yet I can't help but to feel like she was more attractive when she simply didn't give a fuck. That independent confidence was mouthwatering.

Kam has always been genuine, and now she seems fake. I hate fake. Fake women make me think of high school girls who constantly repeat cliché phrases like 'hot' and 'O.M.G'. Even *I* don't make such a mockery of myself. A respectable reputation should be one of classy confidence and style. There is certainly no room in society for degrading behavior such as blind acts of self- inflicted embarrassment.

This newfound falsity makes Kam seem needy. I love her, but I'm not sure how to take it. The confusion makes me doubt myself in general, and our future together. I hate doubting myself, there is too much at stake for that. I've risked everything, and I don't have room for weakness – not anymore. There's only one thing that I *am* completely sure of at this point, and it's this: no other man will ever have her. *That is a fact.*

Gently, I wrap my arm around her waist and let her lead the way. Her nervous trembling hand tightly grips a large metal flashlight. She found it while rummaging through the well-stocked cupboards and drawers in the kitchen. Kam shines it on the ground in front of our feet, lighting up a very distinct narrow walking trail. Hesitant steps carry us into the dark woods. The trees are thick, blocking any trace of the once ample moonlight. Soon we're entirely surrounded by blinding darkness and deafening silence.

There's no need to see Kam's face, I can picture her expression with perfect detail. Her eyes are widened with fear, and her lips are a thin tight line. Anxiety fills the air around her, it's suffocating me. She hasn't been this quiet and nervous since the last time she broke up with me. Normally, she turns into a rambling fool, to the point of spitting and stuttering. Never has she ever been this mute. She's clearly thinking hard about the right words to say. She is scared, and, quite frankly, she should be. I'm freaking out. I've got to break the silence.

"Look Kam, I love you and I always have."

"I know."

That's it? What the fuck!? No "I love you" back?

"I understand you're scared, but I want you to know I'd never hurt you." I lie.

"What about Markie?"

Of course. *I should have known.* That fucking whore is getting between us again. I've indulged in enough sugarcoating and vague pleasantries for Kam's sake. Finally, I'm done with the non-sense. It's do or die. There'll be no more secrets and no more tiptoeing around the truth to spare feelings. Kam loves me, and if we're going to make this work, she'll have to understand. I'll make her understand. She already knows how much I detest that stupid fucking bitch sister of hers. Even *she* thinks Markie is a pain in the ass. Kam will just have to accept the facts.

"What about her?" I demand, trying my hardest to contain the fury, though I feel an uncontrollable impulse rising to a boil in my veins. I'm like an antagonized bull in a tight cage, just waiting for the horn to sound so I can be freed. Even hearing Markie's name sends icy chills of loathing down my spine.

"Please don't hurt her." Kam pleads.

"Kam, we both know that she's got to go." I bark.

Kam's stops our slow stride abruptly, and she turns to face me in the dark. A cold hand slides down my arm and into my palm. A poor attempt at affection, she's trying to coax me against the inevitable. It helps that I can't see her face. That would surely make this conversation much more complicated. *I have to get rid of Markie, I loathe her.* I didn't come this far, and do so much, just to change my mind. Even Kam won't be able to talk me out of it. I had very high hopes for Kam. I can't believe the extent of disappointment I feel right now. There is no guilt inside of me, no remorse. I only feel anger. It's a growing, anxious anger that is surging through my veins.

"I've done all of this for us, Kam. Don't you get that?" My voice is rising.

I squeeze my fingers around hers tightly, it makes her gasp slightly in pain. I don't care that it hurts her. I'm glad   it should hurt, how dare she test me like this? Does she not understand anything?

"You don't understand how much I love you. Markie has gotten in our way too many times. She has to pay for what she's done."

"Hasn't my sister been through enough?" Her voice is croaking, she's clearly fighting tears of panic and fear.

"No!" I shout at her.

"Let's just leave, Brock. You and me. Let's leave Markie and my mom here. We can be together, and no one has to get hurt anymore, please?"

Her pitiful plea falls on deaf ears. What gives her the nerve to question me? She's not in charge, *I am!* I have needs *too*, doesn't she get that?! After all this time and everything we have been through together. I've been everything she's ever wanted or needed and more! I was her friend when she got lonely, I was her fuck when she needed a pick me up. I waited over a year after she broke up with me. Everything she has ever asked of me, I've done it at the drop of a hat.

Pretending to care for Markie while she degraded and ridiculed me for years wasn't easy, and I did it all for Kam. What was it all for, so she can continue to ask more of me? I've even killed for her, and she can't seem to appreciate that! My grip continues to tighten. What a bitch! Kam is a stupid selfish bitch, just like her bitch sister. The simple fact that I've wasted all these years without seeing it only makes me angrier.

"Please, Brock," she cries. "You're hurting my hand."

"You don't understand, do you?" I shout. "Markie doesn't give a shit about you. No one does. I'm the only one who has ever loved you, and this is how you repay me? By barking orders and standing up for the one person that I loathe. Are you really trying to manipulate me like that?"

Kam struggles to break free of my grip. I can't allow it. She can't run off and leave me in the woods, not like this. I can't believe she's even trying. What does she think this is? A sickening realization hits my stomach like a rock landing in a body of water. It makes an undeniable contact, and then very heavily sinks to a permanent place in the bottom of my gut.

Kam will never appreciate me. Just like my mother never did. She will always expect more, and demand for me to do things that go completely against everything that I am. She'll always care for others in her shitty little family more than she does for me. To her, I'm second best. The truth of the matter crashes into my chest, nearly knocking the wind out of me. *How could I have gone this long and not seen the truth in her?* I won't have it. I shake my head back and forth, trying to rid myself of the realization. It won't go away.

Luckily, I've got a good grip, the hold I have on her hand is unrelenting. There is no longer a need for words, I've made up my mind. She won't care about what I have to say anyway, the selfish little whore! And to think, I've loved her for so long, and dedicated so many years to her. The love is still here, but I can't just stand by while she lies and tries to change me. It's one thing to hide who I am, but it's a whole other thing to transform into someone else. This is where I draw the line.

Even Kam can't deprive me of a much-needed kill. Not taking a life that begs to be taken is like leaving an irritating itch unscratched. I've got to kill Markie, just like I have to take a piss when I wake up the morning. It is what it is, and there is no way around it. If Kam doesn't understand that, then she doesn't understand me. If she doesn't understand me, then she can never truly love me. And, if she doesn't love me, then we cannot be together. I rip the flashlight from her other hand and start tugging her violently down the trail.

"Wait, stop!" She begs. "Let's go back to the cabin."

I don't give her the satisfaction of an explanation, she doesn't deserve it – not anymore. Only a hard jerk on the arm is offered, that ought to give her my answer. As always, this is where the struggle starts. I usually love this part, but it feels different with Kam. I make a conscious effort to detach myself. I hadn't planned on this happening, but I can't help it, the rage has consumed me, she's gone too far. Now that impulse is here, and the first steps have been taken, there is no turning back.

I've already enjoyed one kill tonight. Joyce's death was intoxicating. A recollection of the event repeats in mind as I jerk my struggling girlfriend down the deeply wooded hiking trail. I knew that I'd be leaving town before Joyce was found, so I didn't bother with all the plastic nonsense. I watched a thick swarm of police head for the hills behind Evelyn's house, right where I put Peter's body. Like vultures, they raced to squabble over a dead body. I called Evelyn. I told her to stay home, pack a very light bag, and not to open the door for anyone.

I realized it would only be a matter of time before they asked for my help. Considering that pleasant distraction, along with the reassurance of the conveniently stashed Bentley, I didn't even wear gloves with Joyce. I fucked her and then killed her, exactly as it should be. It was perfect, and everything played out in my favor, I was confident that it would. The plan has been set for weeks. One can never be too prepared. Joyce played her part well. She helped me get a car. She gave me something to do while passing the time at my father's house. After all, I did need to look like a wonderful, caring son by spending so much quality time with the slob. Hell, Joyce even gave me a shower fuck before she died.

Kam is different, though. I won't force myself on her as I take her life. I want our last time to have been love making, not a death fuck. I'll remember her for what could have been, had she not decided to turn into a judgmental, skeptical, little bitch. I really had something special with her, we could have been a team to be reckoned with, but not anymore. I'll be making my own choices from here on out, without Kam's altering input. My heart is pounding with compulsive rage. *Fuck this bitch.*

Kam's screams are shrill as she struggles and makes useless attempts to tug her hand free. She is shaking with fear, and she should be, she has it coming. I feed off the fear and let it fuel me, drinking it in and absorbing it through my skin.

"Brock, please don't do this." She sobs.

Her feet fumble and she fights the walk by digging the heels of her running shoes into the dirt. Amidst the forced skirmish steps, she trips. I continue to pull, dragging her along. I reach down and get a better hold. It is a tougher fight to pull her by one hand. I take a firm grip on her hair, right at the base of her scalp. She kicks and starts to scream.

"Shut up!" I command.

We can't risk being heard. Especially by the crippled old man, from the sounds of it, he is just as crazy as the rest of us. Who knows what her screams will bring about? She doesn't stop. *Of course not, why would she?* I should know by now that once panic grips people, their screams are involuntary – And loud, very loud. I turn back to her, she must listen before we're heard.

"Kam!" I shout, "I said shut the fuck up!"

Still, she only grows louder.

I've got to do it. I must shut her up now before we're caught. I tighten my grip on the flashlight's handle and bash her with it. Over and over, I crash the heavy object into her skull. The light of it stays on, allowing me to scan over her once I'm finished. I take a long, mournful look into her smashed and bloodied face. She has stopped screaming, but one leg continues to weakly kick around, like a lost limb. Quickly, compulsively, I make one more powerful blow to the head, and again, I watch. Her leg makes one last twitch before her body goes limp.

"I love you." I whisper into the quiet darkness.

Chapter Twenty-Six

Standing still on the bloodied trail, I listen to the sound of my breath and the steady thump of my heartbeat as it echoes in eardrums. It's too simple, the way I feel. A sense of accomplishment sets in, but it's minor, as if I'm back in high school and just handed over a final essay. The kind of assignment that only took a few short days to write, but I know for a fact I will pass with flying colors, so I want to celebrate. I'm empowered, as I am with every kill, yet it's tainted with an undercurrent of disgust and self-loathing.

It isn't until I start dragging her body reality sinks in. *Oh my God, what have I done? Impulse got the better of me and I killed her. I fucking killed her! The only woman that I've ever loved.* She is dead. *She is fucking dead!* Every other kill was planned. I have always made up my mind beforehand. That's my rule, and it always has been, I have to be sure that it's the right move before I act. I've never killed on impulse, I promised myself as a child that I never would.

I did it, I broke my only fucking rule. I didn't plan this. I didn't want this. Oh my God. Markie is going to pay for this. It's all her fault. I bend down and scoop up the limp body of the woman I love. Her head slumps forward on my chest, blood pours down the front of me. My shirt is soaked through in my favorite shade of scarlet, and for the first time ever, I regret my actions.

The walk back to the cabin is short. Thick trees canopy us and there is a strong scent of rain in the air. I think of Kam's beautiful face and the way she would fill her lungs with a deep breath of this very scent through her nostrils. It's the same dramatic sniff she takes when there is freshly cut grass. Adorable. I take in a whiff, just as she would, and I cradle her limp body in my tired arms. Her legs swing to my side, clipping my blood-splattered pant legs with each step.

Slowly, the silent hinges on our cabin door allow it to swing open, letting us in. My heavy feet drag on the floor. I can hardly lift them, it's as if they've been dipped in concrete. With slumped shoulders and a bowed head, I shuffle through the kitchen, down the hall, and into Markie's bedroom. *Stupid bitch will pay for what she made me do to her.*

I set Kam down in the corner of the room, it's perfect placement for Markie to see her clearly when she wakes. I've made up my mind. I'm going to bleed the bitch out, one slice at a time, for days. Markie will die a slow, painful death. I stand over the hammered lump that is Kam's body, and I can feel the blood on my arms and neck start to crust over as it dries to my flesh.

"Why did you have to try to change me?" I whisper.

It only takes a matter of minutes to tie up Markie and rip off her clothing. She's like an animal taken to the slaughter. *Finally, taken to the slaughter, I've waited too long for this.* The first cut is carved just below the right knee. I don't make it too deep, though, just far enough into the flesh to color the tidy bedspread with a small pool of crimson. It's deep enough to leave an impression. I want her to be afraid and understand the extent of my intentions, nothing more. This is how I want her to wake, instead of the snug position Kam arranged her in.

No sooner than the bedroom door shuts behind me, Evelyn steps out of the bathroom at the end of the hall. Silk sleepwear loosely hangs from her freshly cleansed body, hair drips onto a fluffy white towel in her hand. It drops instantly to the floor in a heap at her toes the second she lays eyes on me.

"What did you do?" She asks, voice trembling.

I stare her down. This is going to be an awkward pissing match between the two of us, I can tell already. The thing about Evelyn is that she's smart, and she'll find a way to get to me without having to kick, scream, and panic like the average woman. *Think fast, stay a step ahead.* She needs to see, I'll have to make her watch so that she knows what I'm capable of. I'm short with her, and I answer abruptly.

"Don't fight this, you'll fucking lose."

"Don't fight what, Brock? Where are my girls, and why are you covered in blood?"

I quickly close the gap between us. With one swift swing of my arm, I make contact with her face. The back of my hand smashes against her jaw, and she falls to a heap on the wooden floor.

I point a finger in her face and lower my voice to an octave above a whisper.

"You will keep your mouth shut, and your hands to yourself. There is nothing you can do to stop this, and if you challenge me I'll go after every other member of this miserable fucking family, but not before I burn you alive. Is that understood?"

Evelyn stares right through me as she pulls herself to a sitting position on the floor. Her loathing eats through my skin, she shoots it from livid eyes. One short nod is offered before she slowly lifts herself, wipes the blood from her lip, and feels her way down the hall. A hand drags on the wall, steadying herself. She disappears into the bedroom containing Markie and Kam. I listen closely, not a peep sounds from inside.

Chapter Twenty-Seven

MARKIE

A painful itch has consumed my wrists and it's nearly unbearable. *Why can't I open my eyes?* My chest is heavy, and I struggle to find air. Only my nose offers intake as I'm unable to open my mouth. *Concentrate, Markie, one breath at a time.* Coaching myself helps, but only slightly. My eyelids feel weighed down. It's a fight to open them, but eventually I succeed. The room is dimly lit, I've never seen this place before. At first, I can smell lilac and fresh linen, but it doesn't take long for a muggy wave of sweat and stale bean burritos to wash it away. I wiggle my fingers, then my arms and neck. The rest of me is numb.

My eyes roll back, and again it is dark. With a disoriented awareness, I try to make sense of where I am and why I can't move. My mind struggles through a mess of jumbled thoughts, and I search for any memory that makes sense. Then it hits me, like a truck ramming a brick wall,

I see his face. Soft Brock and his femininity stick in my mind, only he isn't soft. He is horrible.

The look of his excited evil eyes bounces around my head. I recall the beating he gave me just before our intense escape, and wince at the thought of it. I quickly realize that the ache in my chest and stomach is still there, and still fresh. *Wake up, Markie, you can do this.*

My eyes reopen, just a crack. I try to look around, more frantically than before. *Where the hell am I?* Near objects come into focus, anything further than a foot away is still a blur. I look up my arms and concentrate on the pain in my wrists. They are tied together with a thin, frayed rope. I squint and strain to get a better look. The rope has secured my hands tightly to a fancy metal headboard. Again, I try to move around. This time I'm able to squirm my hips and legs – even my toes wiggle. I look down at my struggling body.

My legs are completely exposed, and I'm lying flat on my back. A thick, light beige comforter is neatly spread under me. The color of it is quickly changing to crimson. A deep rosy flow is escaping my leg, just below the knee. I can't feel the pain of it, not yet. The lower half of my body is too numb to feel anything real. I'm wearing nothing by my underwear and a thin undershirt. Suddenly, I'm very sickeningly aware of my situation.

The ability to move and struggle comes back to me at an alarming rate. *I have to get out. I must get away.* I wriggle and tug at my wrists. Its no use. The hold doesn't loosen, there's no sign of relent. The feeling of my nerves slowly returns, as does my vision. The room I'm stuck in comes into focus, along with the silhouette of my mother and another blurred, but obvious being in the corner. I can't quite sort out the details of who it is. Distorted shapes and shadows are mixed together and swaying through a foggy cloud.

My mother sits on the floor, much closer to me than whoever is stashed in the corner. I focus my eyes only on her, concentrating on her details and small features in effort to make out a clear vision. I try and cry out to her, but my mouth is still unable to open. After a few attempts I realize that my mouth is covered with tape. My screams are coming out as nothing more than a light, panicked hum. I'm unable to draw her attention.

She hugs her knees and rocks back and forth on her tailbone against the wall. She is mumbling to herself with a smooth, and emotionless face. I can't make out her words.

If I make big enough movements, she'll see me, she'll help me, she has to! Why isn't she fighting for me, or trying to untie me? Again, I jerk my restraints. This time the bed shakes and clatters. She looks up to see my fearful eyes staring at her, and she jumps to her feet. I push a muffled scream as loud as I can. My mother only stares at me in fear. I can't tell if she is afraid of me, or afraid for herself by trying to help me. Panic squeezes my neck and intensifies the growing suffocation. I'm weary and my lungs feel weak.

Rather than running to my rescue like a normal mother would do, she begins to pace the floor next to me, and continues to mumble to herself. Her fingernails are shoved between her lips, allowing her to chew on them aggressively between muffled words. Then she stops, stares at the person in the corner, and tugs nervously on her hair by the roots. I take a closer look, straining my eyes to their limit.

Oh my God, it's Kam. In a motionless heap against the wall, my baby sister is completely unrecognizable through the red matted hair and swollen mess of bloody gashes on her face. Her once comfortable running sweats are now covered in chunky mud, and they're soaked completely through with thick coagulated blood. Our mother again begins to pace, she stops only to stare at Kam and then back at myself. She refuses to look me in the eyes. There is no sign of tears or grief on her face. Instead, her eyes squint together tightly in anger.

My backpack sits on the bed by my feet. I distinctly remember the little red zipper bag I had packed. *Thank you, Beth.* I try to reach with my toes, but my leg is very slow moving. It's heavy and nearly paralyzed in place. The scarlet pool coming from beneath my knee is growing and soaking its way up my body through the blankets.

A stinging from the wound kicks in, and the burn of it takes over. *Don't give up,* I tell myself. Again, I try hard to focus on the bag. An inch at a time, I move my bleeding leg. Before long I can feel the cold metal of a zipper as it finally reaches

my toes. I use them to grip it and pull the bag toward me. It tips over, spilling the contents. I try to
rummage through the sample goodies with my
foot.

The image of Phil's face flashes in mind. Memory of his soft eyes and strong jawline stings me
to the bone. *God, I wish he was here.* Why did I
have to be such a stubborn ass? If only I had listened to my instinct to pull the wheel of Brock's
car, or run screaming into Officer Smith's rigid,
unwelcoming arms, I wouldn't be here. I under-
estimated him, even after he beat the tar out of
me in my own closet. I wonder how long I have
been here, tied helplessly to this strange bed. I
remember my mom saying something about a
place up the coast, but I have no clue how far we
are from home, or from anything for that matter.

My toes reach and grab, my leg jolts involuntarily while I rummage. The only thing I seem to
accomplish is spreading my belongings around
the bed, similar to how a toddler would swipe
and spread sand around in a sandbox. I'm frantic,
knowing that if I can get ahold of one stupid item
amongst the mess at my toes, it may save my life.
Nothing. *Please God, let my toes find that stupid*

little bag. I can't get my mind off the thought of that utility knife and exactly how I'm going to have to reach my toes to my fingertips should I get a grip on it.

"What are you doing?!" The sound of Brock's voice bangs in my ears like a gong.

I wiggle and squirm at the sight of him, trying to break free of my restraints. My mom returns to her spot on the floor and doesn't say a word. Brock averts his attention away from me, but only to place blame on her.

"You're just going to let her do whatever the hell she wants?" He demands angrily. "I told you to stay there." He points at her place on the floor. "Don't move or touch a thing!"

I try to scream and cry for help, but the muffled sounds cannot to be heard over Brock's angry, self-loathing rambling. He kneels in front of my battered sister and cries.

"I'm sorry. I am so sorry, my love. I didn't mean to do this to you. It's all her fault. Its Markie's fucking fault. I promise she'll pay for this."

Over and over, he mumbles remorsefully. He brushes a bloodied hand over the exposed meaty flesh that was once her beautiful neckline, then rubs his face roughly and anxiously, smearing her blood all over himself. Just before turning his rage on me, he kisses the top of her bashed in head. He jumps to his feet.

"This is all your fucking fault!"

The gap between us is closed quickly. Before I know it, he is leaning over me with a knife to my neck.

"She chose you!" I can feel the warmth of his breath through the tape that covers my mouth. "I loved her more than you ever could, and she still fucking chose you!"

He stands up straight and shakes his head violently. I'm unable to make sense of his whispered words, but I *can* tell it's self-assuring. He stops and looks me dead in the eye. A mischievous grin consumes his ever-softening face. Brock's demeanor has shifted at the drop of a hat. He switches from aggravated, to confused, to tough, and now he seems giddy, like a kid with an ice cream cone. He's a tantrum throwing child who is easily distracted with a treat. *My torture is his reward.*

His grin slowly grows, and he places the knife gently on my chest. After scouring my tied-up body from top to bottom with those hateful burning eyes, he runs the cold steel slowly across my skin. As soon it reaches the top of my thigh, he presses down.

"I've been waiting for this for a very long time." He leans forward and whispers in my ear. "Then you had to go and fuck it up by making me hurt Kam. You won't die quick, that's a promise."

As the words come out, he presses the knife even harder. The shock of its penetration stings, and I scream. At the top of my lungs, as loud and hard as I possibly can, the shrill sound is muffled inside of my sealed lips. I writhe in pain. The more I struggle, the harder he pushes, sinking the blade into my leg. My eyes close tightly. I can't bear to look into his burning face as he enjoys my squealing under pressure.

A shocking *bang* loudly rings through the room, it explodes into my ear drums painfully, and the pressure in my leg begins to dwindle. My mother's scream is deafening, but not nearly as loud as the shot that stopped my torture.

"NO!" Her voice echoes.

I snap my eyes open in shock, just in time to watch Brock's shoulders slump and his body limp as he collapses. Falling straight forward, he lands across my chest. He's heavy, and the weight of him crushes my already struggling lungs. I manage to take a long draw of humid air through my straining nostrils. Standing in the doorway is a crippled old man. His twisted wooden cane supports his small, hunched over body. With one hand he grips the cane tightly, and with the other he holds a small black pistol. Very steadily it is held, still pointing directly over me.

"Brock, oh my God." My mother struggles.

She jumps to her feet and pulls him off me. He's limp, and it leaves a fresh streak of blood, soaking my top.

"First Kam, and now you." She falls back to her knees, holding Brock in her arms. She couldn't care less about me, tied up, frightened, and bleeding.

I yank violently on my restraints, and with every ounce of energy that's left, I scream through the tape. My rescuer reaches down and with a steady hand pulls it from my lips. Tears stream down my face. There are no words to express my emotions, as I sob uncontrollably. While my mother cries over Brock's dead body, the man picks up Brock's knife that lay next to my fresh wound. He cuts my restraints. A wave of freedom washes over me and I fight the urge to pass out.

I jump to my wobbly feet, and as quickly as my weak, unstable body can move I run to Kam. Our careless mother doesn't even look up or acknowledge me. Why would she care more about that bastard than her own daughter? She's a stranger to me. I glance at her sobbing over my tormentor, and I realize: I have never really known my own mother, and I never will.

I force away the feeling of abandonment, I must, I've got no other choice. I'm in shock and pain, there's no time for heartbreak from that horrible woman. I reach down and wrap my arms around my lifeless sister, placing my fingers on her damaged throat. There is a pulse in her neck. *Oh my God, she is still alive!* The old man's voice is raspy and quiet, but he speaks to me calmly from his place at the bedroom doorway.

"My truck is running. It's just outside the front door."

Is this real? How can this be happening? I'm pained and panicked, but I manage to struggle to

357

my feet. I grab my sister around the waist. As she clings to what little life remains, I pull her out. Her body is heavy, but with the aid of my fear and growing adrenaline, I manage to pull her out of the room. I listen to the sound of my mother and the old man arguing.

"You killed him!" She shouts. "You shot my son!"

"It had to be done, Evelyn. The boy would have killed them both. That girl will be lucky to make it out alive."

They argue like an old married couple. Completely comfortable with one another, yet undeniably spiteful. I continue to pull and drag. Kam is heavy, and both of my legs are wounded. The struggle is borderline unbearable, but I can't give up. Their argument grows quieter as we move farther and farther away.

"I never even gotta tell him that he was mine."

"I am sorry, Evelyn. I truly am."

"You do realize that if my girls leave, this place will be found, right?"

"I've already taken care of that. I only hope your girls can move quick enough. A captain goes down with his ship, Evelyn."

The last of their words grow too quiet to hear. What did she mean by, "He's mine?" I can't wrap my head around it. I regain focus on my baby sister, I must save her. *Fuck my Mom, and fuck Brock, too, they can have each other.*

I fight to drag Kam down a short, unfamiliar hallway, and past a small kitchen. A thick trail of blood is left on the wooden floor, staining it with every tug of her. Out the front door, there is an old running pickup, just as my savior promised. I struggle to drag her limp body across the porch and down a few short steps. Lifting her into the vehicle proves to be an excruciating task.

Blood clots and large chunks of hair stick to my skin, covering me from head to toe. I'm unable to distinguish my sister's blood from my own. *Please God, help me.* Once I have Kam laid securely across the dirty seat of the cab, I climb in myself. With a firm push of a pedal, the tires peel out underneath us, and I refuse to look back. That is, until another gunshot bursts.

Adrenaline drops my heart to the pit of my stomach. I stop the truck. I have passed several cabins, and in front of me now sits a dumpy old shack. I wonder who that shot was intended for. I picture my mother being taken out by my strange old rescuer, or maybe she overpowered him. I realize that anything is possible. *What is this place?* I should go back and check on my mother, but I don't. I can't turn around, not now. A bubbling gurgle sounds quietly from the back of Kam's throat, and I think of the man's words; *I only hope your girls can move quick enough.* Instinctively, I slam the gas pedal back to the floor, following the rocky dirt road as it loops the rickety old house. I have to get Kam to help. She'll never make it if we don't hurry.

A ravaging explosion sounds behind me. I jump in the seat and swerve, barely missing a tree to my right. The noise is powerful enough to rattle the windows of the pickup. In the rearview mirror a mushroom cloud of smoke fills the air, just above the treeline. Flames shoot through the trees toward us. I high pitched *hum* consumes my ability to hear anything but the *buzz* of it.

The realization of what happened hits me like a bolt of lightning. *He blew it up!* The old man just set the cabin, along with everything around it on fire. There's no way he nor Mom could have survived a blast like that. The *humm* in my ears grows louder. *I have to get out of here, fast!* I don't have a clue how far into the woods we are. It won't take long before the fire consumes everything in its path, including myself and Kam. I squeeze the steering wheel with closed fists, taking control of the pickup as it bounces and jolts on the dirt road. It's difficult, as I am growing faint. Blood continues to gush from my leg at a rapid pace and the smell of smoke is beginning to fill the cab. Just as I think all hope is lost, through distorted vision I see the small hint of paved road ahead, along with the blur of quickly approaching lights. *Thank God.*

"Please, stay with me Kam." I place my hand over hers, and her fingers give mine a very light squeeze. She clings to life by nothing but sheer will, and I know I can do the same. "We've made it." I whisper.

Dear reader,

We hope you enjoyed reading *Aggravated Momentum*. Please take a moment to leave a review, even if it's a short one. Your opinion is important to us.

Discover more books by Didi Oviatt at https://www.nextchapter.pub/authors/didi-oviatt

Want to know when one of our books is free or discounted? Join the newsletter at http://eepurl.com/bqqB3H

Best regards,
Didi Oviatt and the Next Chapter Team

You might also like:

Hellbounce by Matthew W. Harrill

To read the first chapter for free, please head to:
https://www.nextchapter.pub/books/
hellbounce-supernatural-thriller

From the Author

Thank you kindly for reading Aggravated Momentum. I appreciate each and every reader. Please continue on and enjoy the first chapter of Search For Maylee.

-Didi Oviatt

Search For Maylee
Chapter One

Autumn drew in a lungful of California air. Although it was thick, it was somehow refreshing. She looked to her side at the sun glistening off small choppy waves on the oceanfront. It sparkled in bright flashes across the horizon. She was really going to miss this stunning morning view. A thin lilac tank-top dampened with sweat in the center of her back. Her feet were growing heavy, but she pushed herself and quickened her stride. Autumn had been running along the beach every day, sometimes a few times a day, for the past three years. She found that running helped to clear her mind, and tiring her body helped her sleep at night.

Every day during this run the thought of Maylee's disappearance raced through Autumn's mind on a loop. Every intricate detail was recalled, in order, exactly as it happened. She remembered what Maylee had eaten for breakfast, and then dropping her off at school that morning. Even the conversation they had haunts her.

"Don't you want some eggs?" Maylee chirped in her perky morning voice.

"Nah, I'll just grab a coffee."

"Whatever Aunt Autumn, you're going to sneak one of those disgusting greasy processed breakfast muffins after you drop me off, aren't you?"

Accusing eyes pierced Autumn's embarrassed face, forcing her to blush. Strange, how such a young woman could find so much fault over an innocent guilty pleasure no bigger than a thin slice of cheese with sausage.

These memories continuously float in and out of Autumn's mind, circling her like a consuming shadow, just waiting for the right moment to swallow her whole. After reliving the worst day of her life, Autumn would clear her mind, steady her breath, and convince herself to focus on the present. It felt like an impossible task to stop living in the past. Maylee was Autumn's niece, and she was seventeen years old when she was taken. Maylee was a high school senior with two weeks left until her graduation. She had her entire life ahead of her.

Now, three years later, Autumn was convinced that if she could just remember any tiny detail, something she may have skipped over, the police would be forced to pry Maylee's case back open. Autumn was more of a mother to Maylee than her junkie sister could ever dream of being – even on a sober day.

It had been nearly an hour since today's run commenced. Time seemed to escape Autumn as the worn-out sneakers laced to her feet moved further down the beach. Her legs were starting to tingle and burn. They weakened and felt like noodles under her wearying body. The intake of air burned her chest, leaving her throat to feel like a charred tree – still intact and alive, but the edges burnt to a crisp. She could feel the color of her face darken as fresh oxygenated blood sped through her veins.

Over the course of the last few days, she had pushed herself even further than her usual run. She would be leaving her beautiful home in Northern California, and moving to a small cramped one bedroom apartment right in the center of Denver Colorado. Every detail of her life would change once again, and it was terrifying.

Autumn fell into a deep depression when Maylee went missing, and she became obsessed with the case. The only time she would leave the house was to go to the grocery store or police station. Her life's purpose became nothing more than to pester Detective Chance, or just Chance, as everyone called him. His full name and title were Detective Chance Rupert Lizhalia III. Clearly, the comfort of being referred to so casually by his first name was developed very early on in his career. The details and progress of Maylee's case were poked and prodded at by Autumn daily. It was a repetitive process until about five months after Maylee had disappeared. At that point, Chance put Maylee's folder on an overstuffed shelf to collect dust.

"We have done everything we can," he told Autumn on that bizarrely hot fall afternoon as he slowly wiped the sweat from his full, perfectly squared hairline.

"So, you're going to throw her away? Just like that, you're done?" Autumn demanded, tears welling.

"Every police station in the country has Maylee's picture." Chance reminded her. "If anyone finds her or comes across anything that we can link to the case, then I assure you, Autumn, you'll be the first to know."

The short conversation had rendered Autumn mute. She stood frozen in shock as he told her to move on with her life. Chance apologized for the loss in such a way that it was clear – Maylee would never be found. Then he brushed past her in the hallway of an over-lit police station and went about his day as if nothing had changed.

Autumn recalled it now as she ran, remembering the cold emptiness in Chance's expression. The excruciating heat of that day hadn't even touched the icy daggers he sent jabbing into her chest. Even his outfit was seared into her memory. He wore a dark gray suit, complementing his tan, and an orange tie.

There was no denying it, Chance was a very attractive man for his age. The stress of the job was surely the culprit of a cluster of wrinkles at the corners of his eyes, although they only added to his enticing façade. Chance was the kind of man that you could take one look at and just know, without a doubt, he could defend himself. His build was strong enough to be noticed, with broad shoulders and a flat stomach, but his eyes were key. They were light gray and deeply piercing, always with a sharp gaze – like an eagle ready to swoop.

The afternoon Maylee's case was practically declared unsolvable and doomed for a cold shelf life, all hope drained from Autumn. Her car was left in the parking lot, and slow dragging feet carried her home, she moved in a blurry haze. Amidst the draining three mile walk to her front porch, the heat transformed into gloom, and before Autumn knew it she was engulfed in rain. The weather as unforgettably odd.

The door swung open, and she collapsed onto the floor, unable to take in air. Anxiety surged through her body in waves, and salty tears streamed down her face. God only knows how long she lay paralyzed on the floor before she got up and ran out the door. Pushing herself through the stinging oversized drops of rain, she rounded a corner and made her way to the beach. Giant deadly ocean swells had never looked so inviting, but she refused stop, continuing to run faster. Step after painful step in the sand, she pushed forward.

Oxygen eventually stopped reaching her lungs, and her legs gave out. Several times Autumn collapsed to her knees and stared into the water while she wheezed and struggled for breath. Each time the *slosh* of wet sand sounded beneath her fallen body, she would pick herself back up and continue to run. By the time she returned home the sky had turned black, and there were no stars to be found. Autumn was surrounded by darkness, a perfect match to the way she felt inside.

A haunting recollection of her own swollen, bloodshot eyes staring back at her from the hallway mirror now left an imprint in Autumn's mind. On that traumatizing day she become a ghost – an empty shell of her once prominent self. Maylee's absence was officially real, there was a sense of finality, a permanence that made Autumn sick.

That night after her first run, the world went completely black. As soon as her head hit the pillow, exhaustion and grief took over, blocking out whatever was left of her subconscious. For the first time in those five miserable months, her body gave up. She had slept an entire night through, deep and dreamless. It was the first night without nightmares and cold sweats since Maylee went missing.

Since that painful day, Autumn continued to repeat that same beachside run. Slowly over time, she's tried to put her life back together. So far that effort has proven unsuccessful.

This would be the day Autumn was going to take what could possibly be the biggest step of her life. Giving up on Maylee was not an option. This move was bound to uncover something. It had to. The winding road came upon a corner and revealed a small deserted parking lot. She was close to home now, with only a few more blocks to go before the first 'For Sale' sign came into view. The signs were pointing in the direction of her striking oceanside condo.

Autumn slowed her stride to a heavy-footed jog until she reached the lawn in front of her newly sold home. No sooner than her sneakers sunk into the freshly cut grass, she bent at the core and clutched her knees tightly, knuckles whitening, to catch her breath. Autumn glanced up to notice the front door had been opened a crack. She squinted over the top of her right shoulder, then abruptly to the left, peering down the road as far as she could see. There were no cars out of the ordinary aside from the large U-Haul sitting a few yards away.

Paranoia was common for Autumn. A constant nagging fear weighed in her chest at all times, she was forever burdened by this. It had taken a full year to convince herself to sell all of her belongings and take this giant leap. She had to be strong, and she had to leave California, for Maylee. With caution in each step, Autumn slowly made her way up to the condo. She peeked into each window, then tilted an ever listening ear toward the crack in the door.

"Oh, for hell's sake Autumn, you're such a weirdo! You're going to pack up all of your shit and take off on some 'save the world trek', and you can't even walk into your own house without panicking!"

The voice was shrill and mocking. It belonged to Candace, Maylee's mother. Autumn exhaled and walked inside. The sight of her sister leaning against the bar that connected the kitchen to the dining room was a lot to take in. Candace was tall and skinny. Too skinny, Autumn noted. One bony leg was crossed over the other and a thick string of smoke lifted into the air from the cigarette burning between her fingertips. She rolled her eyes at Autumn dramatically, and then flicked a long ash onto the floor.

"Candace, do you really need to do that? You know I don't let anyone smoke in my house. You think it's okay to just ash all over the place?"

"Who cares, you sold it anyway."

Candace walked over and ran what was left of her smoldering cigarette under water and dropped it into an otherwise spotless ceramic sink. The condo was empty, making it seem even bigger than usual. Autumn looked around her home, holding back the tears that were soon to inevitably flow — it was only a matter of time. The floors transformed from a dark marbled tile to white carpet in the living room. The ceilings were vaulted and the countertops were black with marbled gray granite.

Autumn had married at a young age and lost her husband in a car accident shortly after. She had only known Keith for seventeen months total. A vow was made to herself when he died, she would never love another and that was final. It'd been eighteen years since the accident, and so far she'd stuck to her promise. Autumn went back to her maiden name, Brown, in an effort to help herself move on from the trauma of his death. Keith had come from money and left Autumn a rich young woman at the time.

Initially, she bought the condo along with a dependable used car. Then she placed what was left of the settlement into a steady monthly income that was meant to last 20 years. Since then, the car had been traded in for a newer model, an end of this cash flow was rapidly approaching, and the condo sold. Autumn was trudging unfamiliar ground as her entire life was growing foreign, and that didn't even include her job.

After the loss of her young love, the years passed and the cost of living grew. Her fixed monthly income was barely enough to pay the bills and keep her fed. Enjoying nights out with her girlfriends, or buying new outfits were rare. A few years after Keith passed, Autumn picked up a job working as a waitress in a small crab shack just down the road from her condo. Surprisingly she absolutely adored it. It didn't bring in much money, but it was enough for the little extras, and it kept her busy.

As Autumn stood across from Candace in her freshly emptied kitchen, her mind wandered to the saddened look of shock on her boss's face when she'd quit. Autumn walked away from the steady job she loved, just over a week before. Candace cleared the tar blockage from her throat, pulling Autumn back to reality.

"How did you get in here?" Autumn asked. "And did you get me that address? I'm leaving soon. I only have a few more things to pack, so I need it. You promised."

"You always leave that window in the back unlocked," Candace said with another roll of her glassed over eyes. "And yes, I have your damn address."

Candace dug a small wrinkled piece of damp paper from her pocket, along with a chunk of dirty pocket lint and a couple of pennies. The goods were slapped onto the empty countertop. Candace then shifted restlessly on her feet, her eyes darting from one side of her head to the other. The look of a wild animal had taken over her face, as if assessing the possibility of an unexpected dash for the door. Unpredictable and permanently on edge, she finally continued in her scratchy smoker's voice.

"I still don't think you should do this. Craig's not a bad guy, he just gets a bad rep because of his record. Maylee's gone because she never paid attention to anything going on around her. It's probably her own fault she was taken, I'm sure Craig had nothing to do with it."

Aside from the obvious itch to leave, Candace was without emotion, utterly careless about Maylee. She spoke as if Maylee wasn't her daughter at all, but some strange girl she'd met on the street. It made Autumn's stomach wrench hearing her sister talk this way about her own child, her flesh and blood. How could she?

The thought of the opened back window was intentionally brushed aside. Autumn didn't even want to know exactly how her sister was privy to that information. The place would be deserted in a few hours, left for the new owners to deal with. The only thing that mattered now was how clearly strung-out and cold-blooded Candace was. A surge of anger flowed through Autumn.

Autumn couldn't stand Candace for the evil woman she'd grown into. The fact that Candace cared more about herself and getting her next fix than she did about her own daughter was sickening. Autumn stormed over to the bar and snatched up the piece of paper. It wouldn't be out of the ordinary if Candace were to change her mind, steal back the address, and make a crazy dash for the door. Frankly, it came as quite a shock to Autumn that her junkie sister had actually followed through on her promise to retrieve it in the first place. Once the address was safely in hand, Autumn finally spoke her mind.

"Maylee hated that man, and the rest of your friends. She was scared of him! She ended up here ninety percent of the time because you were a shitty mom, and your shitty friends are all terrible people. Open your eyes Candace, when are you going to understand that he was the only real lead the cops ever had? Now get the hell out of my house!"

Candace took a step back, shocked at Autumn's outburst. Her head tilted forward allowing her eyes to be shaded by the lowering of her brows. The shifty feet that struggled to hold up her stick-like legs for the first time held still. They had gotten in several fights about Maylee over the years. They brawled more since Maylee's disappearance than ever before. Candace knew she hadn't been the best mom to Maylee, but she would never admit it out loud, and she didn't much care either way. Excuses were constantly shelled out for her behavior as she never even wanted a child in the first place. Candace justified her actions to herself in any way she could.

Autumn wasn't the only one with resentment, as Candace genuinely returned the disdain. For most of their lives Candace hated her sister for being the pretty one, the favorite. A prominent loathing of Autumn's perfection had taken up residence in Candace. There was even a slight anger toward Maylee for confiding in Autumn as much as she did. Candace would leave Maylee for weeks at a time, and then get upset when she would find her at Autumn's house. Maylee was punished whenever her Aunt Autumn was mentioned.

Once Maylee was about twelve years old, Candace finally gave up and no longer asked or showed any concern. Candace couldn't care less whether Maylee came home or not. Candace knew that Autumn's was the only phone number Maylee knew by heart, and that's where she would usually be. There was no point in the chase. Besides, the less Maylee was around, the more freedom there was for her. There were no whiny voices begging for food, or phone calls from teachers complaining about smelly clothes or random bruises.

Candace now stared back at her angry sister contemplating what insult she would throw next. Whether it be about Keith dying, or about their Mom being in a nursing home, she usually thought of the things that would hurt Autumn the most before she spoke.

"You're not going to find her, Autumn. All you're going to do out there is waste what little money you have left and abandon Mom. You're leaving her here to rot while you chase a ghost."

Candace watched closely and fully satisfied as Autumn winced. The fact that their mother would be left all alone pulled fluid to the surface of her eyes. Hannah Brown, Autumn and Candace's mother had lived with Autumn for quite some time after her stroke. Once she became too heavy for Autumn to lift, Hannah was checked into the nicest nursing home within a twenty mile range. Autumn would visit her on a regular basis. Candace, on the other hand, hadn't seen their mother in years.

Autumn watched her sister strut to the door, then turn to look back as she twisted the door's handle. "Good luck on your mission, Superwoman." Candace sneered, chuckled lightly, and walked out.

About the Author

A SIMPLE LIFE: THROUGH THE EYES OF AN
UNEXPECTED AUTHOR.

Growing up in a small town had more than several advantages and disadvantages. Saying that my childhood was sheltered is nothing short of an understatement. Unlocked doors, cleared streets, and the quiet of a trustworthy neighborhood were all welcomed features of my hometown. As a small child I baked cookies with the old lady down the road. I sat next to my kindergarten crush in sun day school, and literally rode my bike in the middle of the road without a care in the world. We didn't have what kids have today. We actually had to use our imaginations to have a good time. There were no smart phones, tablets, or 64s to keep us occupied. We were perfectly content to play with our stick guns and a water hose for hours on end... And I loved it!

Along with my scrapes and bruises I also maintained a simple, happy for the little things attitude, and of course a great tan.

Now that I have made my childhood out to be nothing but cherries and smiles, I have to point out the disadvantages that came with the small town upbringing-- before the world of electronics took over the young mind. One word distinctively comes to mind... Boredom! As I grew into adolescence I no longer cared much for silly toys, dancing, baking, or crafts. I rebelled like many young adults do.With a sever chip on my shoulder and a lack of coordination in the sports department, I spent the majority of my time partying. Nothing too outrageous, mostly close friends,fires, and beer.

As much as I would love to say that living in a small town gave me an overactive imagination and love for books, that is unfortunately not the case. I cared more about having a good time than I did about school. I was voted wild child twice in high school. I cheated my way to passing grades

It wasn't until I was settled and married with a child on the way that I found my love for the literary world. Rearing out of my mid twenties left me a bit more mature, having to find more important things to do with my time than re-occurring nights at the bar. This is when it started - I read one book after another for a few short years, then decided to give writing a bash. I'm completely amazed at the love I developed! Once I started putting the world of imagination that has long been trapped in my overactive mind into a keyboard, the transformation of self began. A new aspiration in life has formed. I want nothing more than to be known as the unexpected novelist who took the literary world by storm!

Aggravated Momentum
ISBN: 978-4-82411-388-7 (Large Print)

Published by
Next Chapter
1-60-20 Minami-Otsuka
170-0005 Toshima-Ku, Tokyo
+818035793528
11th November 2021

Printed in the USA
CPSIA information can be obtained
at www.ICGtesting.com
LVHW042338151123
764091LV00030B/330